The Alchen

By
Eleanor Swift-Hook

Copyright © Eleanor Swift-Hook 2023.

The right of Eleanor Swift-Hook to be identified as the author of this work has been asserted by her in accordance with the Copyright, Designs and Patents Act, 1988.

First published in 2023 by Sharpe Books.

THE ALCHEMIST'S PLOT

The Hague, Late January 1643

From the moment he was formally presented in the days after Christmas, Queen Henrietta-Marie had found Sir Philip Lord perturbing.

He was undoubtedly attractive. His hair was white, not like that of an old man but vigorous and gleaming and those brilliant turquoise eyes could penetrate the private recesses of your soul. He was unsettling.

She knew little about him. She knew he wasn't immune to her charms as he smiled and lingered when she offered him her hand to kiss. She knew he was brave because her brother had said as much, and he had been knighted on the battlefield defending her husband's rights. She knew he was wealthy because he was always immaculately presented. She knew he was said to be a mercenary commander, and that his men called him the Schiavono, though quite what that meant and made him as a man, she was unsure. However, she was very aware that she didn't know his thoughts on anything that mattered. He wouldn't be drawn on politics or religion, was brief and pithy on art and literature and, asked his opinion on men and women of note, he would refuse, politely, to comment.

The only topic on which he was forthcoming was that of the military supplies she was purchasing to take to England. There his opinions often seemed to differ from those of the other military men in her train. Sometimes she was very glad that he hadn't been with her through the long months of selling jewels and carefully accumulating men and munitions. At other times she wondered if he had been there she would have increased the amount and effectiveness of what she was able to provide for her beloved husband. As it was, Sir Philip had persuaded a number of skilled commanders to place themselves at her disposal when before they had hesitated.

He had been the strongest voice advising her against sailing for England in January, saying it was the worst time to make such a crossing when the weather was at its most inclement. Then, when they spent days plunging and rolling through high winds and high seas, tossed around in their filth and vomit in the cabin, it had been he who had rescued her beloved little dog Mitte from being swept away. His hair whipped back by the wind and with a smile that had quite banished her terror, he had taken her hand and given her of his courage.

"You need not fear, majesty," he said. "It is well known that Queens of England are never lost at sea."

If that was so, she had not heard it before. She recalled that he was said to have once been the commander of a pirate ship or privateer, although the details eluded her. Seeing his feral delight in the storm, she could believe him a pirate at heart.

After nine terrible days, they reached the coast, but not that of England. They were in Holland again, two of the precious ships and their cargoes lost. A mass of thanksgiving was held at her insistence, even on that most Protestant of shores, though most could scarcely stand. The priest himself had to be supported by two men, one of whom was Sir Philip, though she had never thought him to be a Catholic. They had to burn their filthy clothes before they could return once more to The Hague.

Dear heart, she wrote to her husband, *I confess I never expected to see you again...I am so stupefied that I cannot easily write more, for I have not slept during nine nights...* Then, nothing daunted, remembering it was well known that Queens of England never perished at sea and thinking of the ship of pure silver she had vowed to Our Lady of Liesse for a safe crossing, she wrote: *I hope to set out again when the wind is good. Sir Philip, who you sent to me, has somehow managed to replace a goodly portion of what we have lost, although how it was paid for, I am still uncertain. Thanks to his intervention, we have ensured the release of a vessel of munitions detained thus far by the calculation of the commissioners representing the rebel parliament here...*

THE ALCHEMIST'S PLOT

Chapter One

Boarding a ship for England from the quay at Scheveningen, for the second time, would be the most courageous thing Gideon Lennox had ever done in the twenty-four years of his life.

Courageous after those terrifying days tossed about on the sea in the *Princess Royale* as the ship became a plaything of the elements. He had spent most of them lying in the cabin he shared with Sir Philip Lord, unable to eat and splattered in vomit. If before he had no fixed notion of the nature of hell, after that experience he was very sure he understood what it might be like.

That Lord had been out of the cabin, working with the crew, encouraging them and putting his life at risk on the exposed deck, hadn't made much impression at the time. Gideon had been too busy vomiting and praying for his life. But the respect in which all the seamen held Lord was evident. As they disembarked, Gideon saw the admiral speak a word to him and heard the captain thank him. Whatever Lord had done, it had helped save the ship, Queen Henrietta Maria, her ladies and Gideon himself.

And Mitte.

Mitte was a small, rather ugly lapdog with huge brown eyes and a short muzzle of whom the queen was particularly fond. And Mitte adored Gideon. Having already suffered problems from having Prince Rupert's dog, Boye, show him affection, Gideon had no wish to repeat the process with little Mitte. He did everything in his power to dissuade the dog or keep out of its way. But he had learned that if he heard the queen lifting her voice and calling Mitte's name, the creature would be somewhere nearby, seeking out his company.

Lord, of course, found it hilarious.

"We must find you a dog," he said. "*Mastiff, grey-hound, mongrel grim, hound or spaniel, brach or lym, Or bobtail tike or trundle-tail...* what would suit? A bulldog, perhaps as you can be so tenacious? Or a clever shepherd dog for your fast thinking?"

ELEANOR SWIFT-HOOK

Gideon wondered why he had offered to travel here with Lord. He could have gone home to England from Paris. He could have spent Christmas in Oxford with the woman who held his heart and soul in her keeping—Zahara. Except, of course, Zahara wouldn't have kept Christmas as she wasn't a Christian. She was a Muslim. The daughter of an Englishwoman, captured from the Devon coast and sold into slavery by Barbary Pirates, and a merchant from Aleppo who had loved both Zahara and her mother.

But religion was just one of the barriers that stood between them. There was also the suffering Zahara had endured at the hands of an abusive man which had wreaked invisible damage on her. And then there was her self-appointed guardian, Shiraz. He had rescued her when, as a child, she had been orphaned by a flood in the city for which he had been named. For all that he was mute, having had his tongue cut out, Shiraz was the most dangerous man Gideon knew, ferociously protective of Zahara and as loyal to Sir Philip as to a brother.

Once returned to The Hague following that first ill-fated attempt to sail to England, Gideon found himself being worked very hard helping Lord to strike deals to purchase as much as they could to replace what had been lost. Being a trained lawyer, Gideon reviewed the proposed purchase contracts and suggested the basis to negotiate better versions. It mostly involved rising early and travelling miles to visit a supplier. Gideon would advise as Lord haggled. In many ways, he was glad for the hard work as it stopped him from having to think of the need to get back on a ship at some point.

They had just returned from one such venture. Gideon, cold and aching from being too long in the saddle and contemplating an unjoyful evening ahead pouring over purchase accounts, wanted nothing more than a good meal. Then he saw something on a pile of documents left for them in their lodgings. He hurried to find Lord who was still in the stables consulting with one of the grooms over the state of his horse's hooves.

"There is a letter from Oxford, addressed to you."

Lord, crouched beside his horse with the groom holding one of the front feet, looked up. "From…?"

THE ALCHEMIST'S PLOT

"From your wife."

Lord was married to Lady Catherine—Kate—even if the marriage hadn't been of a regular kind. It had been by a verbal contract, one which Gideon had recorded and witnessed on the eve of battle. There had been no opportunity since then for Lord to regularise the union. But then these were two people who, Gideon knew, had loved and been lovers for many years with no need for sanction from church or law.

A few moments later Lord was striding back to the house. He had sent a letter to Kate explaining the circumstances before they left Paris in December. Although as Lord had observed at the time, Kate would have known he was being sent to The Hague before they did. She was at the heart of the king's affairs in Oxford, trusted in the councils of Prince Rupert having served the prince's mother, Gideon had recently learned, as a lady-in-waiting for many years.

When they had left Oxford Kate had been bedridden from a bullet wound, the result of her work as an intelligencer for the Royalist cause. Lord and Gideon had gone to Paris to find the physician-surgeon Anders Jensen who had been their only hope to restore Kate to health. Anders went directly to Oxford, but Lord had been ordered here to escort the queen home to England and Gideon had stayed with him. So they had no idea if Anders had arrived safely or how things were in Oxford.

Lord checked the letter, its folding, and seal with the habit of a man used to having his mail intercepted. Then he opened it and read, his expression unrevealing. After a couple of minutes, he glanced at Gideon and then held out the sheets.

"You look like a hungry waif hoping for a crust," he said. "It will be faster if you read it yourself. Have no fear, Kate is too wise to put anything of a delicate, personal moment into any missive."

Gideon snatched it from Lord's fingers.

Anders arrived safe and well a couple of days before Christmas and has told me that he has high hopes he can resolve my injury taken from that bullet. However, he advises me that I need to accept my days of wild riding to the hunt have, of necessity, to be set behind me if I am to be sure to regain and retain the simple ability to walk. I have some expectation now that by the time you return, I shall be able to welcome you upon my feet rather than recumbent if God is willing.

We also have another visitor who has returned from the north where you sent him and is both expecting your censure for failing to conclude the task to which he was set and equally determined that the reason for his failure is one you will condone as I do. Needless to say, the prince is already making good use of him in regard to improving the defences around Oxford.

That would be Daniel Bristow. Philip Lord's friend and most trusted officer who he had sent north to infiltrate the ranks of the man who had destroyed Lord's company, killed his friend and taken most of his best men. Gideon liked Danny and was glad to learn he was safe but wondered what had led him to return if his task had not been completed. However, it was little more than a passing thought as Gideon read on eager for one piece of news and one alone. There were some dense paragraphs about the progress of the war and the hopes that many were placing upon the current negotiations for peace which Kate concluded:

I am not alone in having little faith that these talks will lead to anything, but all must be seen to be done, I suppose.

Shiraz is well, and he asked me to include his greeting. Zahara sends her dutiful and affectionate greetings and trusts you will ensure they also reach the one she would most wish to receive them.

And that is all. You know already you are my heart and my soul and no words of ink on paper could ever encompass what is between us, so I will not essay an attempt. I know you will come back to me because God is not so cruel as to offer me the restoration of life without you, which would merely be as death in life.

Kate.

THE ALCHEMIST'S PLOT

For a moment the words blurred in Gideon's vision. It was so little, but it meant so much. Zahara was safe and well and was thinking of him. He realised he had been gripping the page too tightly and, relaxing his fingers, returned the letter to its owner.

His heart was both lighter for knowing Zahara was well and heavier for knowing it would be some time and a sea voyage before he could be with her.

Indeed, when the time came to board it was that one thought which gave him the courage to step from shore to ship. He had no choice. He had to do it so that he could see Zahara. He knew from the faces of the queen's ladies and those of her gentlemen who were on the ship, that he was far from alone in his anxiety. Most were whey-faced, and one was even sick with terror and only persuaded aboard by the queen saying stoutly that it was well known that Queens of England were never lost at sea so all on the ship with her would be quite safe. Gideon had never heard any such thing said before, but hoped the queen was right.

He stayed on deck as the shore receded and was joined by Philip Lord, leaning on the wood, hair blowing like a white banner in the wind.

"Are you alright?" he asked, his tone solicitous.

Gideon kept his teeth gritted and nodded.

"As much as it may surprise you," Lord went on, "the most hardened of the crew felt shaken by that last attempted crossing."

"Even you?" Gideon asked.

Lord's turquoise gaze moved from the coastline to study Gideon as if trying to understand why the question was asked.

"To be honest," he said. "I was too busy to be shaken. But had I been a passenger and not allowed a role working to keep the ship afloat, I suspect I would have been. We were fortunate."

Gideon drew a deep breath and let it out again. If that was being fortunate…

"Is it likely to happen again?"

Lord turned so his back was to the rail and looked up at the sky.

"I can't promise you it won't. But I would say it is unlikely. Though that doesn't mean we'll make Newcastle with no issues. Wind and weather this time of year are never certain."

Which was honest if not as reassuring as Gideon would have liked.

"At least the queen is convinced she is safe," he said. "Apparently, there is a long-standing tradition that says no queen of England can drown at sea."

For some reason that made Lord throw back his head and laugh.

"Then we have nothing to worry about," he said and clapped a hand on Gideon's shoulder before walking briskly away.

Lord was right.

Both in his prediction that they wouldn't encounter the same severity of bad weather as they had on the previous attempt and also in saying that they might not make it safely to Newcastle with no problems.

"Bridlington," Lord said when Gideon asked where they were anchoring. As a Londoner, Gideon's knowledge of the northern parts of England was hazy at best. "Well, Bridlington Quay to be precise. It is like the Piraeus to Athens, with Bridlington itself inland a mile perhaps from the quay and its harbour."

"And where in all England is Bridlington Quay?"

"In Bridlington Bay, of course."

Gideon opened his mouth to ask again but Lord relented.

"About halfway between Scarborough and Hull."

There was one key fact Gideon knew about both those ports.

"Scarborough and Hull are held by Parliament. Bridlington—?"

"Is too small for it to matter either way. There's no garrison and we have men enough with us to occupy it. Besides, the country about holds for the king. With luck, we can land and be halfway to York before anyone is aware we are here."

That time Sir Philip Lord's predictions were less accurate.

To begin with they had to wait to enter the harbour until a company of cavalry had arrived to ensure the queen's protection. Inevitably it had been Sir Philip Lord who had taken it upon himself to go ashore and see to the dispatch of messengers in person. He returned grim-faced.

"If we had any hopes of secrecy for the landing there is none now. Had I been heard we would have started unloading the munitions by now, but those voices that consider the queen's safety is best served by keeping us all from shore, seem to be in the ascendant."

"I thought you had command?" Gideon protested. "Wasn't that the point of the king sending you to the queen in the first place?"

Lord managed a cynical smile.

"Command is always in the hands of power, in this case, her majesty herself. I have no authority to overrule her, and she is subject to persuasive voices from all sides. And it would indeed seem sensible to await some troops on shore to secure the landing—if one didn't know that land attack is not the biggest danger here." He shook his head. "That is the problem with soldiers, they always forget the sea."

They finally began to disembark in the late afternoon of the second day when a detachment of cavalry arrived from York. There was little problem landing the principal passenger and her retinue. Accommodation for the queen and her immediate household had already been arranged. Whether the owners of the large house by the quayside were honoured or horrified to be asked to leave their home so the queen and her household could occupy it, Gideon had no idea. Either way, knowing Sir Philip Lord, they would at least have been compensated for the inconvenience. Lord himself was also accommodated in the building, although he made it clear he didn't expect to make much use of the room, so Gideon was settled there instead.

"There's no time to start today. We will be unloading from first light," Lord explained, "We have to land the troops first, then the supplies and I want to ensure everything is ready by then to minimise the delay—organised both shipboard and on land. I will sleep once we have everyone and everything ashore."

"What can I do?" Gideon asked.

Lord gestured to the bed in the room he had just commandeered.

"Get a good night's sleep. There will be work enough for you tomorrow when I will need every able-bodied man to help get the cargo from ship to shore and stored safely."

Roused soon after first light, Gideon found that Lord had meant his words. Every man he could muster was unloading and a number of the local women too. Even the queen's dwarf, Jeffrey

Hudson, who at under two feet tall made himself useful securing ropes,

They worked all day but there was still more to be done when Gideon went, exhausted, to bed. He was woken by Lord shaking his shoulder. It was still dark and by the candle Lord held, Gideon could see his concern.

"It seems Batten has found us after all," he said. "You'd better get up."

"Batten?" Gideon was still sleep hazed and blinking.

"The man Parliament has made Admiral of the North or some such title. He has four converted colliers and is bringing them in on the tide. At high water, we will be in easy range for his cannon and if we don't get them unloaded, he will be trying to sink our ships. Thank God we got the troops off yesterday, they can defend the unloading. Batten might even have sufficient troops with him to attempt a landing. I need to go and see Admiral van Tromp. If he moves his squadron, it will force Batten to withdraw."

The navy, such as it was, had fallen under the control of Parliament since the start of hostilities. Gideon knew that a large part of the reason that the Dutch Admiral van Tromp had been sent to escort the queen and her precious munitions, despite all the Dutch protestations of neutrality, was to protect against just such interventions.

Lord was getting changed as he talked and by the time Gideon was dressed, he was gone. Gideon made his way to the quay where Lord had already taken a small boat out to the Dutch flagship. Individuals and groups from the work parties of the previous day were being roused on Lord's orders, even in the dark.

When he returned from the Dutch ship remarkably quickly, tight-faced and tight-lipped, Lord urged everyone to greater speed before giving his full attention to the troops he had available to protect the unloading and defend against a possible landing of troops from the Parliamentarian vessels.

Then suddenly it was clear they were not planning any kind of landing. The ships were preparing to open fire upon the shore. Just before they started Lord was beside Gideon.

THE ALCHEMIST'S PLOT

"I've sent some men to the queen's house," he said. "I need you to go after them and make sure the queen and her household understand the urgency and are out of there. One of those ships has placed itself so its guns could bear on that house. There are ditches behind the village, I've given orders to get the women and non-combatants in them. That will be the safest place."

Gideon had no time to wonder why Lord had sent him on such a vital mission, but it meant Gideon was almost at the house when the first of the shots began. A man collapsed a few paces in front of him, a step away from the shelter of the building. Gideon dropped to a crouch to offer aid, but there was none he could give. Where the soldier's head had been there was now nothing. A ball fired from the ship had taken it.

It was still dark, perhaps five in the morning and the noise and chaos were intense. He knew then why Lord hadn't come for the queen himself. No one else had his powers of leadership and command to keep the work of unloading progressing apace under the lethal assault. Every soldier who wasn't already set to guarding the queen was needed to defend the munitions ships, those unloading them and the buildings in the village where the supplies they had unloaded were being stored.

When he reached the queen's house, the soldiers already there recognised him and stepped aside. Screams came from inside the house and almost as soon as he opened the door people pushed past him in panic. On the stairs, he encountered someone he recognised. Henry Jermyn. a favourite of the queen who held an appointment as her chamberlain and secretary. Gideon had heard malicious rumours that their relationship was closer still, but he doubted the truth of them.

"Where is the queen?" Gideon demanded.

Jermyn seemed not to hear him and perhaps he had been unable to as a cannonball found a target that rattled the house at the same moment. Leaving the panicked man, Gideon hurried upstairs and banged on the door to the queen's rooms. One of her ladies opened it enough to tell him her majesty was up and would be dressed in just a...

Gideon didn't allow her to finish.

"Her majesty," he said, wedging a foot in the door so it couldn't be closed on him, "needs to leave *now*. This house is under attack, and she is at risk every moment she remains here. There is no time to dress, a warm cloak will have to suffice—for her majesty and for all of you. Please be quick. Soldiers are waiting to escort you to a place of safety."

He decided announcing that they would be sheltering in a ditch was unlikely to encourage speed, but the roar, whine and crash of the cannon were incentive enough. Less than a minute later the queen herself emerged, bundled up in an all-enveloping fur-lined cloak.

"Monsieur Fox," she said, greeting him in French showing no sign of fear or distress. "I do not like the music they are playing for me. If you would be kind enough to escort me from here, I would be most grateful."

Surprised and immensely flattered that she knew his name, even if his assumed one, Gideon bowed and led the way downstairs. Then with a tight knot of soldiers about them and the queen anonymous amongst her ladies, they went as fast as he could chivvy them, to the relative safety of the land beyond the village. It wasn't out of range of the guns or even of the musket fire. A man was shot dead just yards away as they reached the ditches on the edge of the fields behind the last of the houses. Gideon wasn't sure if these were dug for drainage, irrigation or perhaps even carved by a stream. In the cold of a February dawn, it made little difference. They were simply frozen mud.

There were a few men there. Those such as Jermyn, who had avoided the unloading work on the previous day and now pretended to regard their duty as the personal protection of the queen, even though Sir Philip Lord had provided a very adequate military escort. Gideon bit back the words he wanted to say and decided that as the queen was quite well enough provided with protection, his duty was to rejoin those trying to unload the munitions.

He was scrambling out of the ditch when someone caught his arm. It was the queen herself, her face distraught.

"Mitte," she told him. "Mitte is still in the house."

THE ALCHEMIST'S PLOT

Gideon's heart sank.

"I will fetch her," he promised. But that wasn't enough.

"She will be too scared. I must come with you so she will not be afraid."

It was then Gideon knew a moment of pure panic.

"But your majesty—"

"Come." She hooked her arm through his as if it were the most natural thing in the world that she might do so. "We must hurry. Little Mitte will be so scared with all this noise."

Having no choice, Gideon gestured to the nearest of the soldiers who joined them to provide an escort back into the maelstrom of shot from both muskets and cannon. The queen was close to running. Much as Gideon could appreciate her concern, the thought that this rescue mission for a lapdog might cost the life of the queen herself or one of the men with them left him feeling sick.

Dawn had come and in the stark light, Gideon could see where one of the ships had placed itself opposite the house and was set to bombard it. It occurred to him this was no chance choice. Someone must have betrayed that the queen was staying in the big house by the quay, and this was an attempt on her life.

That was when he pulled up short in the shelter of one of the other houses.

"Majesty, please let me do this. Mitte and I are good friends, I promise you. I will bring her to you if you wait here. But those guns, they are meant for you and if you are seen to go into the house you will bring more danger to little Mitte as well as to yourself."

It wasn't his finest or most persuasive speech. The queen, her eyes wide and her long hair unbound under the hood of her manteau, surveyed him. Then she nodded.

"Please find Mitte, Monsieur Fox."

She was so sincere Gideon understood how the questing knights of Arthur's court must have felt when charged to undertake some heroic deed. He made a swift bow, then ran for the house, aware that every step left him exposed to the guns on the ship that was riding the tide so close to land.

"Gideon," Lord's voice came from beside the house. He was at the head of a group of men, clothes filthy and a musket in his hands. "I told you to get the queen to—"

"Mitte," Gideon explained and ducked into the house. Unbelievably he could hear a burst of laughter from Lord. It coincided with a lull in the bombardment, sounding out of place and inappropriate, but somehow also the most real and human thing in the chaos.

Gideon ran upstairs calling for the little dog.

His shouts were rewarded by yaps and scrabbling at the door of the queen's chambers. He opened the door and a small cannonball of brown and white fur launched itself at him. The room itself was a mess, discarded shifts and dresses lay over the furniture, and a box of the queen's correspondence had been emptied over the floor, some ripped into strips by the claws of a terrified and desperate Mitte who had relieved herself over them in her fear.

As Gideon bent to scoop up the little dog, he caught sight of a seal on one of the undamaged letters. This one was yet to be opened as the seal was intact, but the design on it sent a sudden shiver through his entire being. Without even thinking of the possible consequences, he picked up the letter and slipped it into his doublet, then with Mitte in his arms, her head buried in his chest and shivering, he left the house taking the stairs two and three at a time on the way down.

THE ALCHEMIST'S PLOT

Chapter Two

The nightmare ended by mid-morning.

As the tide fell it forced the Parliamentarian ships out to sea to avoid the risk of shoaling. Then—and only then—to Sir Philip Lord's expressed disgust, Admiral van Tromp sent a stern message to William Batten that if he did not cease firing upon the queen and withdraw, the Dutch would have no choice but to regard them as an enemy.

The queen seemed to accept van Tromp's excuse that a morning mist had been the reason for his inability to intervene, but Gideon suspected that she was offering diplomatic belief. The queen, he had come to realise, was very much her own person and not ruled by anyone. Whilst she would consider all counsel, her decisions were her own. She insisted that she would return to the house as soon as it was safe to do so, saying she would not give rebels the satisfaction of driving her out.

Lord hadn't demurred, merely establishing that the house had adequate protection. Then, Gideon noticed, he took the time to ensure that the dead would be buried and the injured tended to before he ordered the unloading of the supplies to continue apace. With the risk from the Parliamentarian ships lifted, Lord joined the work himself, even stripped to his shirt and hefting supplies alongside Gideon at need, as he had the day before.

After dinner, Lord changed into some degree of finery. He was, Gideon learned, supposed to escort the queen inland. A member of the local gentry had come forward to make his house available to the queen offering both more secure and more comfortable accommodation than could be had in Bridlington Quay.

The queen wasn't easy to persuade.

Gideon was with Lord when, surrounded by her small retinue and having thanked the gentleman who had offered her accommodation, she declared she wouldn't wish to leave the precious munitions she had brought from abroad and had been landed with her at such cost.

"I am the general of these men," she said. "If I stay, they will keep their courage and defend the supplies even if we are attacked again."

It was Henry Jermyn who coughed and spoke what all there were thinking. "I believe you will find, majesty, only men can be generals of armies. Your safety is what is paramount to the soldiers, not your presence. You are more like the banner of the army, our glorious royal standard, the colours for which we all fight." He lifted his arms as if in adoration as he spoke.

The queen's face didn't fall, but her whole body stiffened.

"Indeed, Secretary Jermyn, only men may be generals," Lord said, and all eyes moved to him. "But women may still lead armies. Boadicea led her tribesmen to fight Rome, and Joan of Arc led an army to defend France, to name but two."

That was met by an awkward silence. Because for all they fawned on her, these were men who had no wish for the queen to be given any voice in what was done now. Back in England, to their minds Gideon could see, she was no longer needed as the active diplomatic figurehead they had required her to be when abroad.

"Then what rank is there for a woman who leads an army?" The queen asked.

Lord answered her at once, speaking before any of the others could. "A female supreme general must be a generalissima," he said and gave her a neat military bow rather than one due to a monarch.

The queen's eyes widened a little.

"Then I shall be the She-Majesty Generalissima of this army," she decreed. "Until we reach my husband."

"It is wise to reserve command to yourself," Lord said, which earned him a few hard and hostile stares from the other men.

That was when Gideon realised Lord hadn't been patronising the queen or pampering a royal ego. He had been buttressing royal confidence by making it plain that he felt her more capable than most of the men who paraded around her proffering their opinion. From what he had seen of her intelligence, courage and poise, Gideon found himself in some agreement.

THE ALCHEMIST'S PLOT

"If you will trust me to see to the safety of the supplies here on your behalf, Generalissima," Lord added, "I will bring you a full report when they have been landed and stored, together with the arrangements for moving them, subject to your approval."

The queen looked at him in appraisal. She wasn't tall and had to tilt her head up to meet his gaze.

"You have my trust, Colonel Sir Philip Lord. As you defended my husband's honour in battle, I look to you to defend these supplies which are almost as precious. Until my husband's chosen commander, the Earl of Newcastle is here to ensure their safety."

The last, even Gideon could see, was a necessity. It would be impossible to allow a mere knight, albeit a knight banneret, authority over an earl.

Lord acknowledged her instruction as a colonel to his commander, not as a courtier to his queen.

It was only then she consented to leave Bridlington Quay and as she had given him command of the forces defending the supplies there, plans were changed. Lord was to remain whilst the queen appointed Jermyn to lead her escort. From the looks he was giving Lord, Gideon decided that Sir Philip might have won over the queen but in the process had made himself an enemy in Harry Jermyn.

That evening, after supper, when Lord returned from reporting to his She-Majesty Generalissima in her new lodgings, Gideon finally managed to get Lord on his own. They were staying in the house by the quay. Lord, as the new local commander, had moved to occupy the once royal suite. Gideon found him there and was allowed within. Closing the door behind him, Gideon held out the unopened letter he had taken from the same room earlier that day, its seal visible.

Lord accepted it, then with a deepening frown turned the letter in his fingers to read to whom it was addressed. Then his expression became incredulous.

"You stole a letter from the queen?" Lord sounded torn between hilarity and despair. "Gideon, you do realise that is more than sufficient grounds to get you hung?"

"I saw the seal," Gideon said, doggedly. "It is the same symbol that was on the wrapping of the blank pages we found in the secret chamber in Howe Hall. I believe it to be a mark of the Covenant."

It had been several months since he had learned of the shadowy conspiracy of powerful men who had shaped Lord's life from pre-conception onwards. Men who believed that he carried the bloodlines of Tudor and Hapsburg. They had raised Lord to believe that one day he would rule, not just England but a new empire where the divisions between Catholic and Protestant were resolved into a single creed that embraced and stood above both.

Gideon had only ever met two men, both now dead, who had been a part of it. Sir Bartholomew Coupland and Sir Richard Tempest. They had hired him to find Lord and deliver a message, fully expecting and intending that Lord would kill him. It had been Gideon's good fortune and a testament to how little the Covenant men understood Philip Lord, that instead, Lord had employed him. So when the documents that proved Lord's heritage might eventually be found, Gideon could apply his skill as a lawyer to authenticate them.

But Gideon hadn't forgotten the seal he had seen on the document bag they had found in Howe Hall. Howe, which had been Sir Bartholomew's stronghold and the place where Lord had grown up as a child.

The seal had a circle with a dot in it, and a semi-circle or crescent above, drawn as if looped through the circle rather than placed on its circumference. Under the circle and touching it was an equal-armed cross and the bottom arm of that sat at the centre point of two curves, formed as a child might draw the wings of a bird or the waves on the sea.

Lord turned the letter back over and studied the seal, stepping closer to the fire and holding it up to the candle on the mantle shelf so he could examine the detail.

"It is their mark," he agreed. "The man who created it called it the *Monas Hieroglyphica*—it was a summation of his esoteric philosophy and represented his ambition for religious reunion under a single ruler. The Covenant, which he helped found,

THE ALCHEMIST'S PLOT

adopted it." Lord shook his head. "I was raised to believe I was the living embodiment of that symbol."

Gideon wondered how that must feel. Somehow it wasn't a question he could bring himself to ask. Lord had been brought up never knowing his parents, told he was the legitimate descendent of a child born secretly to Queen Mary and Philip of Spain. Brought up to believe that he was the one chosen by God to bring peace to the world by ruling over it.

"What is it supposed to mean?"

Lord rubbed his thumb over the seal. "The central circle is the sun, the crescent above is the moon, the cross below represents the four elements—fire, water, earth, and air—and the arches at the bottom are a stylized form of the astrological symbol for Aries. But what it means is..." Then he looked up at Gideon. "You are not a rash man by nature. But this? Stealing the queen's unopened letters?" His tone was far from censorious, being closer to amused admiration. "This is more something I would expect from Danny or Kate."

"The queen wouldn't know," Gideon said. "If I had thought for a moment she might, I wouldn't have touched it. But Mitte had upended the case with many of the queen's letters in it and had been scrabbling to get out of the room and even managed to piss over some. There were several pages shredded beyond any recognition. If the queen or anyone else recalls this one letter they will assume it was one of the victims of Mitte's terror."

Lord looked at him. "I saw that, and I believe you have the right of it, but even so I feel ashamed that you are falling into felonious ways under my influence." But he didn't sound ashamed. If anything, Gideon thought, he sounded rather smug. "If it's something vital to the queen then it can be 'discovered' by me in the room and taken to her tomorrow." He turned it again in his fingers and studied the writing. "I don't recognise the hand."

"You could open it," Gideon suggested and took the chair by the hearth. His legs ached from the work of the day.

"If it were not addressed to the queen's own majesty, I would be wary to do so, but I doubt even these men would be so vile as to seek to attempt to poison her."

He opened the letter, his gaze scanning over the contents. Then he shook his head and began to read it out aloud.

"*Majesty, I trust you will forgive my temerity in sending this to you and I apologise for the means by which it is delivered.*" Lord glanced at Gideon. "One has to wonder how it was sent."

"If it came from London, by a merchant?" Gideon lifted a finger as a thought occurred. "Perhaps it came through the hands of one of the parliamentary commissioners at The Hague?"

"If so," Lord said, "that would explain why it has remained unopened. I cannot imagine the queen would be eager to assist any petitioning her through such offices." He looked back at the sheet in his hands and continued reading. "*There is a man in your service who has cozened himself into your majesty's good graces and those, I believe of his majesty, your husband also. His name is Philip Lord. Although he might travel under another name, you will know him by his distinctive appearance as he has white hair and eyes the colour of turquoise. You may not know, but he was a traitor to England selling secrets taken from the very chambers of King James to the Spanish—enemies of both France and England—through the aid of Don Diego Sarmiento de Acuña, Count of Gondomar and he has fought against England and English interests many times since. If you doubt my word, I have evidence both of his perfidious nature and of his treason. I would hope your majesty will take swift action to ensure this dangerous man is arrested and dispatched before he can wreak further harm in these troubled times. I remain your majesty's most humble and loyal servant, Sir Isaac Ruskin.*" Lord frowned. "The name seems familiar."

He folded the sheet and looked at Gideon, who had felt the blood drain from his face when Lord read out the name.

"Sir Isaac is the father of Ellis Ruskin, who we met in Paris. I know Sir Isaac. He was a friend of my father. He's been Recorder of Westminster, a Serjeant-at-Law." Gideon drew a ragged breath, "I've worked for him on several occasions. He is upright and godly, compassionate and fair—an honourable man and—" Gideon broke off realising what he was saying, what the existence of Sir Isaac Ruskin's name on a letter bearing that seal must mean.

THE ALCHEMIST'S PLOT

It was a realisation that severed him adrift from the most solid moorings of his life. If a man like that, a man he had admired and respected, could be part of the same vile conspiracy as had bred Philip Lord like a bloodlined horse or dog, then he no longer knew who he could consider just and righteous.

Lord said nothing and took a pace over to the hearth, dropping the letter into it and watching it flare up with flame.

"Is anything in it true?" Gideon brought himself to ask, at last.

"My appearance?" Lord suggested, then shook his head. "I began my career fighting against English interests, but that was many years ago and it's never seemed to trouble anyone before. As for the charge I had correspondence with Gondomar having met him when he was still in London. The last part was true, I did meet him. I think I was twelve at the time and I understand he found me disquieting. I was a very arrogant and imperious child. I had correspondence with him if you count sending a formal letter of thanks. The rest, of course, was pure fantasy. Someone was arranging to send secrets to Spain through the good offices of the Count of Gondomar. They wanted to curry favour with the Spanish king and show how much a Spanish match would benefit the Habsburgs. The same man who wanted the Spanish Infanta to marry Prince Charles. Or did until he experienced for himself at first hand the scorn of the Spanish court. Then he wanted war with Spain as grand and florid revenge."

"The first Duke of Buckingham?" Gideon guessed.

"George Villiers. Yes."

"Do you think after all this time you can prove it untrue?"

Lord shrugged.

"If there is evidence still in existence." He took the poker from its stand and pushed the last bit of the paper into the embers. "I doubt the queen would have paid the letter much heed, but it is possible my enemies at court might have used it against me. You did well to steal it. Thank you."

"But you are pardoned so it makes no difference."

"I am pardoned," Lord agreed. "But it makes a difference. It is yet another reason that I need to go to London."

Gideon stared at him, feeling a cold chill prickle the hair on his arms that had nothing to do with the temperature and everything to do with a sudden foreboding.

"London?" he echoed. "You cannot intend to go to London. Not at this time. Perhaps after the war when things are safer there and—"

Lord interrupted him. "Things will never be safer there for me than now."

"Why not? You have a pardon from the king. When he is restored to—"

Gideon was silenced by a shout of laughter.

"And what if he is not? What if England becomes captive to its own Parliament instead?"

The thought was so strange that Gideon struggled to encompass it.

"Even if Parliament wins, they will need the king," he protested.

"As a puppet, perhaps."

"But the peace negotiations—"

Lord shot a hand towards the window.

"You have seen what we brought with us from Holland?"

"Yes, but—"

"And yet you think the king plans to negotiate?"

"From a place of strength," Gideon suggested. But he already knew the queen would hear no talk of peace or accommodation with those who dared to oppose her husband, and most of the king's councillors were men of war like the princes.

Lord shook his head. "I'd like to hope you are right," he said heavily. "But I see nothing more than delaying tactics in these peace talks. The king is hearing news of success every day— Hopton in Cornwall, Rupert in Gloucestershire, Newcastle here in Yorkshire—why should he negotiate?"

"Then perhaps it won't be long before the war is over if he is doing so well," Gideon suggested.

"Perhaps. And perhaps not." Lord shook his head again but more slowly this time. "Either way it's a risk I cannot take. It seems everything I need to know is in London. It was always my intention to go there, ever since you and I rode from Howe. But other matters have prevented it." He gestured to the fireplace. "That letter shows the Covenant are set to undermine me with the king any way they can. By good fortune you intercepted it, but this won't be the only attempt they make. Were they to succeed it's not just myself who would suffer the consequences. It's never just myself. It will be Kate and Zahara, you and Danny, Shiraz and now Anders Jensen. Even those who are my men like Roger Jupp and Argall Greene. Anyone and everyone who could be thought to have offered me support. The one advantage I had over the Covenant was surprise and the chaos of this war, but now the surprise is gone, and the letter shows they are preparing their counter. If I delay too long, I may lose the shield of chaos." He sighed. "There is a reason I have not returned to England before this. You must never underestimate the ruthlessness, power, and guile of these men."

Gideon had seen at first hand the callous thoroughness the Covenant brought to its work. Howe Hall with its secret chamber where a tormented creature had been made to live out a life for the sole purpose of bringing forth another generation. That Philip Lord had broken free spoke to the nature of the man. But then Gideon realised he had been missing something that should have been obvious. Philip Lord hadn't broken free; he had been expelled.

"The Covenant can't have wanted you to be declared a traitor?"

Lord looked at him sharply.

"Of course not. They were ambushed by it as I was."

"So why didn't you go to them for help?"

Lord said nothing. His face closed, expressionless. Then he gave a brief laugh.

"You need to understand I was very arrogant and thought myself, at the tender age of fifteen, a wise and worldly man. In some ways I was, compared to many the same age, but I was also naive. I believed Villiers—dear Steenie—was a friend and had my best interests at heart. When he came to me close to panic in apparent fear for my safety, I did not stop to think. I went with him. It was only when I was left alone in the Netherlands, but on the wrong side of the border, I realised what had happened. But then it was too late."

"And the Covenant? They made no effort to assist you?"

Lord crossed to one of the chairs and moved it closer to the fire where Gideon was sitting, brushing at the cushion to remove some dog hair before he sat.

"They might have, had I told them where I was. I would like to say that I had seen through their wiles, but at that time I believed I was regarded as a traitor by all in England. I didn't yet understand what the Covenant was. So I avoided England, Englishmen and any I thought might know me. I changed my name, changed my nationality. I did what many youngsters escaping trouble do and joined the nearest army." He gave Gideon a brief, tight smile. "It wasn't that hard."

Gideon wondered how hard he would have found it stranded in a foreign land at such a tender age with no resources except his own wit. He somehow doubted he would have fared as well as Lord even if he had joined the nearest army. He wanted to ask more, to ask how Lord had managed to hear from King James, how he had learned the true nature of the Covenant, but it was getting late and there was something much more urgent he needed to know.

"As soon as we return to Oxford, Prince Rupert will expect you to take back your military duties and then you will be given no more time to yourself until this war is won or lost. So how do we get to London? I can't see any easy path at the moment."

"You are, of course, correct. Which means the solution should be as obvious to you as to me."

That made little sense.

Then it did.

A sickness gripped Gideon's guts with a hollow clawing.

"You mean not go back to Oxford? Zahara is there. Kate is there." He knew he must sound close to anguished. "Surely you wish to see Kate, know how she fares? Know if Anders has—"

"By God's wounds, Gideon," Lord's voice burst across his. "What kind of man do you think I am? Of course, I want to see Kate, there is nothing in this world I would wish to do more. She is my light, my heart, the soul of my soul. But..." He paused and drew a shuddering breath. "But as you said yourself, if I go back to Oxford I will not be allowed to leave again until this war is done and by then it might well be too late for all the reasons I have already mentioned and many more that I have not gone into. *I* have no choice," he placed careful emphasis on the pronoun. "You may return to Oxford if you wish."

It was asking too much. To go to London with Lord and risk all that would entail was already more than Gideon was sure he could do. But to do so without seeing Zahara again…?

For the first three months he had known her they had been in close company. They had seen each other every day, worked together, talked together, exchanged looks and glances. Known the agony and the bliss of being in each other's company and yet not being able to be more than that. It was now almost as long again, and he hadn't seen her at all. Yet not an hour went by that he didn't think of her.

His neck bowed with the pain of it. Then a thought pushed through the dark emotions as the new shoots of spring might push through dark soil. He lifted his head and met Lord's gaze.

"You have an idea." Lord didn't make it a question.

"I do," Gideon agreed. "One of us needs to go to Oxford, to find out how things stand there and to reassure both Kate and Zahara that all is well with us. You cannot without being expected to resume your military duties in full. I, however, have no military duties to resume. You might have forgotten but my last employment in Oxford was as part of Lady Catherine's household, I wasn't employed in any military capacity at all. There is nothing to stop me from returning to Oxford and leaving again."

Lord nodded and a smile formed on his lips as he saw the ultimate direction of the line of thinking Gideon had put forward.

"And were you to return to Oxford it would of course be expected that you had with you an escort of a reliable servant."

"I would indeed," Gideon agreed.

At which point Lord's smile became a wolfish grin.

"I can see my efforts in your education have not fallen entirely on stony places, though I do sometimes think them fallen among the thorns of your obdurate principles."

The lift in Lord's mood was marked.

"But I don't see how you escape the responsibility you have here," Gideon said. "I thought the king made it your duty to see to the safety of the queen and the men and cargo she brought with her."

Lord looked unperturbed.

"When Newcastle arrives, which I doubt will be too long at all, I'm sure her majesty will be happy to allow me to return to my duties at the prince's side. At that point, I think I can in good conscience, entrust the charge of both queen and cargo to the earl. Until then we sit tight."

"You have thought how to explain your slow return to Oxford? I'm going to guess we could be some time in London."

Lord shook his head.

"I am counting on the fact that whenever I return the prince will fall on my neck with joy and forgive any delay. I doubt he will punish me. Whatever his faults he is never captious towards others. Besides, Kate would never allow it."

"The prince knows of your supposed treason and, I presume, of your innocence in that, but does he know anything of the rest? Of the Covenant?"

"The prince," Lord admitted, "neither knows nor cares about my guilt or innocence in the matter of treason. To him, it is all ancient history either way and either a youthful misdemeanour on my part or an unwarranted calumny by my enemies of the time. For him, the matter was finished with the issuing of the pardon. About the Covenant—there are less than a handful now living, other than myself and those who are sworn to serve it, who know enough to understand why I need to uncover the truth. His highness is not one."

"So who does?"

"You. Kate, of course. Zahara and Shiraz."

"Mags told me he knew."

Lord avoided Gideon's gaze. Mags was another mercenary commander. The one Danny Bristow had been sent to deal with, who had wormed his way into Lord's company then betrayed Lord and left, taking most of his men.

THE ALCHEMIST'S PLOT

"Mags was born in Howe," Lord said as if that explained it. Perhaps it did.

"Does Danny know?"

Lord considered. "I'm not sure," he admitted. "He knows I've been hunted, but I think he always put that down to the small matter of treason. I have never spoken to him about it. It is not a safe thing to know. Kate knows because she is the keeper of my soul. Zahara and Shiraz know because they have lived too close to me for too long now not to know. You only know because you were thrown into it by Coupland, and I have had to keep you close and change your name to ensure your safety ever since."

Which was a small revelation to Gideon. He was trying to think of a suitable response when Lord yawned and stretched deliberately.

"We should sleep," he said. "There is more work tomorrow."

Chapter Three

The next day brought more work. It also brought an unexpected visitor.

Captain Sir John Hotham, the son of the governor of Hull and a Parliamentarian commander, sent a flag of truce on the pretext of exchanging prisoners. Upon being granted safe conduct by Sir Philip Lord, he was admitted into Bridlington Quay.

"Oh, it's yourself," Hotham said as he was shown into the room Lord had made his own. "I'd heard you were back, but you know how it is. Never believe what you hear. You told me that once as I recall."

Lord sent the men with Hotham away and closed the door. He had told Gideon to stay when they had been brought word of Hotham's flag, saying he would find it educational. So Gideon was there playing the servant to have an excuse to observe.

"As that was a lesson I learnt at some cost, I have been keen to pass it on," Lord said, crossing to the hearth. "Is that why you came? Because I'm sure we have no prisoners of yours." Lord took his seat, gesturing that Gideon should serve them both with wine.

Hotham was a large man, of an age with Sir Philip Lord, but with a florid face and a nose that looked large for the rest of his features. He was sitting in the chair Gideon had occupied the evening before and seemed to fill it more completely.

"You may not," Hotham agreed. "Newcastle has. And I've some of his he might like back."

"I'm sure so. But you could have sent to York at any time, so don't expect me to believe that is what this is about"

Hotham shrugged. He seemed unperturbed at being accused of dissembling. "Why not? It's no lie."

"But it is also not the whole truth, is it, *Captain* Hotham?" Lord put emphasis on the rank. "It must sting having to take orders from the likes of Ferdinando Fairfax and his offspring." Then he paused and drew in a sharp breath in parody of a man having an epiphany. "But you haven't, have you? Doncaster, Cawood Castle—and that right after the Fairfax Treaty of Neutrality had been signed promising no military action. I'm not up to date, is there anywhere else you have taken on your own initiative?"

"If you know so much about it, you tell me why I came." Hotham slurped at his wine, looking curious more than defiant.

"I think it is less 'why' than 'how much'," Lord said. "Did you want me to take the opening negotiation to her majesty? Or was it that you wished to kiss her hand yourself?"

"Things change," Hotham said as if that were an answer or an explanation, but Gideon could see it as neither. Lord, however, nodded as if it made perfect sense.

"They do. But are you any more willing to ride pillion behind a Cavendish than behind a Fairfax? For that is what it will amount to."

Hotham drained his cup and made a brief gesture to Gideon who moved to refill it.

"For the right price," he said as Gideon poured the wine.

"Which is?"

"My father to be a viscount, I'll be a baron and we'll take twenty thousand pounds of the money you just brought back from selling off the royal gewgaws."

Gideon nearly dropped the jug he still held and turned away to hide his face as he put it down. How could the man be so venal? And to ask so much?

Lord said nothing. He sipped his wine, watching Hotham over the rim as he did so.

"And for that, the king gets Hull and...?"

"Is Hull not enough? There are good supplies of arms and munitions there and it controls the trade into Yorkshire."

"I have bad news for you," Lord said after a short pause. "The queen is not here. If you wish to be presented, you will need to accept my escort. Assuming she is willing to receive you. Do you wish me to send and ask?"

"See the little queen herself? Well, I've seen her husband and then her son begging leave to get into Hull, so why not? She may think my offer a fair one even though you don't."

Lord got to his feet and picked up a sealed note from the mantle.

"I thought you might wish it." He beckoned Gideon over like the servant he was pretending to be and gave him the note. "See this dispatched to her majesty at once, then ask for dinner to be served to myself and my guest here, while we await a reply."

When Gideon went back to the room to help serve the meal, he found Lord and Hotham exchanging tales of their mutual past. These were war stories of the kind he had never heard Lord resort to before, but which were the meat and drink of every old soldier of whatever social rank that Gideon had ever encountered. He slipped from the room once his task was done and left them to it. Charging another to serve them, he went to help with the physical labour.

He didn't notice when they took horse to see the queen but saw when Lord returned alone at twilight. He appeared uncharacteristically dispirited when Gideon went to his room to ask how things had gone.

"You get used to that kind of thing in the wars across Europe," Lord said, pouring himself some wine as he spoke. "Men selling their towns, their troops, their loyalty. But I had somehow hoped not to find it here. Whatever it might be that brings Englishmen to blows with each other, brother against brother, father against son, is it all just greed and vanity?" He shook his head in disgust. "By God, if you have to go out and slaughter your next-door neighbour the least you can do is have the decency to kill him in hot blood, for what you truly believe, rather than for such sordid and tawdry baubles as gold or titles. Where are the principles and the passion?"

It was a strange philosophy for a mercenary commander. Gideon was about to say as much but then thought of the principles and passion he had heard so often expressed in London in the months before the country fell into war.

"For many, it is that. Perhaps for most," he said, not sure if it would bring any response. When there was none, he asked: "Will the queen pay him?"

"I have no idea and I'm not sure I wish to know. I have played my part, the rest is for the likes of Newcastle to see through if he can." Lord had already emptied the best part of a jug of wine and was filling up his cup again. "Talking of whom, the earl should arrive tomorrow, and the queen is invited to stay the night at every house between here and York. It will be a slow progress. Therefore, I have secured permission for us to leave as soon as the earl arrives. I led her majesty to believe that like Hotham, I prefer not to ride pillion. She was gracious enough not to insist." He took a drink and then gestured towards the door. "You had better get an early night. I want to travel fast when we go."

Gideon knew from experience that Lord drinking and in such a mood wasn't a man to trouble with. He withdrew to his own chamber and spent the time before sleep distracting himself from the cares of the day with a copy of Richard Johnson's *Tom a Lincoln*. It was the unlikely adventures of a son born out of wedlock to King Arthur and the daughter of the Lord Mayor of London who was raised by a shepherd in Lincolnshire.

Then he put out the candle and lay in bed for a while thinking of Zahara and wondering if she was thinking of him, before murmuring his prayers for her safety and wellbeing.

The following morning the Earl of Newcastle arrived together with what seemed to be a fair portion of his army. They came shortly before midday and were in sufficient strength that Sir Philip Lord took his leave of the queen in good conscience. Gideon had no requirement to make a formal farewell and waited with their horses, already packed with their necessary possessions and chosen by Lord from those available for speed and endurance. It was two hundred or so miles to Oxford. Having good horses, able to sustain a decent pace, would make a substantial difference in how long that journey took.

Lord emerged from his final leave taking tight-lipped and subdued. It wasn't far from the door of the house to where Gideon stood with a soldier holding the horses, but it took Lord several minutes to cross the distance. He was intercepted again and again by those wishing to bid him farewell or ask him something. Being who he was, he both found time to offer an ear and a word to all and yet managed to keep moving in the direction he was taking. It was a skill Gideon had observed in him before and, as before, he thought how like a royal progress it appeared.

ELEANOR SWIFT-HOOK

He would make a good king.

The thought came from nowhere and shocked Gideon. Not so much in its outlandishness as in its truth. Perhaps it wasn't so surprising. Lord had been brought up to his guardians' expectations of kingship or greater, and he had spent much of his adult life in places of high command. Gideon pushed the idea away. Aside from the fact it was treason, and the role of king was already taken, the very last thing the present turmoil needed would be the complication of a pretender to the throne.

Lord took the reins of his horse and accepted a leg up from the soldier who had held them, who after moved to offer the same courtesy to Gideon. To ensure speed of travel, Sir Philip Lord had taken care to shed the trappings of his rank and to eschew the retinue that he would be expected to have. They set out then, accompanied by six men, lent on the insistence of the queen to escort them on their journey.

They completed most of the distance to York that day, in the pre-spring sunshine of a bright February afternoon. If Hotham had patrols out, they didn't encounter any and in the evening, stopped at an inn in the village of Stamford Bridge.

The following day took them through York and then south to Tadcaster, which showed signs of a desperate battle to capture it from Parliamentarian control some months before, including its hastily repaired bridge. After that, they moved into territory that wasn't securely held so they ate a quick dinner there before heading on to spend the night as guests within the impressive walls of Pontefract castle.

Lord woke Gideon before dawn the next day.

"It's time we took leave of our escort," he said. "From here we will travel faster and safer alone."

A short time later, they headed south as master and servant as pink and blue tints heralded the rising sun on the horizon to their left. It was then that Gideon discovered Lord's time spent in swapping war stories with Hotham hadn't been wasted. After they had left Pontefract behind them, Lord took the time to darken his hair and beard, then before they went on, he held out two documents for Gideon. One was a letter of safe passage signed with a flourish by Colonel Sir Philip Lord declaring that the bearer was on his business and should not be detained. The other was similarly worded but signed by Captain Sir John Hotham. It seemed Lord had secured something of value in return for his service as a go-between.

"For the love of God do not confuse them," Lord cautioned. "Keep them in separate places so there is no chance you might produce the wrong one."

Gideon protested that he wasn't so foolish, but after the first encounter of the day, he was reminded of how hard it could be to keep a clear head under such duress. As the man playing the master, he was the one who had to engage the soldiers of each side in conversation and seek to assure them that he wasn't any variety of enemy agent or sympathiser and on business too pressing to be persuaded into joining either army.

As it turned out, they were most often left alone provided they went off the road to allow soldiers to pass and, even if challenged, Gideon was usually not required to do more than answer brief questions as to his name and business. But over the next three days as they travelled south, he had to produce one or other of the passes on a handful of occasions. Once he found his hand in his doublet on the wrong side and had even touched the paper before realising the mistake. Fortunately, the soldiers saw nothing amiss, no doubt assuming he had forgotten where he had placed the safe passage.

As they neared Oxford, Gideon had needed to produce Sir Philip Lord's signature more and more often. Their last encounter was as fortuitous as it was unexpected. A troop of cavalry came from behind heading at speed towards the city. Gideon and Lord moved off the road to let them pass, but instead, a shout went up and the small cavalcade came to an efficient halt as one of their number turned back towards them.

Tawny hair pushing out from beneath his hat, as unruly as it had been on their last encounter half a year before, Danny Bristow grinned at Gideon.

"I thought it was you," he said, glancing at Lord, in his servant's place behind Gideon with no sign of the recognition he must have. "Sara will be pleased." Then his eyes danced with forgotten but familiar mischief. "So will Kate. But come, let's get you through the gates and into the college to see them. We can talk then."

Taking that warning, Gideon made no attempt to ask anything and just fell in beside Danny, who seemed happy enough to talk for the three of them. His theme was the progress of the war and as he went on, it occurred to Gideon that he wasn't just hearing idle chat and gossip, he was hearing the report of an officer to his commander. In a succinct and often humorous way, Danny was bringing Lord up to date with the most recent developments that he might want or need to know, whilst not even acknowledging his existence. He kept up the account as they were waved through the gates. Danny was clearly a familiar figure around the defences, needing no word or warrant to pass in and out of Oxford.

The city itself was a heaving anthill of people, nothing like the bustling but peaceful and prosperous city Gideon recalled from his youth, nor even the same city he had left to go to France three months before. There was prosperity to be seen, but the filth in the streets reminded Gideon of some of the most odorous areas of London. This was a city with people packed in greater density than he had seen them be even in Paris. It was a Sunday so there was little open trade, but still large numbers of people filled the streets.

Mounted and with an escort of soldiers, they were able to pass through with people stepping aside.

"Of course, the prince wants Bristol as soon as we may and no doubt expects myself and de Gomme to provide the means to crack that nut, but I think it's a project that will need to wait for the summer— and here we are. You were fortunate I was out and about today."

They had turned into the college gates, passing the guard and into the familiar stables. Then all other thoughts were crowded out by the one that mattered the most. Soon he would see Zahara and know if she had missed him as much as he had missed her, know how she fared and if all his thoughts and prayers had somehow touched her. It seemed almost too much to hold in his heart

Dismounting, he reached to remove the bags from his saddle and was startled when Lord took them from him, before recalling that he was the master and Lord the servant and that here of all places that role had to be maintained. It was a needed but unwelcome reminder that whilst they had come to a place of safety, there was still a requirement for wariness and subterfuge.

Danny appeared beside him and clapped a hand on his shoulder.

"You look as if you could do with a drink. Bring your man and we will see what there is. We're crowded now, though Anders managed to find his own rooms in the town by the mysterious alchemy physicians seem to have, but with six of us in the three rooms already it'll be a cosy fit."

"Six?" Gideon did some rapid addition—Zahara, Kate, Shiraz, Danny and Martha, the servant girl they had rescued from a manor house before it was plundered and burned. Then who would be a sixth?

Danny just grinned and led the way up the stairs through the crowded college, often pushing through where there were groups of people talking or making elaborate bows and apologising when the individuals were those of any rank. Gideon followed and behind him, carrying their luggage, his head down, came Philip Lord.

Zahara. Zahara. Her name was the beat of Gideon's heart. It was all he could think now and although Danny was saying something about sleeping arrangements, he didn't hear the words and nodded agreement or understanding or whatever was required.

When they were at the door, Danny knocked. Kate's voice called to them to enter and then the door was open.

Three women sat together, their chairs set by the window. Clad in gowns of varying degrees, they looked to Gideon's eyes like a bouquet of flowers. Kate sat in the middle, her hair in dark red ringlets, wearing a maroon and black satin gown. Then his heart seemed to shift beneath his ribs. Zahara, hair covered but with escaping strands the colour of fresh apricots, dressed in golden russet wool. With them, not Martha whom Gideon had first assumed it must be, but a woman with the sea-water eyes and white hair of Sir Philip Lord, clad in watchet blue silk. For a moment it was a tableau, their faces all turned towards the door, joy and delight rising in each.

"Look what I found cluttering up the streets of Oxford," Danny said brightly. "A malignant pair if ever I saw such."

His words seemed to break a spell. Lord dropped the bags by the door and strode forward, none denying his right to be first. But before he could cross the room Kate rose to her feet and he paused mid-stride. It was Kate who walked to him then, her steps tentative as if uncertain of her own strength. Lord's eyes were fixed on her face as one starved might look upon a banquet.

"Feed apace then greedy eyes,
On the wonder you behold..."

He let her come to him, only opening his arms when she reached him. Then, embracing her, he buried his face in her hair. Gideon had to blink a couple of times. When they had last seen Kate, she had been unable to stir from her bed.

Zahara slipped from behind them, her smile as gentle and warming as the sun on a spring morning. Gideon wished with all his heart he could hold her as Lord held Kate. She took both his hands in her own and gripped them, which was suddenly more than enough.

"I have missed you so very much," she said and at that moment Gideon's heart knew its true homecoming.

Lord stepped back, his arm still encircling Kate and turned to face the third woman in the room who stood, looking a little uncertain.

"Mistress Lavinstock—Christobel if I may? I am going to assume Danny is responsible for your presence, but by whatever means you came and whatever brings you here, you should know you are most welcome, and I am glad to see you again."

Christobel made a graceful curtsy. Gideon looked between the two and knew he wasn't the only one there marvelling at how alike they were. Beside him, he could see Danny grinning as if he had worked it as some magic trick.

"Thank you, Sir Philip." Christobel's voice was strong and of a timbre that reflected Lord's in a feminine tone. "I have been made very welcome by your wife."

"There is a story for you to hear behind Christobel's presence," Kate said. "But you must eat first and Anders will come to see how

THE ALCHEMIST'S PLOT

I fare. He told us how you both redeemed him from false charges in Paris."

Zahara released Gideon's hands with evident reluctance and then, shyly daring, leaned in to kiss his cheek chastely before stepping back. "I will find Martha and arrange for food," she said and left them. Gideon was too stunned to follow, his whole face feeling warm from the touch of her lips.

"Christobel, forgive me, I am being rude to neglect a simple social duty," Lord said, "This is Gideon Lennox, although he is known as Gideon Fox for reasons too complex for me to explain at once. He is a lawyer by profession and my friend by his deeds."

"Not just *your* friend," Danny said and crossed over to Christobel to stand with her. She looked up at him as if she was appraising or assessing his motive. A moment later she smiled, as if satisfied.

"You have the right of it, of course," Lord said. "Gideon, this is Mistress Christobel Lavinstock, who I am confident is a long lost relative, but quite how long and lost I think we are both unsure."

"That is another conversation to be had," Christobel said. "Perhaps if we can share what we know we might find some way to uncover the mystery of it."

"Perhaps so," Lord agreed, then looked thoughtful. "You are not here under any duress?" He glanced at Danny, who bridled.

Christobel looked between the two. "I'm here because I choose to be here," she said. "But also because I have no choice but to be here. Daniel rescued me from being held prisoner by a man who compelled me into marriage. If I were to go my own way, I would fear being returned to him by force." Something in the way she spoke his name made Gideon wonder if she regarded Danny as more than just her rescuer.

Lord looked again at Danny who nodded.

"The delightful Sir Nicholas Tempest."

Lord's expression changed then, becoming cold.

"And he still lives?" The question was aimed at Danny and held accusation.

"I had no idea before he sent me to Howe, and after…" Danny lifted his shoulders. "After it seemed less important than getting

Christobel to a place of safety, and this was the one place I could think of."

"You should have—"

Kate moved in the circle of Lord's arm.

"Philip, Danny did what he could," she said, reaching a finger up to touch his face, and Lord seemed to come to himself. He lowered his head for a moment then looked back to Danny.

"Of course, I know that. I am just—" He shook his head.

Danny gave him a rueful look.

"If you knew how much I wish I had when the chance was in my hands."

"Myself also," Lord said. "I too had the chance and had I acted then, this would not have even transpired. My anger is at myself."

"No," Christobel said, her voice firm, "I wouldn't have anyone become a murderer on my account. There must be legal redress for such a crime." She looked at Gideon, her gaze as disconcerting as that of Sir Philip Lord. "You are a lawyer, sir. It was a lawyer who created this entanglement so surely a lawyer can release me from it?"

Gideon had no idea of the circumstances and so could promise nothing, but this wasn't the time to say that.

"If there is anything that can be done legally, I will gladly undertake the task," he said and was rewarded by a small tight-lipped smile.

"Thank you. I will find a way to pay you for the work."

Lord opened his mouth and Gideon was sure he saw Kate place a slippered foot over his riding boot, at which point he closed his mouth again. It served as sufficient warning for Gideon not to say anything further too and he inclined his head in the way men of his profession did when the unpleasant necessity of payment was mentioned.

At that point, Zahara returned bearing platters of food with the other two members of the household, Martha and Shiraz.

Once the welcomes were done and the food was served, conversation was set aside in favour of eating. For Gideon, the greatest delight was to have Zahara sitting beside him and almost every time he glanced in her direction it was to see she was glancing at him. The ring he had left her was on a chain about her neck. It was a swivel ring, its blazon worn. The one thing Gideon had from his mother and she, from her grandfather. When Zahara saw him looking at it, she slipped the chain over her head and held it out.

"You gave this to me to keep safe until you came back," she said.

Gideon shook his head and closed her hand over it.

"I gave it to you to keep," he said, then found he couldn't hold her gaze.

"You are going away again," she said, "with the Schiavono."

The Schiavono. The name that was almost a title by which Sir Philip Lord was known across Europe as a commander of both mercenaries and corsairs.

"Yes," Gideon said, his heart aching at the thought.

"I have to go to London," Lord said and for a moment Gideon thought he had overheard them, or perhaps his attention had been caught by the ring and he understood the import of Gideon's gesture. But then he realised Lord was speaking to the others. "Gideon will come with me. I will need his skills if I can find what I am looking for. Besides, he knows London well."

"So do I," Danny put in. "I'll come with you too."

"No." Lord was insistent. "It will be dangerous enough for two of us, I have no intention of allowing anyone else to take the risk."

"I rather think that is Danny's choice," Kate said. "If I were restored to full health, I would come with you whether you wished it or not."

Danny lifted his cup in a silent toast to Kate, then he drank and put his cup down. "I won't travel with you if you would prefer that I don't." He sounded indifferent. "But I am heading to London anyway as I have unfinished business with someone there."

Lord frowned at him.

"Mags is in London," Danny said simply.

Gideon would have liked the chance to learn more. Lord had sent Danny to kill Mags, the man responsible for the death of Lord's friend and officer, Matthew Rider, and who had lured to his side many of the fighting men Lord had brought to England. However, before Gideon could ask, Anders arrived and the gathering regained its previous celebratory atmosphere.

It was good to see Anders had put back on most of the weight he had lost whilst enduring imprisonment in Paris for a crime he hadn't committed. He had recovered his old confidence and calm too, reassuring them that he had managed to remove the bullet from Kate, with assistance from Zahara, and the wound was healing well.

"But, as I already explained to Lady Catherine, I cannot promise miracles. There has been damage done. If she can walk again, that might be all God allows and to God's council chamber we have no key."

Kate smiled at him.

"And if that is all God allows, I will still be most grateful to you," she said.

Later, as Anders was leaving, Sir Philip Lord took Gideon, Danny, and Shiraz outside with him. There was nowhere within the crowded college buildings that could offer any privacy, so Lord led them outside.

The air was cold but with the first hints of spring, and around the courtyard could be heard laughter and snatches of conversation. Lord's tone when he spoke was business-like.

"I'm not saying this in front of the women because as far as I am concerned, they are all free agents. Even my wife. They are not in my pay, but all of you are." Shiraz lifted his chin at that, and Lord drew a breath. "All of you except Shiraz are in my pay," he amended. Shiraz inclined his head, satisfied. "But all of you, including Shiraz, are under my command and authority."

"We are also all your friends," Danny said, pointedly.

"I hope so, and I hope that friendship will survive what I am about to say."

That sent a cold shiver through Gideon that he could feel resonating like a rumble of distant thunder through the others as well. He recalled a night when Sir Philip Lord had used words as weapons to try and slice away the bonds of friendship and feared this might be more of the same.

THE ALCHEMIST'S PLOT

"I do not think you could say anything that would change my feelings towards you," Anders observed. "But it troubles me that you feel it might."

"Me too. Besides, I'm used to it. So you may as well just tell us." Danny's voice had an edge to it.

"I intend to go to London on my own and make enquiries there myself."

"You already told us that," Danny observed.

"You miss my point then. I said 'myself.' I do not intend to take anyone else with me."

There was a cold, shocked silence in the wake of his words.

"But you already admitted you need my expertise," Gideon objected. "If you find the documents you seek, you will need them authenticated."

"And I already told you I am going to London for other reasons," Danny said. "It makes no difference to me whether you are going or not. I have my own work there."

Shiraz was shaking his head, his hands moving in the gloom.

Lord lifted a hand at the protest.

"This is not something that is up for discussion. I have decided. Danny—if Mags is in London, I will deal with him. And Gideon—should I, as I expect, find anything that requires your expertise I shall bring it back here to Oxford for you to study. You do not need to be in London for that."

"What has brought this change of heart?" Danny demanded, his tone heated.

"You will be needed here to take on the oversight of the company. On a temporary basis, I hope, but permanently if I should not come back. There is no one else I can trust. Argall and Roger are both good men, but they are not of the calibre required to manage and command the entire company and all its assets." Danny tried to speak but Lord snapped at him. "And that is not a request, that is an order, Lieutenant Colonel Bristow. Gideon, you will aid Danny as he might require and continue assisting Kate in her intelligencer's work, whilst also trying what you may to help Christobel in freeing herself from her marriage."

Gideon was torn between feeling pushed aside and diminished and yet in some measure delighting in the realisation that this meant he would be able to stay with Zahara. Danny was fuming and drew a breath, but it was Anders who spoke first.

"I do not see what this has to do with me. I have never had any intention of going to London. My work for you is here."

"That is true," Lord agreed. "Shiraz also, his task is to ensure the safety of the women here. But you are in my employ and as such, in my absence, I am intending part of the burden of the administration of the company will fall on your shoulders. I'm confirming you in rank as major, so you can assist Danny as he needs."

Anders was frowning but gave a reluctant nod.

"After all you have done for me, sir, it is the least I can do in return."

Shiraz made some urgent hand movements and when he finished Lord sighed.

"Thank you, Shiraz," he said, his tone making it clear he was far from grateful for the intervention. "Whilst I appreciate your concern for my safety, I can assure you I have no more need of nursemaids having left petticoats and their strings behind me many years since." Gideon heard Danny suck air in through his teeth.

Then Lord let out a breath in a long sigh.

"It's late and we are all tired. I will hear your objections tomorrow. I'm not going anywhere for a few days. I want to spend some time with Kate first. Anyone who thinks they have a valid contribution to make will be able to do so. You know I always listen to my officers—and more so to my friends."

He made a brief bow, raising his voice with a servant's intonation.

"Goodnight, sirs."

Then he turned sharply as if he found their company too difficult to endure and was gone.

THE ALCHEMIST'S PLOT

Chapter Four

Danny exploded first. "Of all the high-handed, stubborn, overbearing, pompous—" He closed his mouth as if unwilling to let more words escape.

"But it is as he says," Anders pointed out. "He is the one in command and we have all trusted his will and judgement up to this point. As a physician, I can assure you I see no trace of any sudden weakness of the mind. If anything, the opposite. I believe he has very good reasons for this, even if he is not sharing them. I would remind you that every person is a fool in somebody's opinion."

"Oh, none of us would challenge his mental acuity," Danny said. "Just his overweening arrogance. We all know why he's doing this. It's because only Sir Philip bloody Lord is allowed to risk himself in this venture. He's decided it's too dangerous for the rest of us."

Shiraz made a gesture which needed no translation.

"One thing is plain, there is nothing more to be done tonight," Gideon said, suddenly weary. He'd been in the saddle for too many days and that, together with the emotional impact of being reunited with Zahara, had taken its toll.

"Indeed so," Anders agreed. "I need to get back to my lodgings and Shiraz has kindly said he will escort me. Oxford has become a dangerous place after dark."

Danny bade them goodnight and stalked indoors still in high dudgeon, leaving Gideon to make his own farewells.

Anders explained he was staying in the house of a fellow physician and promised to return the following morning to see Kate. "Though in truth, there is little I need to do for her now. Zahara is managing what can be done to ensure the healing, and God and Lady Catherine's strength sees to the rest. But it will be good to talk to you again, my friend." He gripped Gideon's shoulder as they said goodnight, then he walked off with Shiraz.

Gideon watched them go before retracing his steps into the college buildings. Accommodation was limited in the three rooms set aside for Lady Catherine and Sir Philip Lord. Gideon wasn't at all surprised Anders had sought his own rooms.

Kate had been sharing her bed in Lord's absence with Zahara. Christobel had been in one of the other two rooms with the maid Martha and, with Lord's return, Zahara had moved to join them. Danny and Shiraz occupied the only other room and that was where Gideon was to sleep.

He entered the suite of rooms in some trepidation because the mood Danny was in, it wouldn't have surprised Gideon to find he had continued the argument with Lord. But if he had wanted to do so he would have been disappointed. The curtains around the Lord's bedstead had been pulled closed giving Lord and Kate such privacy as they might have in what was the most public of the three rooms, being the one with access to the outside world. Gideon didn't linger and crossed to the door of the room he was sharing.

Danny was sitting on the side of the bed pulling his stockings off when Gideon entered the room. As well as the tester bed he recognised, a new bed stood by the far wall that hadn't been there when he'd left for France.

"Kate bought it for Shiraz," Danny explained. "We get to share."

Danny was a man who struggled with sleep so that wasn't the best news.

"A bed is a bed," Gideon said, stoically.

"And now you know why we all adore Philip," Danny said. "His temperate, obliging and collegiate manner sets him apart from the conceits and imperiousness one expects to find in a military commander."

"He did say he would listen to us tomorrow," Gideon pointed out.

Danny shook his head. "He did, didn't he?"

Gideon said nothing and got undressed to his nightshirt and quickly into the bed as he had no wish to be inveigled into a game of cards. But for once Danny seemed as keen to sleep as Gideon himself because he too climbed into bed and extinguished the candle. Gideon said his prayers in the dark, as always, focused on Zahara. He wondered if she prayed to her god for his welfare as much as he prayed to his own for hers, then realised that in her view they prayed to the same God but in different ways and somehow that felt right.

Comforted by the thought, sleep came swiftly, even before Shiraz returned from escorting Anders. Instead, he was woken from a dream in which he was running away from something unseen and shadowy. A hand gripped his shoulder.

"We need to go," Danny said, sounding impatient. He was dressed already. "Don't make me wait long. I was for going without you, but Kate insisted."

"Insisted? On what?" Gideon struggled to sit up and shook his head to clear it. "Where are we going?" He reached for his clothes as he asked. Shiraz was absent from his bed.

"London, I suspect."

"But I thought…"

Danny sighed and handed him a new pair of stockings.

"His imperiousness, Sir Philip Lord decided to take leave of his wife and his friends in the middle of the night. I can't say it is entirely surprising, although I misjudged. I expected it'd be tomorrow night, not this one. I assumed after so long an absence he would have wanted to spend at least a day with Kate. My mistake. But then that was no doubt what he was counting on—that we would all think that."

Gideon did battle with his points, hooks and eyelets, then wondered if he was over or underdressed for the task ahead. He had somehow imagined when they were to go to London it would be in a planned and orderly way with such things well thought out.

"Are you sure this is wise?" he asked, slipping the baldrick holding his sword over his coat.

"Of course, it isn't wise," Danny protested. "How can it be? But it's less wise to allow Philip to go alone to London."

That was when it hit home to Gideon what Lord was doing and suddenly the urgency was upon him too. A few minutes later he was in Kate's room where she was standing barefoot, clad in no more than her night shift and manteau. Reading a letter by the light of a candle because the thin dawn rays were still much too weak for such a purpose.

"Listen to this," she said as Gideon and Danny entered the room. *"My dearest love, forgive me—I have too grieved a heart to take a tedious leave—I would give anything to be able to stay with you now and face no more than the hazards of war, which we both know well. But this matter is that which strikes at the root of all I am and until that is resolved in some manner, I cannot be free to even know if I am the man I believe I am or that you believe me to be..."* She threw the sheet down. "As if I care—as if any of us care who his forebears might be. As if his parentage changes him in any way that matters at all. As if—"

Zahara came in then, similarly clad to Kate, her hair loose like a wave of soft apricot gold about her shoulders. She crossed to Kate and put an arm about her, drawing her to sit down.

"You know it is not just that," Danny said. "He's after getting the yoke of it all from his neck. And I've seen some of it now. I've seen how far and deep it runs." There was a bitter note to his voice that sounded bleak. "And that's why I know he can't do this alone."

"You think he can be freed from it?" Kate asked, her face haunted.

"I don't know," Danny said. "But I do know if he is to stand any chance of doing so, he needs help. You did right to wake me."

She would have stood again, but Zahara's hands were set on her shoulders and Danny must have seen her intent because he crossed to her and dropped on one knee, taking her hands in his like a knight making an oath before the statue of a saint.

"I promise I will find him and do my best to bring him back. Or failing that, I'll aid him in what he is insisting on doing."

Kate managed a smile.

"You are a good man, Danny and a good friend." Then as he stood, she held out a hand towards Gideon and he moved to take it. "And you are a good man and a good friend too. Philip is blessed to have you both—I am blessed to have you both."

Zahara stepped forward and with a naturalness that took Gideon off guard, embraced him briefly, her body separated from him only by thin linen, then before he could respond in any way she had slipped away and back to Kate.

THE ALCHEMIST'S PLOT

"Shiraz will have the horses ready," she said.

Danny made a bow to Kate. "Please tell Christobel..." He seemed uncertain how to finish and shook his head instead.

"She will understand," Kate assured him. "She is more like Philip than I think either of them quite yet realises." Then, "Gideon, there is a purse of coins in the desk. Can you take it, please? You will need money for your journey."

Kate held up a hand to forestall any protest and Gideon, who had scarcely a penny to his name at that point, found the purse and stowed it safely.

They left. For once the college halls and stairs were empty apart from some early rising servants who stepped aside to let them pass. Shiraz was waiting with two horses. One was the dun Danny had been riding the day before, the other was an old friend, the bay Gideon had inherited from him.

Before they left Shiraz made some of his rapid hand gestures and Danny nodded.

"I will," he said. "You can be sure of that. Look after the women."

Then they were riding from the college and through Oxford, heading south for the London road. No one questioned their leaving although it no doubt helped that Danny knew both the gate guard and the word of the day. They received the reassurance of being told that a messenger bearing the signature of Sir Philip Lord had indeed already left. As the sun had lifted its face over the horizon, they were covering the ground at a canter.

"He has at least an hour on us if the men at the gate were correct," Danny said when they slowed to let the horses rest. "He told Kate that he was up early as he needed to write some urgent messages so he could then rest for the day, and she believed him and slept. When she woke again, he was gone."

"Can we catch him?"

"If he is set on avoiding us, I would doubt it," Danny said grimly. "So we will have to hope not."

A memory stirred in Gideon's mind.

"I may know where he is going—or at least one place he will go. A place he mentioned would be connected with these enemies who seek him."

Danny looked at him sharply.

"You know something of the Covenant?"

Gideon nodded, surprised. "Sir Philip seemed to think you didn't."

The sun had come up to make the day one of the gems of new springtide, fresh and bright, with the sense of newness sparkling like the dew on the grass. It was unseasonably warm riding in the sunlight and Danny pulled off his hat to wipe at his brow and ruffle his hair before restoring it again.

"I met two gentlemen who serve it. It was the only reason I stayed with Sir Nicholas Tempest. I knew whatever it was, it posed a bigger danger to Philip than Mags. Although he too has been sucked into the very bosom of the Covenant. It is information Philip needs, but he gave me no chance to share it."

Sir Nicholas Tempest was the nephew of Sir Bartholomew Coupland and the man who had inherited his Howe Hall estate and baronetcy. It was news to Gideon that Danny had been with Tempest and not with Mags.

"So where do you think we should look if we can't catch him on the road?" Danny asked.

"He'll be looking for proof of his heritage." Gideon said with certainty. "He thought they might be in a house in Mortlake."

"The only place of note I know of in Mortlake is the tapestry works," Danny said. "They were set up in the house once owned by the mathematician John Dee. He died... when...?" Danny screwed up his face in concentration, freckles wrinkling. "He must have died around the time Philip was born." Danny groaned. "Come on, we must try and get to him before he reaches London."

Gideon set his bay to match the speed of Danny's mount and they took the road towards the capital. The first part of the journey was still in lands controlled by the king, but the closer they got towards London the more disputed the territory became. Gideon realised that they would need to sleep in a place under the control of Parliament that night and then head into London itself the next day.

Soon after midday, as they were approaching a wayside inn, Danny cursed loudly and then laughed. Following his, gaze Gideon saw a man sitting at a table outside the inn, a jug of ale or wine before him. He had nut brown hair, and was clad as a professional man, with a paunch such as one of his sort might often develop over the years, from too much time sitting at a desk. He had a smart broad brimmed hat sheltering his eyes from the sun as he watched the road. Had Danny not remarked him, Gideon would never have realised who it was.

Sir Philip Lord.

A short time later they joined him at his table.

"Since you have to be here, I am glad it is both of you," he said by way of greeting and then looked at Gideon. "I did wonder if Danny would bring you."

"I wasn't going to," Danny admitted, scratching at his beard.

"Kate?" Lord hazarded.

Danny nodded.

Gideon fought back the curl of anger that was tightening his chest.

"If you wanted us with you, why did you just ride out?" he demanded, aware of the need to keep his voice low so as not to attract attention. "You could have waited. Kate was—"

"I do not want you with me and didn't intend to wait for you," Lord said, tone cutting. "I would much prefer to go alone as I planned. But having set out, the more I considered the matter, the less chance I knew there was that my orders would stand. Danny, I knew, was going to come after me whether I wanted it or not, even if in clear contradiction to my specific orders. That being so it is safer that we travel and act together rather than risk drawing danger upon ourselves and each other by pursuing things separately and perhaps at cross purposes. In other words, since you will not leave me, I am forced to accept your company whether I wish for it or no." He looked at Danny, his expression cold. "I trust you already have an alternative employer in mind because, after this act of mutiny, you are no longer on the payroll of the company. If I give a direct order, I expect it to be obeyed. You know that."

That fuelled Gideon's anger afresh.

"How can you—?"

"I don't hold you responsible," Lord said, his gaze switching to Gideon. "You would have been obeying the orders of others anyway. But Danny has no excuse— and I hope you both like pigeon pie because I asked for enough for three." He said the last as a serving boy came over with the promised food and extra cups.

Danny looked unabashed and when they were alone again, helped himself to both food and drink.

"If you are set on turning me off, Kate has said she will take me on," he said, his tone placid. "She needs someone to do odd jobs now she is unable to ride about the countryside. Or of course, I could carry on with the prince. He would love to have me as well as de Gomme. He's said so a few times. So don't worry, I'll not starve."

"I had no reason to think you would," Lord said. "However, I am interested in who you intended should run the company if neither of us returns from London?"

Danny stabbed a knife into the pie.

"Christobel could always dress up in breeches and pass herself off as you," he said. "She and Kate between them would do a better job than we have been."

Gideon gasped at the audacity and came close to choking on his mouthful of ale. Lord, by complete contrast, started laughing, almost doubled over on the table with mirth.

"By God, Danny, only you could suggest..." He eventually managed to suppress his laughter and took a swallow of ale so he could talk. "Alright, you win. You may keep your job. Providing we both get back from London alive."

Danny grinned back at him and lifted his cup in a silent toast. Gideon felt excluded from something between them, an acute awareness of the brotherhood of the blade which had a depth that must surely always override any other form of friendship.

"We need to find somewhere we can talk openly," he said, needing to feel he still had a role to play. "I think if we are to be effective, we all have to have some clear notion of what we are seeking to achieve in London." Then sensing a hesitation in Lord, he added in a low voice, "Danny tells me he knows of the Covenant from encountering it."

Lord shot a quick glance at Danny whose expression confirmed the truth of Gideon's words.

"You didn't think I stayed with Sir Nicholas Tempest because of his youthful charm, surely? I was cleaving as close as I could to the little turd because he was dragged into some issues with two men who claimed to represent an organisation that could make my life very good or very short, depending on my choices. Men who introduced themselves to me as Gabriel and Michael, and who I worked out had you as their focus. So, I stuck around to try and learn more."

Lord's eyes narrowed. "You didn't say anything of this in your messages."

"Ciphers can be broken—even ours. We know at least one of my letters to you was lost; I wasn't willing to take the risk."

"You could have told me yesterday."

"Between supper and bed? Strangely enough," Danny said, "I thought I would have an opportunity to tell you today. For all that this matters, other things do too. I had no wish to spoil your reunion with Kate."

Danny's mild gaze held Lord's ice crisp one. To Gideon's surprise it was Lord who looked away first.

"I am chastised," he said, spreading his hands in defeat. "Humbled to my knees. I hope that makes you both very happy."

"It does," Danny said, stabbing at the food on his plate. "But it's Kate who you will need to go to on humbled knees after this."

That sobered Lord, who had the grace to look peccant.

"I would be happier yet," Danny went on, "If I knew your plans for when we reach London. Gideon said something about Mortlake."

Lord glanced at Gideon, but a bit to Gideon's surprise there was no censure in the look. "You remembered? I have to say I wasn't sure you would—or even how seriously you took my ramblings at that point."

"After what we saw in Howe, what you said made too much sense," Gideon admitted. "I will confess I still don't know if it is true, but I am very sure now, as you said at the time, that there are men who do believe it to be so."

"Believe what?" Danny asked.

Lord lowered his head and drew a deep breath. "This is not a conversation for here and now, although I agree it is one we must have soon. Let's eat and when you are finished, we should be on our way. Two gentlemen at law returning to London with our servant. You will need to lose the more obvious military trappings Danny, but that aside you are the only man I know who could go about dressed in taffeta and velvet and yet still seem the servant."

"I don't wear taffeta and velvet," Danny said. "Apart from anything else, once you have seen and handled the finest and the best, everything else seems as the cheapest wool frieze by comparison, so it makes no difference what to wear."

"Spoken like a true draper's son," Lord said,

"Mercer's son, if you please. We always marked the difference by the degree of warehousing involved. Although my father liked to say that a draper was to a mercer what a kersey was to a broadcloth."

"From mercer to mercenary, it has a poetry to it too," Lord confided. *"The braver they are, the sooner are mercers undone."*

"I think that's the mercenaries," Danny said dryly.

The conversation continued in a like vein as they finished the meal, and it was only when they were again on the road that Lord seemed inclined to consider anything more serious. They rode fast to begin, then slowed to rest the horses. Riding three abreast on the road, Lord in the middle opened the conversation.

"I would know of your encounter with the Covenant," he told Danny. "Before that, I would know how it is you came by Christobel. The last time I saw her she was the mistress of her own holding in Durham, although playing unwilling hostess to Sir Nicholas Tempest and his company of horse. She freed me from her cellar where he had me locked. We had no chance to converse. I had planned to visit her when I was able, but circumstances didn't turn out in a way to allow that."

THE ALCHEMIST'S PLOT

"You didn't mention her." It was Danny who spoke, but Gideon would have said the words if he had not.

"No, I didn't," Lord agreed but gave no explanation. "You rescued her from a forced marriage to Sir Nicholas. Did he force her in other ways?"

The casual way he asked the question made Gideon's stomach clench. Danny shook his head, his expression closed as if he was sitting on a powerful emotion.

"I didn't tell her—and wouldn't have her know it—but I think that is why he wanted her in York. He had been to see his father, Sir Richard, and came back to order me to go and fetch her. My impression was that he was under some pressure to do so. I don't think he cared for her much one way or another at all. This was all the will of the Covenant." Danny broke off and shook his head. "It is an evil thing. I felt the cold breath of it on the back of my neck enough to know that. And even men like Tempest are victims of it."

Lord looked at him. "You are not going to tell me you feel some sympathy for Tempest?"

Danny shrugged. "Sympathy, no. But there were moments when I could see the shape of a half-way decent human being in Sir Nicholas struggling to break free. He saved my life a couple of times, set against the many I had to act to preserve his. Then each time I thought I'd got through, thought I'd maybe managed to reach him, he'd do or say something, and I realised it was just a flash in the pan. But would he be the man he is if the Covenant hadn't twisted and warped him to fit its purposes?"

"Regardless, he *is* the man that he is," Lord said, his tone unforgiving. "It is in the nature of his kin." He drew a breath. "You saved Christobel from a fate worse than death—"

"I saved her from death," Danny said, his tone bitter. "She was set on it and had to be watched all day and night at Howe to keep herself from it. That morning when I arrived, she had managed to find a knife and bestow it under her bed." He stopped and it was clear he found what he was saying difficult. "She admitted to me that she planned to use it in the dark to escape her fate. If I hadn't come to Howe that day..." He suddenly seemed to find it too hard to go on.

That made Gideon draw a breath of shock. There could be few sins more terrible than taking your own life before the time God had allotted. It was a horrific thought and he struggled to see in Christobel as she had been in Oxford any trace of the kind of self-hating spirit that must be required to lead to such an evil act. Surely Danny was mistaken?

Lord just shook his head as if hearing of a great sadness, his eyes on the road ahead. "For that, you have my gratitude. She may well be my only living relative. I am hopeful our sojourn in London will discover if that is so. Then you will be able to take the answers back to her as well and, gentlemen," he went on, tone sharper than before. "Have a care."

Emotions still reeling, Gideon followed Lord's gaze. Approaching them was a large body of cavalry, either a full company or the best part of one.

"Friend or foe?" Lord mused.

Danny was frowning, eyes squinting from under the brim of his hat. "My guess from where we are is that it has to be 'foe'. But either way, we would be wise to be off the road and out of their way."

It was something Gideon and Lord had done a dozen times or more on the way from Bridlington to Oxford, and the three pushed their horses into the fringe of trees that stood on one side of the road, offering a degree of concealment as much as allowing the oncoming cavalry full use of the road.

But that wasn't enough this time.

They had been seen and, for some reason Gideon was unable to fathom, their decision to move from the road was taken as something suspicious because horses were set into the trees from further down the road as well as breaking into a canter to reach them.

"We stand, gentlemen," Lord said quietly. "For now."

Gideon wondered how they could change their minds after the event. Once surrounded, they would be at the mercy of these troops, whoever they might be. But he could see that if they tried

THE ALCHEMIST'S PLOT

running it would lead to the same end. At least this way they might have some chance of talking their way out of it.

Lord had straightened in his saddle and adopted the look of a man much put upon. Danny managed to convey the appearance of someone made uncomfortable by the intimidating presence of armed men. Gideon decided his own unfeigned demeanour of nervous wariness was the best to maintain.

"Hold," Lord shouted as the soldiers closed about them. "There is no need for such importuning rudeness. Who is your officer?"

Gideon felt his stomach shrivel at the imperious tone. Surely these men would take it amiss to be spoken to so dismissively?

"That would be me."

The horses about them stepped aside to allow the speaker to approach. He was well dressed and well mounted, no more than Gideon's age and he eyed the three with some curiosity.

"Who might you be, sir?" Lord was the epitome of an outraged English gentleman. "How dare you detain us thus?"

The other man's jaw tightened, and Gideon was sure Lord had misjudged.

"I think, sir, you are the one who should identify yourself. Running from my men was not a wise move."

"Running from your...?" Lord made a noise that managed to embrace both incredulity and indignation. "We were not *running*, sir. If we had, you can be assured we would have been across the fields and away long since. We gave you the courtesy of leaving the road so you and your soldiers could pass."

That put a chink of doubt in the officer's expression, but it was a chink that he covered. "Your name, sir? My patience is not limitless."

Lord bristled

"Neither is mine. I am Theophilus Bassington and if you have any knowledge of such matters, you will know that I have been assisting in facilitating the negotiations with Charles Stuart to bring an end to these wars so you and your soldiers can all go home again."

"You can prove that?"

"Good grief, sir. Do you expect me to carry state papers in my saddlebags?" Lord made a disparaging gesture flicking a fisted hand towards the bags he mentioned. "I am returning to London upon an urgent family matter, and I didn't think I would need to carry personal proofs with me. Not even the enemy have required such or doubted me. It is beyond belief that I should have to undergo such an interrogation from... from...?"

"Major Paston Appletree and I do require some proof since you were attempting to evade my men."

Gideon blinked. It was a distinctive name, not a common one, and he had done some work once for a man of that name, but that had been an older man by far. Lord lifted his chin and in response, Danny moved one hand towards his coat as if to scratch an itch. Gideon had a very bad feeling about what might be coming and spoke quickly.

"Major, forgive me, I believe I know your father, Sir Paston Appletree. I did some work for him two years ago, a question of a dispute over land ownership, an estate near Winchelsea."

The officer shifted his gaze to Gideon, who was relieved to see Danny's hand had stopped reaching into his coat.

Gideon went on quickly. "I doubt many would know the deeds had been left behind in Calais when your great-grandfather was a resident there."

"You speak of my late uncle," the major said. "I was named for him." The tension had begun to evaporate. "What is your name?"

"I'm Gideon Lennox." It was very strange to be using his name again. He had become used to being Gideon Fox, the nom-de-guerre Lord's men had given him. "This is indeed Theophilus Bassington. We are travelling together."

"Lennox? That was the name on the documents when we received them."

The major seemed much less certain now and Gideon pressed his advantage.

"Sir Paston, you have been assiduous in your vigilance, and I understand our gesture of politeness could be taken as a deliberate retreat to avoid attention. But had we indeed been intent on such

THE ALCHEMIST'S PLOT

we wouldn't have waited here by the road for you and your men to pass."

"You are too generous to the man," Lord snapped. "It is clear to the dullest mind we are honest men and no threat and yet he treats us as if we were infiltrators and malignants. I shall report this to the committee, and they will take it to the house."

Appletree swallowed hard and made a curt gesture to his men. "Release them, they are free to go."

"So we can be stopped on the road by the next bunch of cut-throats in uniform?" Lord demanded. Gideon stared at him in disbelief. They had the good fortune to be able to turn the tide in their favour, why keep on?

The Major sucked in his breath and made a small, very stiff bow in the saddle.

"You need not concern yourself. I shall send an escort with you to ensure such a thing does not happen again."

Which was why they arrived in Westminster the next day unmolested, having been able to pass without question through the outer defences of London.

Chapter Five

"No one, but no one has Theophilus as the first name they think of," Danny protested. "Thomas or William, I could grant you, but Theophilus?"

They were sitting in a private room in The Bell, an inn on King's Street in Westminster. It was one of the older inns in the city, having been there for over a hundred and fifty years and sat on the fame of antiquity to an extent that Gideon thought still didn't justify its prices. But then he wasn't the one paying.

"It was the first name that *I* thought of," Lord insisted.

Danny laughed. "Let's be glad you didn't light upon Endymion or Bulstrode." Then the amusement faded from his face. "I know that talking of less agreeable matters is bad for digestion, but it's getting late, and we should have in mind what we need to do tomorrow."

Lord took a drink of the rather fine Rhenish wine they had been served.

"First," he said, "we need to ensure we are all aware of what we are here for and share what we know."

For all having an escort had speeded and smoothed their passage to the capital, it had also meant they had been denied the necessary privacy needed to discuss their affairs. Here they had that. Gideon doubted they would be the first—or the last—conspirators to sit in this very room and talk of secret matters.

Conspirators.

It was an ugly word.

Were they that?

He felt a tightening of his throat at the thought, then reminded himself that far from being conspirators themselves they were there to unravel a conspiracy.

"You should tell me what you know of the Covenant," Lord said, his gaze on Danny, who sighed and sat back.

"It's not much in the telling. I went with Sir Nicholas to his father's house near Durham. We met two gentlemen there who

THE ALCHEMIST'S PLOT

gave me no names, but Sir Nicholas seemed to think they were called Gabriel and Michael. They interrogated me thoroughly on my knowledge and relationship with you. I, of course, stuck with the line that we had fallen out and they seemed content to accept that. Then later they summoned me and told me that I was to stay with Sir Nicholas and ensure he did what they asked of him and protect him with my own life if need be. They were very interested in Mags, and they were also keen to tell me that if I could secure you, I would be rich beyond the dreams of most. They also made it plain that if I chose not to walk their path, they had a long reach in every corner of the kingdom and most abroad as well. If I had been the kind to be intimidated, they would have done a good job of it."

"Who were these men?"

Danny looked thoughtful. "I could draw sketches of them if you wanted, but they never gave me their proper names."

"Please do, it might be they are familiar to one of us and it would be good to know the faces of our enemies." Lord's lips tightened. "But you have more?"

"I do," Danny agreed. "They gave a message in code to Tempest. The seal on it was Dee's odd symbol, the *Monas Hieroglyphica*. No need to look at me like that! I've read some of his works, he shared my passion for mathematics and ciphers. Anyway, the message was supposed to be something for Tempest to pass on to Mags. But it was set as a test, for me or Tempest or the both of us. It was written in a dense cipher and the writer seemed to think Mags would know him. Signed himself 'Michael' so I assume was one of the two who spoke to me, but I also think that wasn't his true name."

"Michael?" Lord said the name reflectively. "The Covenant was always governed by five men. Four had titles which were the names of the archangels—Michael, Raphael, Oriel and Gabriel— each with a specific function. Oriel was the treasurer, Raphael was the archivist, Michael was in charge of the armed force and Gabriel, of those who served as informers or spies. Above them was the one who held command over the whole Covenant. Had I kept to their plans, that would be me today."

Danny was staring at Lord with an odd look on his face, almost as if he was seeing the man he knew well for the first time. "Perhaps it is your turn to tell me what you know."

For a moment Gideon thought Lord would refuse, but then something in his expression changed and he shook his head.

"You are right. You need to know. I'm sure you suspect much already."

And so it came out, the tale Gideon already knew scraped back to its skeleton. The plan the Covenant had to establish an empire of a reunited Christendom under the rule of one whose bloodline would have a claim to most of Europe. How the conspirators had taken the secretly born and deformed child of Queen Mary and Philip of Spain and harvested its precious Tudor and Hapsburg blood into a pedigree line of which Sir Philip Lord was the final legitimate heir. It took little time to tell for the magnitude of its impact.

At the end Danny shook his head and laughed, leaving Gideon with the impression that he had long suspected there was something extreme in Lord's past even if he hadn't known the details.

"Good God, Philip, I always knew you were a right royal bastard, but I never thought it might truly be so."

"The problem being," Lord said, "these people believe I am not a bastard at all—except in the metaphorical sense where I doubt they would differ with your assessment of my nature."

"And Christobel?" There was a sudden tension in the atmosphere at Danny's question.

Lord spread his hands. "I know as much as you."

Danny stared at Lord hard for a moment then nodded. "When you find out the truth we will know then."

Lord inclined his head in assent and Gideon had the feeling some kind of bargain had been struck between the two.

"That would explain why Michael was keen to secure the allegiance of myself and Mags," Danny went on, "They have succeeded in that last, by the way. They found his price."

Lord's brow creased in a frown. "You had better tell me."

THE ALCHEMIST'S PLOT

Danny sighed. "It's not pretty to tell. The Covenant has thrown in its lot with Parliament. They promised to confirm Mags as Baronet of Howe. I think that's why Tempest was after Christobel. Producing a child—an heir to their insane conspiracy—that is the only card he had left to play." Danny pointed a finger across the table. "They want her or you. Without either their entire game of thrones is no more than a charlatan's sideshow of thimblerig, with nothing at all under any of the thimbles."

"It is nice to feel so wanted." Lord took another drink of his wine.

Gideon had listened carefully, sure that he was missing something important.

"But if they side with Parliament, I don't see how the Covenant can hope to engage them with the notion of reuniting the Christian world. Right now, there seem to be enough issues just keeping the Presbyterians in line with the Independents."

"If the matter of religion is still high on the Covenant's agenda I would be surprised," Lord said. "The notion of replacing the current king with a new ruler, however, thus securing their power, that would make more sense to me as a realistic goal."

"And that means they have to look to the Parliamentarian faction," Danny pointed out. "The other lot have the place of a king already filled, complete with an heir and a spare." He tilted his head to one side and looked hard at Lord. "Have you thought this through? Are you sure you don't want to take up their offer? You'd not be as bad a king as most."

His words stole the breath from Gideon's lungs, and he had to gasp in more air. And yet it was the same impulse he had when they were in Yorkshire. Was it that unthinkable?

Lord said nothing for a moment, then placed his cup down with care on the table and refilled it. *"The devil taketh him up into an exceeding high mountain, and sheweth him all the kingdoms of the world, and the glory of them...* Am I tempted?" He smiled and lifted the cup to his lips. *"Give me a staff of honor for mine age, but not a sceptre to control the world."* Then he drank the cup off and put it down again. "If that was a test, do I pass?"

Danny shrugged. "It was just a thought."

Gideon released a breath he hadn't realised he had been holding. Until this moment he had not been sure that some part of Sir Philip Lord wasn't set on the shining prize of England's crown as Mags had once suggested. Few would have blamed him if he had been. Lesser men had tried to seize it with far less legitimacy and Danny was right, whatever his faults Lord would be a better king than many if he chose to rule.

"But why not?" The question asked itself before Gideon could prevent it.

Lord looked at him steadily.

"If I thought you asked that to suggest I should reconsider I would be troubled," he said. Then he sighed. "It is perhaps not so easy to explain. You must realise I was raised to be a king—an emperor even—and so perhaps I have more insight than most into what it would mean. I know enough of kingship, have seen enough of it, to know what I would be forced to become. I would not wish that for myself, or for the world or for my friends."

In the silence that followed Gideon recalled the darkness he had witnessed in Sir Philip Lord, the cold and ruthless brutality of which he could be so capable—and then Gideon thought he understood.

"If we have moved that counter from the gaming table," Lord said, refilling his cup, "perhaps we can see what remains."

"If you have no interest in being king, what does it matter who you are descended from?" Danny asked. "Why put yourself—put all of us—in hazard to find these proofs?"

Which was a good question.

Lord didn't answer at once, sitting with the cup between his hands and staring into it.

"If only it were that simple," he said at last. "Yes, the proofs will tell me who I am and that is something I feel a need to know. Like any man, I would know my parentage. But more importantly, this is the best way to draw the claws from the Covenant. It would remove the sword of Damocles they hold above me, shatter their conspiracy once and for all and place my destiny in my own hands." He looked at Danny. "It will make us all safer, especially

THE ALCHEMIST'S PLOT

Christobel who at the moment seems to be as much their target now as I am and less able to defend herself by far."

Danny lowered his eyes and gave a brief nod, accepting with reluctance what Lord said.

"And what of the treason charge?" Gideon asked. "Now you are pardoned, does it still matter? That is unrelated to this with the Covenant."

Lord's gaze switched to him.

"Is it?"

Gideon struggled to see how the two could be connected.

"How can it not be? You said yourself that the charges ambushed the Covenant as much as they did you."

Lord put his cup down on the table.

"Were I to somehow uncover the existence of a conspiracy going on in the highest of circles," he said, "I might think that to remove the lynchpin of it in a manner that would ensure it could never be replaced would be the best way to destroy it. By sullying that which lay at the heart of the conspiracy and thus discrediting the whole, I might hope to deal with it once and for all. Which is what transpired."

His words were met with silence.

"But who?" Danny asked.

"A man who wished to gain more influence with the then royal favourite and had no taste for a Spanish match for the English Prince Charles, had the knowledge and skill to manufacture a case, and reason to know what he was spoiling for the Covenant at the same time."

"That narrows the field," Danny said. Then his expression changed. "You already know, don't you?"

Gideon had been thinking hard.

"Bacon or Coke," he said. "It would need to be someone of their standing, and both would have had cause to seek favour with Buckingham at that time. Sir Francis Bacon had been thrust from power and knew he couldn't redeem himself and Sir Edward Coke was…" He looked at Lord, suddenly certain. "It was Coke, wasn't it?"

"Yes. I believe so," Lord said. "Bacon was aligned with the Covenant."

Gideon shook his head.

"Bacon? I don't see how...? He was well known as being the mentor and creature of Buckingham."

"Lord Verulam was a student of Machiavelli," Lord said. "He was keen to protect his own interests and material prosperity so would feather his nest with the plumes from many birds. But he was committed to the Covenant long before George Villiers was even born. Bacon was one of the men I was educated by so I can say that with some confidence. He wrote his work *The New Atlantis* for my edification and never intended it to be published. I think he hoped to shape my malleable young mind to his ideas on science so that when I came to power, he could be as the Father of Salomon's House. Although I am not sure he was ever in the Covenant's inner circle. On the other hand, Edward Coke, to the best of my knowledge, opposed it and all it stood for just as he opposed Bacon and all his works. He must have been pleased to see me tainted and discredited and at the same time be able to gain himself a little more hold on Buckingham."

"But if he knew of the Covenant, he would have exposed it." Gideon was struggling with the idea of Sir Francis Bacon, a man whose writings he admired, being implicated in any way in the darkness he perceived emanating from everything to do with the Covenant.

"If he had any evidence, I am sure he would. But knowing of something and being able to prove it is, as our present plight demonstrates, a very different matter. But being allowed to act to destroy something he saw as heinous, why would he not do so?"

"Then he would' have kept the documents relating to such deeds very secret or destroyed them."

"I am sure so," Lord agreed. "He wasn't a foolish man. But two days before he died, when he was bedridden and in no place to protest, the then Secretary of State arrived and removed every document from his house on orders of the Privy Council."

"You should tell it all," Danny said, filling his cup, and then lifting it to Gideon. "When you know him better you'll be able to spot when he is stringing out a tale as if in ignorance to test your knowledge of it."

Lord laughed. "The Secretary of State at that time was a gentleman called Sir Francis Windebank and he is presently in exile in Paris."

Gideon blinked.

"Then—"

"Yes. I did," Lord said, holding up a hand to stifle Gideon's words before he could voice them. "Whilst you were pretending to be a water-seller and balancing your bucket and hoops. Amongst others present when I was playing tennis was Sir Francis Windebank. He told me that as far as he knew the papers he took from Coke's house were unsorted, thrown into a box, and left in the Paper Office. I am sure he exaggerates, but I need sight of that box and its contents."

"And this Paper Office is somewhere in London?" Danny asked, looking between Gideon and Lord.

"Yes," Gideon said. It was something no lawyer in London would be unaware of. "The Paper Office is in the Holbein Gate."

"Not far then," Danny observed. "The King's Gate is just down the road from here and the Holbein is just through that and on the other side of the Privy Garden. What are we waiting for? We could be there in ten minutes."

Lord sighed. "Sarcasm is not helpful, Daniel. But yes, part of my reasoning in being here is that it is close to the Paper Office and where I need to be to try and gain access."

"That'll be far from easy," Gideon said, thinking of the few times he had managed to get into the upper rooms of the chequered Holbein Gate that guarded the entrance to the main buildings of the Palace of Whitehall. "You would need authorisation from a high officer of state or one of their secretaries." Then he stopped talking as he realised something else. "On the other hand, I have no notion of how matters stand now."

"You could find out." Lord didn't make the words a question and Gideon felt an all too familiar tightening in his stomach.

"If by that you mean I would know who to ask, then yes. But to do so would mean admitting I am here in London and if I am, how do I explain why I wouldn't return to my former lodgings?"

"Because," Lord said, "you are engaged in some matters of the greatest secrecy and import to one of the committees. It worked in Paris."

"Paris," Gideon pointed out, "is not London. Besides, if I were involved with one of the committees, no matter how secret, I would also have access to someone who could sign me into the Paper Office."

"That does not follow at all. In clandestine matters, those who are seeking information will go to great lengths to ensure they are not known to be the ones seeking it." Lord's tone turned speculative. "Your friend Ellis Ruskin should be back in London by now, perhaps he would help?"

Gideon was aghast. "You will recall he is the son of Sir Isaac Ruskin, the same Sir Isaac Ruskin who sent that letter to the queen I stole?"

"You *stole* a letter to the queen?" Danny echoed, sounding incredulous.

"Gideon stole the letter because it bore the *monas* you spoke of before," Lord explained. "Don't look so shocked—I blame your influence upon the innocent lad, for I have always offered him a model of probity to which he might aspire. Anyway, this letter from Sir Isaac claimed he had proof of my treason." Lord's expression changed to one of discovery. "Oh, as I recall Gideon mentioned he is a member of the Order of the Coif as well. That could be useful."

"And what, pray, is the Order of the Coif?" Danny asked.

Lord pulled a face. "A pretty legal conceit. It is because they are called 'serjeants-at-law', so they are given a facade of military convention. As well as the title of serjeant, they have their own Inns and rights and privileges that set them apart from other humbler barristers. It occurs to me that such a man might even have access to the Papers Office." Lord looked meaningfully at Gideon.

THE ALCHEMIST'S PLOT

"You don't know what you are asking of me," Gideon said, ice water running through his veins. He was struggling with the way Danny and Lord seemed to make light of everything, turning even the most serious and perilous of issues into some kind of joke. Then it struck him that this was how they dealt with danger—diminishing it with the inventive wit that ran in both men as their blood, and they were including him in an old and well-practised intimacy.

"You are wrong. I know exactly what I am asking of you," Lord said. "After all, isn't that why you came to London? To help me with your local knowledge and contacts?"

Gideon closed his mouth hard and said nothing. He'd thought he would be asked to look at documents. He hadn't expected to be asked to do anything like this.

"And such is what we get by way of gratitude," Danny said, lifting his hands in mock exasperation. "Don't let it get to you, Gideon. It is what we must suffer for our audacity in daring to offer our assistance."

"You will recall I didn't ask you to come," Lord said, tone acid. "But since you are both here it seems the least you can do is be useful."

"And whilst Gideon is rubbing shoulders with the legal equivalent of an order of chivalry, how can I 'be useful'?" Danny asked. "Do you still want me to find Mags?"

Lord pondered. "The first question we need to answer about Mags is whether he is a prisoner or a free man."

Danny frowned. "Why would he be a prisoner? He was free when I last saw him, if badly injured, and under guard for his own protection. He may even be dead, but we don't seem to have that kind of luck."

"Assuming his health was restored, his degree of freedom would depend on his attitude to the Covenant. At the least he is, from what you have told me, a useful blade to hold against the throat of Sir Nicholas, even if he lives a cripple. And at the most, if he recovers his strength, he is a name—a force—who can pull troops from the continent as well as mine can, if not better."

"And pull troops from you too," Danny added, a bitter twist to his tone.

"You pulled quite a few back," Lord assured him.

Gideon was unsure he'd grasped the point Lord was making, but then Mags wasn't his concern. There was one other issue though that was.

"When do we go to Mortlake?" he asked.

The other two looked at him. Danny with curiosity and Lord considering.

"And where?" Danny added. "The tapestry works? The place that used to be Dr Dee's old house?"

Lord sat back in his chair, the fingers of one hand splayed idly over his cup of wine.

"My understanding is," he said, "that the tapestry works have been pretty much shut down thanks to the war. There is little demand for expensive woven works of art when all your plate and jewels are being sold to fund the purchase of men and weapons."

"So there will be no one there?" Gideon asked, wondering if that meant they would be obliged to break in like thieves.

"Oh, I am sure there will be someone there," Lord assured him, "My point is more that they might well be eager for a commission, even if it is only a small one."

"They might not be allowed to work on such," Danny said. "There's probably some ordinance from parliament declaring tapestries an ungodly luxury."

"Let us avoid giving them any such an idea," Lord said. "Especially as I think Sir Theophilus Bassington—"

"Wait, he has a knighthood now?" Danny sounded amused.

"He has a baronetcy at the least, perhaps even a baronry," Lord said, considering. "Somewhere unpronounceable to any English tongue in Wales or—no, forget that, in Northumberland, with a cold bleak castle that needs a warm tapestry."

"He will need to be a very rich baron to buy their work."

"Barons can be wealthy. Besides, Sir Theophilus wants a single tapestry, not a series of six on some mythological or Biblical theme. He might even wish his face immortalised in wool and silk rather than on canvas."

THE ALCHEMIST'S PLOT

Danny laughed. "He is as modest as the man who portrays him then."

"When do we go?" Gideon repeated his question.

"Tomorrow," Lord decreed. "You will be my legal and financial advisor. Danny is my servant and bodyguard."

"Then I don't need to act a role," Danny said. "Just be myself."

"I am endeavouring to allow you both to have parts in this play for which you are well suited. I, however, shall struggle to portray an overbearing, arrogant, insensitive, pompous—"

Danny picked up an apple from his plate and aimed it over the table at Lord's head with unerring accuracy. Lord snatched it from the air and took a bite.

Chapter Six

The following morning, they went to Mortlake travelling on the river. Having left their horses under the care of the ostler in the Bell, they caught the rising tide from the Westminster Stairs. The journey upstream was pleasant enough, the air being crisp but not too cold as the sun was shining. Gideon was glad for it. After the excesses of a hard winter, it was good to have the promise of returning warmth.

The river was busy with travellers and trade, and they had a view of the building of the defences which Danny took great interest in. For much of the way there were grand houses, dipping the hems of their skirts, their grounds and gardens, into the river, and between were fields and forests.

It was a very different scene to the Seine where Gideon had been struck by the amount of industry that seemed to take place on or beside the river. Here it was as if a giant hand had swept aside all obstructions and left the way clear for travel and commerce. In one way, he reflected, that was quite true as it had been the powerful royal hand of the last King Henry who in decreeing that the river should be freed of all impediments had removed and put a stop to any such developments.

Their wherryman seemed more taciturn than most of his kind. Perhaps, Gideon thought, it was because of the self-important presence of Sir Theophilus Bassington, who sat with his hands folded on his impressive stomach and kept up a steady monologue upon the dire state of the nation, the lack of respect of the younger generations for the older and the various treatments he had been recommended for the onset of gout. In brief, Sir Philip Lord was enjoying himself. At one point he even broke into verse:

"Thames the most loved of all the ocean's sons
By his old sire, to his embraces runs;
Hastening to pay his tribute to the sea,
Like mortal life to meet eternity."

THE ALCHEMIST'S PLOT

As Bassington's servant, Danny was grim-faced, but his eyes danced with hilarity and now and then he would say something couched in a dour mien to prompt or provoke a fresh outburst of righteous indignation from his supposed master.

Perhaps, it was simpler for Lord and Danny to play out such roles, but unlike Paris where Gideon had been able to pretend to be whoever he wished, in London he could be recognised. At least the chance of encountering anyone he knew in Mortlake was vanishingly small, neither business nor leisure had ever taken him there before.

Mortlake was a peaceful-looking and pretty little town some ten miles or so upstream from the city of London itself and right on the banks of the Thames. It lay close to the Richmond Palace deer park, less than a mile to the south that had been a favourite royal hunting ground. By the time they landed, it was midmorning and Lord asked the wherryman about the times of the tide, then paid him off with an excessive tip.

It wasn't hard to locate the tapestry works as they were close to the river, their grounds backing onto it, flanked on either side by houses that did likewise. From that rear view, at first impression, it struck Gideon that the original building had been a single house that had grown by extensions and swallowed up those beside it. He could see how such a structure would offer the space and size of rooms that must be needed for a commercial tapestry weaving venture.

There were three floors beneath a slate-tiled roof in a style that was perhaps fashionable a century before, with cross-layered brickwork creating a hatched pattern over part of the frontage. It was occupied domestically as well as commercially because a group of children played in the grounds and linens were laid out in the courtyard. That was open to the rear but had a stable and another couple of outbuildings the purpose of which was hard to discern at a distance, to one side.

Gideon became aware that beside him Lord had gone very still. His back to the river, he was looking at the house as if at the portrait of someone he had once known but who was long gone.

Then Gideon remembered the evening of revelations in the old mill in Weardale.

There is a certain house in Mortlake, if it even still stands, where I was born.

Then this, surely, was that 'certain house'. Lord drew a breath then they walked on, taking the road up to the highway which fronted the house.

From the front, the impression of being a row of houses bound into one was even more acute, but the main entrance seemed to be a solid, metal-bound door.

"How interesting," Lord said. "It looks as if the weavers themselves live here."

He lifted a fist to rap on the door but before he could do so, the door opened, and a young man walked out carrying a carved wooden book stand that blocked his view. Lord stepped aside and the man looked aghast.

"I ask your pardon, *meneer.*"

From within came the sound of raised voices speaking in Dutch, a language Gideon had become most familiar with during his time in The Hague.

Another man appeared, much older and shouting what sounded like imprecations at the man clutching the stand, who turned and tried to gesticulate to show they had company, but only succeeded in dropping the stand. It was Danny who caught it as it slipped from the young man's fingers and set it on the ground.

Gideon realised he shouldn't be so surprised to find that the tapestry works were occupied by Dutch weavers and that the finest English tapestries were created and produced by Dutchmen. He had heard that the United Provinces tried to bar any of their skilled weavers from leaving the country, but whatever inducements had been offered when the tapestry works were set up had been enough to persuade some to leave their homeland and settle here on the banks of the Thames.

The man who had been carrying the bookstand was much the same age as Gideon, but the one who came out shouting was much older, in his sixties. He had very bright eyes and a grey beard that whilst shaped into the fashionable form, had been allowed more

THE ALCHEMIST'S PLOT

latitude than normal, covering more of his face as a result. He saw Lord, standing aloof and with eyebrows raised, and closed his mouth quickly.

"Forgive me, *meneer*, this boy is taking something I asked him not to," he said, making a bow. Then he glared at the younger man. "We will talk of this later, Jan. Please for now bring that back in."

For a moment Gideon thought Jan would refuse, but then he huffed a sigh and picked up the book stand again, pushing past the older man who had to step aside to allow him to enter the house.

"I am here to discuss a commission," Lord said in his finest Sir Theophilus tone of indignant outrage. "I would have sent ahead to make an appointment, but my time is limited in London. If now is not convenient I will come back next time I can do so which might be some months and—"

"A commission?" Instantly the older man's attitude changed. He studied Lord with an astute gaze, eyes shifting to glance at both Danny and Gideon before settling back on Lord. "But of course, please do come in, sir. You *must* come in."

He stood aside as he spoke and held out an arm to guide them into the house.

"I apologise. We are in some chaos," their guide said, leading them up a flight of stairs, "Please come, I will show you the looms."

Gideon had a feeling that in better times they wouldn't have received such a rapid and effusive welcome. Then he found himself drawing in a sharp breath as they came into a huge room that was the entire width of the house, which had to be about twenty feet by Gideon's reckoning and was at least three times as long with a door at the far end. The room was higher on one side lifting to the rafters, with a gallery over the other half. There were tall and wide windows letting in bright light and illuminating six large looms, their rollers held in wooden cases, each filling a large portion of the space available. Gideon decided they must each be over ten feet wide, and they were built up as high as the ceiling, which was plastered, with a ridge of rafters visible that supported the floor above and seemed to anchor the looms as well. Only one of the looms had any work on it and Gideon could see the cartoon from which the tapestry was being created set by the warp threads.

Philip Lord gave a sigh of satisfaction.

"True *haute-lisse* looms, I have come to the right place."

"But of course, *meneer*. We are the best. The finest in the world." Their guide made it sound so matter of fact that there was no sense of any boast in his words. He gave Lord a bow. "Phillips de Maecht, I am overseer and director of the tapissiers here at the Roy—here at the Mortlake Tapestry Works." He must have decided that not knowing the allegiance of his potential client it would be unwise to advertise their royal connection.

"Sir Theophilus Bassington," Lord provided, "Baron Kyloe. You will have heard of me; I have been the member for Berwick."

De Maecht nodded with interest as if he had indeed heard of the Baronry of Kyloe. Gideon wondered if such a place even existed.

"And you are interested in our work here?"

Lord strode across to the one loom being worked and stood as if admiring it.

"Lady Bassington, you understand," he said. "She was most insistent that I come here. Said nowhere else will do."

"Of course, I understand, my own dear Jannekin is much the same way about some things. So might I ask—?"

He was interrupted by a tap on the door and a large florid-faced woman in her middle years, with appled cheeks and crystal blue eyes, came in. By her dress, she was a servant of some variety, and she bobbed a curtsey at the Phillips de Maecht. Gideon felt his ribs tighten, making it hard to breathe as his heart stood still in his chest. He had to exert every ounce of willpower to keep still and quiet, whilst reciting a silent prayer that she wouldn't look his way.

"Did you want me to wait until you are done to clean in here, sir?"

"Oh, yes, that would be better. Thank you, Hester."

Hester glanced at Lord, bobbed him a curtsey too and went as she had come, leaving Gideon drawing in a deep and grateful breath of air whilst giving thanks to God for his protection.

Danny, who was beside him, gave him a look of concern and enquiry. But there was nothing Gideon could say at that moment.

THE ALCHEMIST'S PLOT

There was no way to explain that he knew the woman who had just come in claiming to be a maidservant called Hester, but he knew her from elsewhere and under a different name. The last time he had seen her she had been accusing him of a murder she had been responsible for.

Lord and de Maecht seemed not to have noticed anything amiss because their conversation turned to tapestries, materials, time to produce and, inevitably, the cost. The conversation went on for quite a while and Gideon was unable to stop his stomach protesting that dinner was overdue.

Almost as if the sound reminded Lord of Gideon's existence, he turned to him.

"I should have presented my man of business, a lawyer too, Gideon Lennox." Cursing inwardly at the casual granting of his name, Gideon made the necessary bow.

"You will excuse us Mr de Maecht," Lord said then. "I would dine and return to discuss the details later."

"I would invite you to dine with us, *meneer*, but my wife is indisposed and still very distressed. You will have heard I am sure of our tragedy and scandal."

"I have not been in London for some weeks," Lord said, sounding bored rather than intrigued.

"Oh?" De Maecht seemed nonplussed. "Well, I fear you will hear of it soon enough I am sad to say; it is all they are talking about in this town. My brother-in-law, one of our weavers, took his own life last week—but my wife will not accept it. She insists he was murdered."

"*Murdered?*" Gideon spoke the word before he thought.

De Maecht looked embarrassed.

"It is what she thinks, but it is not possible. He hung himself on the loom in an upstairs room and he had locked the door before he did so. The key was still in the lock on the inside. But my dear wife…" He pressed his hands together as if in prayer and shook his head sadly. "Well, he was her brother so I suppose she would think that way."

"Did he have some reason to take his own life?" Gideon asked, then realised it was far from appropriate to do so. Perhaps had Lord not been offering a commission, de Maecht would have brushed his question aside or refused to answer, but instead he shook his head.

"That is the very point my wife makes. That he had none and if he had he would have told her. And it is hard to see why Gerhard would have done such a thing. He was content here more than most." He lifted his shoulders in an eloquent shrug. "But things have been very difficult for us with the war getting in the way of trade." He turned back to Lord. "Of course, my son and daughter-in-law would be delighted to have you stay to dine."

It struck Gideon that the man was so desperate for custom that he was afraid if he let them leave, they might not return to make the promised commission. Lord waved the offer aside with a gesture that implied whatever the director of tapissiers or his family might dine on wouldn't be fit fare for a Bassington.

"I made enquiries before I came and have been assured that the Queen's Head is a fine hostelry, and I am sure it will provide a decent repast."

De Maecht showed them back down the stairs and out of the house, promising to have some samples and possible designs ready for their return that afternoon.

They crossed the road to the church and were walking towards the inn, which had a clear sign showing the face of Queen Elizabeth over its welcoming door. Gideon glanced back at the tapestry works.

"Something disturbed you," Danny said quietly.

"Mention of murder disturbs most people," Lord observed in a similar undertone. "Gideon is simply as most people. It is you and I who are the exceptions. *Murder be proud, and tragedy laugh on.*"

"No. It wasn't that," Gideon said and something in his voice made them both look at him sharply.

"Then we had better wait until we have privacy," Lord said and led the way into the inn.

A short time later they were settled with some difficulty in a private room. The hostess had been most insistent that the room was reserved for a gentleman who was staying in the inn, but Sir Theophilus Bassington was having none of that. By a careful mix

THE ALCHEMIST'S PLOT

of furious bluster and emollient coin, Lord secured them the use of the comfortable room and a fine meal of roasted woodcock.

"So let us see what we have," Lord said once they were alone, "Danny?"

"It would be very easy to get in," Danny said. "The windows are all casements and one in the weaving room is broken. It is pushed closed and could be pulled from the outside—the third one in from the end we entered. The brickwork is uneven enough I could climb it and from the rear, there is a courtyard to access."

Gideon knew he must be staring. Danny, it seemed, had been studying the house from the moment they first saw it with a view to breaking in. But that revelation was submerged beneath his own urgent news.

"We have a different problem," he said.

"Something, as Danny observed, disturbed you," Lord said, cutting into the bird on his plate. "And not just the notion of murder."

"The woman servant," Danny said, in a tone that displayed he was sure of his assessment. "What was her name? Hester?"

"That might be what she is calling herself here," Gideon said, his voice tight. "It might even be her name. But the last time I saw her it was in the village of Pethridge in Weardale, going by the name of Mistress Goody and she was accusing me of involvement in witchcraft and murder."

Lord paused with his knife poised above his plate and gave Gideon a sharp look. "I never had the opportunity to meet Mistress Goody, though I heard a great deal about her. As I recall, she was the one who arranged the killing of the witchfinder, Fanthorpe and was hand in glove with Constable Brierly to make it seem the women accused were guilty of witchcraft."

Gideon's mind had taken him back to a taut moment when he had been accused of the murder himself. "I was left with the impression that she was the one who was in charge, not Brierly—although I think she bowed to his local knowledge."

"And Brierly was Coupland's man, even if he played his own games," Lord said.

"Then perhaps Mistress Goody wasn't there under orders from Coupland himself. Perhaps her orders came from the same authority that governed Sir Bartholomew."

He met Lord's direct and speculative gaze and held it, confident that the other man wouldn't miss the implications.

"If so," Lord said, "we do indeed have a problem."

Danny was frowning.

"Forgive me, but I must be missing something here. It's all very well for you two to reminisce about the good times you had together in County Durham last autumn, but you seem to forget I wasn't there."

It was, Gideon realised, the one part of the tale Danny had yet to be told and took less time to tell than Gideon thought it might. The weight and impact of what had happened in his own life as a result of it, added more to his own perception of the narrative than the stark events. Lord told it succinctly, from the time he had encountered Gideon in Maggie's Alehouse through the accusations of witchcraft directed at three innocent women and how that had unravelled.

For his part, Gideon was just grateful that Lord glossed over how at the time they hadn't been on the best of terms—and that Gideon had been convinced the witchcraft was real and even halfway persuaded that Lord himself was in some way implicated. It was embarrassing in the extreme to recall that now.

In the retelling, Gideon realised how far he had come from the rather naive and innocent man he had been just six months before. What was it Lord had called him then? 'Giddy One'. That was it. And on mature reflection, he could see how well deserved it must have seemed to Lord, even if it had been irritating beyond bearing for Gideon himself at the time.

"What about this Hester?" Danny asked when the account was finished. "Or Mistress Goody, or whatever she might be called? What's she doing as a servant here in Mortlake?"

Lord returned his attention to his food as he spoke. "I would think that rather obvious," he said. "If she works for the Covenant as seems most likely, she is there to find and remove the same documents we are seeking."

THE ALCHEMIST'S PLOT

"Yes, but if so, it suggests the Covenant might only recently have had cause to consider there is anything there to be found," Gideon put in. "They have had years, decades, so why look now?"

Lord frowned and sat back, his fingers drumming the table.

"Perhaps because I have returned to England. Before no one was going to look, why should they? Whatever was there was safe enough, presumably—buried, hidden, concealed."

"So why would this Hester not have taken the documents already?" Danny asked, frowning.

"Firstly," Lord pointed out, "we have no notion of how long she has been working there and secondly there were changes made to the internal structure of the house to make it a meet place for a tapestry works. It might be that the Covenant do not know where the documents are to be found now."

"There is another possibility," Gideon put in, not liking the thought that had occurred. "It could be that the documents are long gone or were never in the house in the first place and Mistress Goody is there because, as you said, the Covenant knows that is somewhere you will think to look." He locked his gaze with Lord, who frowned.

"You have a point," Lord agreed. "But there is one thing that could suggest the Covenant don't know where to look and are still searching—"

"The murder?" Gideon suggested, speaking over him.

"The murder," Lord agreed. "If indeed it was a murder as Jannekin de Maecht seems to think and not a self-killing as the world is viewing it."

"Why?" Danny asked, his freckles wrinkling in puzzlement.

"Because if *mevrouw* de Maecht's brother found the housekeeper behaving strangely, tapping on walls or attacking the fixtures and fittings, he might well question her behaviour," Lord said. "But that is speculation. We need knowledge. Perhaps I should offer the services of my man of law to look into the matter. Suicide or murder, either way, it could provide the perfect excuse for someone to poke around in the unremarked recesses of the house."

Gideon felt his stomach tighten.

"But there is Hester—Mistress Goody. She will know me."

Lord nodded. "I am counting on it. You are not like poor Gerhard, a weaver who never wielded anything more dangerous in his life than a well-loaded bobbin and was probably in his declining years if the age of his brother-in-law is anything to go by. You are young, strong and have a passing knowledge of how to use that very fine sword you wear."

"None of which makes me feel reassured. How can we be sure there are not more of the Covenant's employees on the premises?"

Lord was eating as he considered, then having cleared his plate, cleaned his knife and sat back in his chair. "What if I leave you Danny?"

Danny shot a surprised look between them, then shrugged.

"How would that be explained?" Gideon asked.

"I am sure we will think of something." Lord made a dismissive gesture with one hand and reached for his cup with the other.

"Perhaps we should see if it is even possible first," Gideon suggested. "It might be that Phillips de Maecht has no wish to encourage his wife in her ideas of it being murder. Then we would be hard-pressed to do things that way and would need to resort to climbing in through a window instead."

Which was how things were left when they finished their drinks and departed the inn to make the short walk back to the tapestry works.

It was obvious before they reached the door that there was something very wrong. A crowd had begun to gather outside the building, and it took Sir Theophilus Bassington at his loudest and most demanding to force a path through. The door itself wasn't locked and as no one challenged them, Lord led the way inside, gesturing to Danny to close the door so others didn't decide their entry was a signal that all could do so.

They had made it up the stairs and into the weaving hall before encountering anyone and then it was two women who were clinging together in floods of tears. It was clear Lord saw that as no reason not to approach them for information but as he strode over the far door opened and Phillips de Maecht himself came through it, looking shocked and distressed and as if he had aged another ten years since they saw him that morning.

Lord changed direction away from the women and intercepted de Maecht.

"What has happened?" Lord demanded. "Why are there crowds outside and women crying?" It was brutally insensitive and somehow it made little difference to Gideon to know that Lord was acting how the self-centred Sir Theophilus would act.

"You must forgive us, please, *meneer*." De Maecht seemed to have some difficulty getting his breath to go on. "I will have to ask you to come back another day. There has been another death. Jan Engles, you met him when you first arrived, he was carrying the bookstand, he was…"

"Did he take his own life too?" Lord asked, frowning. The impact was crass and callous to a degree that Gideon found hard to bear. It might be an act to Lord, but for these people, this was real life, real tragedy. He stepped forward, but one of the women spoke first, grey hairs escaping from her headwear and the lines of a full life lived on her face.

"No. he didn't, whatever they may say. And neither did my brother Gerhard. Someone killed them both. We have a murderer amongst us, and he needs to be uncovered before more of us are killed."

ELEANOR SWIFT-HOOK

Chapter Seven

Not even the forceful Sir Theophilus was able to prevail against the men of the tapestry works, who came in behind Phillips de Maecht and insisted again that they leave. But as Lord argued in the most inappropriate and unfeeling manner, Gideon was able to speak with the woman who had declared the deaths to be murder.

"My name is Gideon Lennox, and I am a man of law," he told her, guessing from her words that this was Jannekin de Maecht. "If there is an injustice here, I would like to help see it set right."

Her eyes were the soft blue of forget-me-nots, and their gaze seemed to cling to Gideon, for some moments. She nodded then as if she had decided he was trustworthy but said nothing and let the other woman with her lead her away.

A few minutes after that they were outside the house again and back on the Barnes Elms road. Lord's brows were lowered in a thunderous expression which served to clear their path and Gideon was unsure if that was Sir Theophilus or Sir Philip who was angry. On the journey back along the river he decided it was both.

"That went well," Danny said as they went up the Westminster Steps. It was late afternoon, and the sun was ahead of them. New Palace Yard was as full as ever of human activity. Men and women coming and going in coaches in front of Westminster Hall. The Great Conduit fountain, where people came to collect their water, cast a long shadow with its onion-shaped roof. They walked past the shops and taverns and through the Gate House which was just opposite The Bell. Lord stopped outside and heaved a sigh.

"I am not good company. I will dine in my room and speak to you in the morning."

Gideon wondered at that, but Danny gave a brisk bow, maintaining his role as their servant.

"I'll share with Mr Lennox tonight then, sir."

Lord nodded. He had the look of a man with a crashing headache who knew he still had a book of accounts to settle before he could rest.

THE ALCHEMIST'S PLOT

"Very well," he said.

Then he was gone leaving the two of them standing in the street.

"He looks ill," Gideon said, worried that it might be so.

Danny shook his head. "I've seen him this way before and I'm sure you have too if you think back. Leave him be. He'll appear tomorrow rejuvenated—a male Aphrodite emerging on a giant scallop shell from the foam." Then he rubbed his hands together. "But for us, the night is still young, and the pleasures of the capital await. It's been too long since I was in London. The question is, where do we start?"

Gideon wanted to say that he had no wish to go out anywhere. A meal followed by a good sleep would suit him well. But there was an unholy excitement about Danny, and he had a feeling that left to his own devices, Danny could get himself—and thus them all—into trouble.

"The only places I know in London wouldn't suit your tastes," Gideon said.

"You might be surprised. I've *very* broad tastes. You must have friends here who you might wish to see after so long?"

Gideon made a decision that in retrospect wasn't the wisest, but in the moment made perfect sense. After all, if Danny was held to the need to focus on their work, then he would be much less inclined to run wild.

"We could call on Ellis Ruskin," he said. "But if we do, you'd need to keep in your role as my servant."

Danny shrugged.

"If that's your idea of fun, far be it from me to say no to you."

Gideon opened his mouth then saw the light dancing in Danny's eyes and closed it again.

"I thought that we could get one thing sorted at least," he said.

"We might at that," Danny agreed, his gaze becoming speculative.

"No," Gideon said firmly, "Ellis doesn't play cards."

Ellis Ruskin had rooms in a side street beside Lyon's Inn and they took a coach from where several waited in New Palace Yard, heading for Charing Cross and on towards Holborn where the Inns of Court and Chancery were all located. The place Gideon, until last summer, had come to think of as his home.

"I must," Danny said almost wistfully, as they went past a heavy chain pulled across a side street, "have a closer look at the defences before we leave. And there is a man working here I need to visit. His name is James Wemyss. I'd like to persuade him to abandon London for Oxford, but if not, he has some interesting new ideas around artillery that I have to catch up on."

Gideon struggled to imagine how the words 'interesting', and 'artillery' could fit in a sentence together. Catching the over-eager tone of an enthusiast, Gideon changed the subject, lowering his voice although the driver would be hard-pressed to hear what they were saying over the horses' hooves on the cobbles of the streets.

"You need to know that Ellis is under the impression I am employed by one of the parliamentary secret committees," he said. "He recognised me in Paris, and I had to come up with some reason for being in the house of the king's agent and in company with Sir Philip Lord."

"Everyone always needs a good excuse for being in company with Philip," Danny agreed. "But this might work well if he believes you are still thus employed—and me also. We might be able to get what we need from him tonight."

Gideon was still thinking about that when they came to a halt. Stepping from the coach, the road was exactly as he remembered it, but somehow it had changed.

Then he realised the change wasn't in the street, it was in himself. He was seeing this street with new eyes, eyes that had seen the streets of Newcastle and Durham and the high houses of Paris. Eyes that had seen the mysteries of Howe Hall, the siege of Wrathby and the brutality in the baggage train at Kineton. These were the same close-pressed houses, leaning in to shake hands above the street and the same two or three that had been demolished and rebuilt with more modern and flat-fronted facades. But the man who now stood by one of those newer houses and knocked on the door was no longer the man he had been the last time he knocked upon it less than a year ago.

THE ALCHEMIST'S PLOT

The woman who answered the door, round, smiling and in her middle years, knew him at once. "Oh Mr Lennox, it is so good to see you again. I'll tell Mr Ruskin you are here, he'll be delighted. Come in and wait in my parlour and your servant is welcome too. Come in, come in."

"It must be nice," Danny said as they waited in the small parlour, "to have people welcome you like that. They usually greet me with screams of rage or a clean pair of heels."

"I didn't notice Christobel doing either," Gideon observed with deliberate mischief and was rewarded by Danny closing his mouth and turning to study the small shelf of books by the window. Gideon's attention was taken by a collection of pamphlets on the table by the fireplace.

He was reading one, which seemed to be a justification of rule by the two houses of parliament without the need for a king when the door opened, and Ellis was there. He looked as he had in Paris, down to the same troubled and harassed expression.

"Gideon, what on earth are you doing here?"

Gideon dropped the pamphlet back onto the table and stepped forwards with a smile.

"I am in London on some business and thought to see you as I am here."

But the dark expression on Ellis' face remained.

"I have a visitor," he said, lowering his voice. Then he glanced at Danny and frowned. "A visitor—on business." He put an odd emphasis on the last word and Gideon nodded, understanding.

"There is no need to worry, Adam here is my man in all things and a strong supporter of the business we are both engaged in."

A flicker of relief lifted Ellis' features.

"I was hoping to persuade my guest to head out to supper, perhaps you would join us?"

"That would be very pleasant," Gideon agreed, hoping the insincerity didn't show.

Ellis smiled then, but still looked strained. "If you would like to go ahead, we'll be eating at The Rose and Crown."

ELEANOR SWIFT-HOOK

The Rose and Crown was just around the corner from Lyon's Inn and was a tavern which Gideon knew well. So having taken his leave of Ellis he set out at a confident pace.

"Adam?" Danny hissed. "Do I look like an Adam?"

"I haven't met enough to know," Gideon said. "It was the—"

"—first name you thought of?"

"No, the second," Gideon lied. "But upon giving the matter a moment of consideration, I decided that Unless-Jesus-Christ-Had-Died-For-Thee-Thou-Hadst-Been-Damned might be a bit much."

Danny looked at him. "On reflection, I think Adam is a good name."

Gideon laughed. "Exactly so. But if you wish to invent a surname for yourself, let me know and I will use it."

"What shall I be? Butcher? Baker? Tanner?" Danny danced a step sideways to avoid two men who were standing talking in the street. "No. I have it. Brewer. I always wanted to be a brewer." Then he turned.

"Isn't that your friend?" There was a sudden edge to his tone.

Gideon looked back and saw Ellis with another man, standing on the corner of the turning to Ellis' house, engaged in a heated discussion.

"Yes. But I don't know the man with him."

"I do," Danny said. "And he knows me. Change of plan. You sup with Ellis and his companion, and I keep out of sight. Tell them I was taken ill, or you had to send me on some business or—"

He broke off as the man with Ellis made an angry gesture and strode off in the opposite direction. Ellis stood still as if in doubt whether he should follow or not, then pulled his cloak around his shoulders and turned away.

"It seems Adam Brewer might get to sup in the warm after all," Danny said. "I wonder what he said to upset his angelic friend." He turned and walked on, the sign for the tavern in sight ahead of them.

"Angelic?" Gideon asked, a dark suspicion forming in his mind.

"The only name I was given for him was Gabriel."

The words confirmed the suspicion. A Covenant man.

THE ALCHEMIST'S PLOT

"Did he see you?"

Danny shook his head. "If he had I suspect his reaction would have been very obvious and very different. I think whatever was exercising him with your friend Ellis was mercifully distraction enough."

They reached the door of the tavern.

"Perhaps we should make our excuses and leave," Gideon suggested.

Danny looked at him in surprise.

"But I want to see if Ellis will play Gleek."

"Gleek?"

"It's a kind of three-handed version of Piquet."

"Ellis is not a gambling man," Gideon said, rather desperately. "Don't even suggest it."

"That's a shame."

Danny reached out to open the door, but instead turned fully, pushing past Gideon to run back the way they had come. Confused, Gideon stayed where he was. Then he saw the two men who Danny had stepped aside to avoid had gripped Ellis between them. They seemed to be forcing him towards a coach that had just pulled up nearby.

Gideon ran in Danny's wake, sword drawn before he had crossed half the distance. By that time Danny had put one of Ellis' two assailants on the ground and the other was reaching for something under his cloak. Fearful it might be a pistol, Gideon barrelled into him.

The first man had rolled to his feet and took off running. The second wasn't so fortunate. Danny had a blade to his throat before he could rise. But the coachman had driven the horses towards them. Danny jumped back just in time. The man on the ground had no chance. He was trampled under the horses' hooves then there was a horrible noise of shod hooves and metal-rimmed wheels, grinding flesh and bone against cobbles and a scream that started but was never finished.

Ellis pressed back against the wall, the back of his hand against his mouth, his face transfigured with horror. Gideon crossed to him, slipping his sword back as he went, whilst Danny went to examine what lay in the road.

"Are you alright?"

Ellis nodded, but he looked pale and ill. Gideon managed to step aside just before he vomited, holding Ellis' cloak away as he added to the filth in the street.

"Dead," Danny said. "Whoever those men were, they weren't keen for anyone to know who employed them."

Ellis had managed to collect himself enough to step away from the pool of vomit. A crowd had begun to gather.

"Those coaches are a menace. The poor man stood no chance. Knocked down and trampled."

"He was down already. Someone had a sword."

"Who's sent for the constable?"

Danny pushed Gideon towards the tavern.

"We should go, sirs," he said in a carrying voice. "This accident in the street isn't our affair."

For a moment Gideon thought Ellis would protest, but instead, something inside him seemed to collapse and he stumbled along, supported by Gideon.

Once in The Rose and Crown, Gideon commanded a private room and settled Ellis at the table with a restorative drink of aquavitae. The spirits brought some colour back to his face.

"I can never thank you enough," he said when his power of speech returned. "Those men said I was to go with them, or they would kill me. One had a knife pressed against my ribs. But you…" He trailed off looking at Danny who stood at the far end of the table as might be fitting for a servant.

"I just did my job, sir," Danny said. "Mr Lennox said to do so."

Ellis switched his gaze to Gideon.

"You were attacking those men with your sword too. I saw that. Where did you learn—?" He stopped and drew a sharp breath. "No. I don't think that's something I even want to know. This war has changed us all so much." He shook his head. "But again, thank you."

"Do you know who those men were?" Gideon asked.

Ellis shook his head. "I've never seen any of them before."

THE ALCHEMIST'S PLOT

"I noticed you argued with someone. Was that the man you had planned to bring with you to supper here?"

Ellis looked nonplussed as if he had forgotten that had been his stated intention. Then he nodded. "But I didn't get to ask him. He was much caught up in other affairs and unwilling to listen to me. He wanted me to go with him and when I refused… Well, if you saw him then you saw what happened." Ellis sighed. "It's good to have you here, Gideon. I need a friend I can trust to keep my confidences and who I may call upon for advice."

Which seemed strange as they had never been close friends. But then Gideon had never had any close friends, always set apart by being too Scottish or too English, too conformist or too radical. Then it struck him. Now, for the first time in his life, he had those he could trust, who valued him for who he was—who were indeed his close friends. The strangeness of it silenced him.

"I can wait outside if you wish, sirs?" Danny said.

Gideon found himself hoping that Ellis would refuse the offer. He had the distinct impression that freed from Gideon's company Danny would take the chance to indulge in his own idea of entertainment, of which a game of Gleek might be the mildest iteration. But instead, Ellis reached for his purse and pressed a coin on Danny.

"You should buy yourself a meal and a drink, with my gratitude," he said, then added another coin. "Please ask for food and wine—a decent one—to be brought to us here."

Danny thanked him with a bow, then grinned and winked at Gideon behind Ellis' back as he left the room. It reminded Gideon that Danny had done what was needed to progress their task and with an effort he made himself focus on it.

"What is troubling you?" he asked as the door closed behind the departing Danny.

Ellis sighed, his expression forlorn.

"My father expressed the wish that I should concern myself in what he calls 'matters of gravity'. As if the existence of civil war is not grave enough and my involvement in that not all-consuming. The man I was talking to is one of my father's confederates in this enterprise, whatever it may be, and he was keen to persuade me to commit myself as my father requires. He wanted me to go with him to see something which, he said, would make me change my mind. When I told him I wasn't intending to do so, he began calling me a blind fool and declaring that there are matters which transcend differences in politics and religion and these are what I should be investing myself in."

"Of what might he speak?" Gideon asked, sure he knew but wondering if Ellis did.

"Trade, of course," Ellis said as if Gideon was being slow. "What else but trade? It's all most of the city cares about—money and making more of it. I'd thought my father above such, but since he began investing in financing these new colonies and settlements and such like, he has wanted me to join him."

"Trade?" Gideon echoed, hoping the surprise wasn't too evident.

"As I said, what else could it be? Now he wishes me to take some oath of secrecy and sign a document binding myself to some covenant so I can inherit his share in the project in time."

Gideon realised he must be staring.

"You have no knowledge of what it is he wishes to involve you with?"

"Indeed not," Ellis sounded dismissive. "It is as with all matters of money. They believe their knowledge is wealth, so they protect it with binding oaths and legal shackles on the tongue. They no doubt believe they know the location of a gold mine in Virginia or have found an island where a new variety of tobacco grows faster than weeds or whatever. So, of course, they will not share unless someone has first bound themselves to eternal silence."

"And you do not wish to be a part of that?"

"I'm not a merchant," Ellis said. "I wish to remain a lawyer and become a member of parliament when I may so that I can be part of the mighty changes that will come when this war is won. Until then I serve John Pym in whatever he asks of me, and the trade of my father and his friends can go to the devil for all I care."

Their conversation had to break then as the meal arrived. Gideon was grateful for that, more because it gave him a chance to reflect on what Ellis had said than because it quashed the beginnings of hunger. It made sense that Sir Isaac would have kept Ellis apart

THE ALCHEMIST'S PLOT

from the Covenant to date. It wasn't the sort of conspiracy of which Gideon could ever see Ellis approving. He was against any kind of monarch unless constrained by parliament. He was strong on the notion that power over the nation should never be at the whim of one man. Gideon knew this because he had heard Ellis express such views often enough. Then another thought occurred.

"You say that man your father sent to speak with you wished you to go with him?"

Ellis was chewing still, so he nodded but didn't speak.

"Then he would have had a coach, perhaps, close at hand?"

Now Ellis was staring at him. He swallowed his mouthful and chased it with a gulp of wine.

"Are you suggesting that those men who tried to make me go with them…? And that coach which—which…?" He stopped talking, eyes round with horror. Then he dropped his knife to the table with a clatter and slumped back. "Oh, dear God, please. That cannot be so."

Gideon wondered what words of comfort he could offer.

"I'm not sure," he said, which was at least honest. "But it's a possibility at least."

Ellis groaned. "It's more than a possibility. That man, Mr Gabriel, told me that if I didn't choose to join them then I might be compelled to do so. I thought he meant my father would threaten to disinherit me or some such ploy, but now I see he meant it very literally." Then he buried his face in his hands. "What am I going to do?"

"Are you so sure you have no wish to join your father in whatever enterprise he is undertaking?" Gideon asked.

Ellis lifted his head and met Gideon's gaze, his own miserable. "I was sure before. This only serves to make me more so. That he even chooses to associate with such people. I mean, I know he and I in recent times have seldom agreed on much in recent times, but I always believed him honest, upstanding and godly by his own path. But this…?"

"Perhaps he didn't know of it."

"Perhaps not. I hope not." Ellis looked anguished at the thought. "But at the very least he has been party to it both by associating with such men and by pressing me to join him. It was at his request I met with Gabriel today." He looked over at Gideon and his eyes had a brightness which suggested he was close to being overwhelmed by emotion. "What am I to do?"

Gideon thought for a moment, considering what Sir Philip Lord would suggest.

"If I may counsel you as a friend, I would suggest that you don't go home tonight," he said. "These men seem capable of going to any extreme and having failed to seize you, they might well be waiting for you to return to your lodgings. If you have friends in a place of power, such as Pym himself—and there is no one with greater power in London than he has—you should seek shelter with them as soon as you may."

"But I have no wish to say what has happened. It would reflect badly on my father, and I have no wish to do him any harm."

Gideon refrained from pointing out that Sir Isaac wasn't so scrupulous towards his son.

"Then ask if your employer has lodgings closer to hand so you can better serve him. I think if it is seen you are under his protection, they might leave you alone. Apart from anything else, they wouldn't wish to draw attention to themselves from a man who has the power to hold them to account for their actions."

Ellis nodded and Gideon was pleased that he looked more thoughtful now, less stricken.

"There is someone I could stay with, perhaps. They had a room to rent last week and asked if I knew of anyone who might like to take it. It is in a house in Channel Row. It would be more convenient for me anyway as most of my work is now in Westminster."

That made Gideon open his eyes wide. Most of the houses there were impressive affairs belonging to the wealthy and titled.

"Can you go there tonight?"

Ellis considered for a moment then nodded.

"I believe I would be welcome. I can think of some excuse if one is needed."

"Then do so and send to have your things collected tomorrow." Gideon realised there was one more thing. "Also write to your

THE ALCHEMIST'S PLOT

father setting out what happened and making it clear that you have no wish to be involved in his affairs and should he press you further in any way you have lodged a deposition which will be released should anything befall you stating the same."

Ellis frowned.

"You say I should *threaten* my father?"

"It is less than he has done to you."

That made Ellis draw a tight breath. "I just thank God you were here," he said. "I don't care to think how things might have turned out if you hadn't been. My father has involved himself with madmen. They are obsessed with their enterprise and care nothing for the law."

Gideon kept his mouth closed and just nodded. He felt it would be undiplomatic to point out that Ellis himself was aligned with those many might see as equally mad and unlawful. Instead, he finished the last of the wine in his cup and got to his feet.

"I'll come with you to Channel Row to be sure you get there safely and are taken in by your friend. I don't like the thought of you being unescorted at the moment."

"I wouldn't take you out of your way," Ellis said. But the words were pure politeness. Gideon could see the relief in the other man's eyes as he stood and picked up his cloak.

"I assure you it's not a problem," Gideon said. And it wasn't since Channel Row was a road that led from New Palace Yard, not much more than a stone's throw from The Bell. But he saw no reason to tell Ellis where he was staying.

"Then I'm very glad to accept your company and that of your man." Ellis went towards the door then stopped and turned back. "There must be something I can do for you in return."

Gideon made sure to take a moment or two before he replied as if he were considering the matter.

"There is no need, we are friends after all. But if you wish to be of assistance, do you happen to have any access to the Paper Office in the Holbein Gate?"

Chapter Eight

Danny was sitting in the common room of the tavern close to the door of their private room. As Gideon emerged, he got to his feet and swept up the cards from the table and apologising to those at the table with him, scooped a pile of coins into a pocket.

"Gleek?" Gideon asked.

"Put."

"Put what where?"

"Put is a game of bluff," Danny said.

"Then you must be good at it."

"I am. Very."

Ellis was frowning. "It is an iniquitous game. It encourages liars, cheats, and gamblers to prosper and defeats the honest man."

Danny shaped a small bow towards him in response. "I'm impressed that you are so well acquainted with the game, sir."

Gideon spoke up to prevent any escalation.

"We are going to escort Mr Ruskin to—" Something in Danny's expression, the inflexible smile perhaps, warned him in time and he changed what he was going to say. "—his lodgings."

Danny inclined his head. "As you wish, sir." Then he glanced towards the door. "If you two gentlemen would like to walk ahead, I will be right behind."

Gideon had no idea what Danny was intending. There must be someone in the tavern who he felt posed some threat. Gideon had no choice but to trust his judgement

Ellis' frown had deepened.

"I'm not sure—"

Gideon propelled him towards the door. "We should go."

They had almost made it out when the inevitable happened. This was a tavern where Ellis and Gideon were well known. A voice hailed them before they could reach the door and by the time Gideon had managed to free them from their solicitous acquaintance, Danny was beside them.

THE ALCHEMIST'S PLOT

"We should go quickly, sirs." He glanced at Gideon.
"Where…?"
"Westminster."
Danny nodded. "Then the steps I think, sirs. We'll take a boat."
"Are there—?"
"Some gentlemen seeking to follow us? Yes, sir. I delayed them, but we still need to hurry."

It was into the evening, and they strode through darkening streets. As they reached the Temple Stairs, they heard sounds of running feet and neither Gideon nor Ellis needed any encouragement to increase their own pace, taking the steps at a dangerous speed. Half-prepared to stand and fight on the foreshore if need be, Gideon was relieved that an empty boat was there. Its waterman called out as they reached him.

"Westward-ho!"

"Westminster Steps," Gideon said, clambering in, keeping his voice low so their pursuers would miss hearing their destination. "Go now and don't stop anywhere else." Ellis followed and Danny was last, the sword in his hand encouraging the waterman to go. Once they were heading upriver, Gideon saw a group of six men standing on the foreshore looking after them. Feeling much relief, he settled back in the wherry.

They reached the Westminster Steps without further incident and Danny parted with a fair portion of his winnings to compensate the waterman for having his wherry appropriated. Then they escorted Ellis to the house he was heading for on Channel Row, but which turned out to be very close to New Palace Yard and on the corner of a small cut-through alley.

"You must come in," Ellis insisted.

Gideon had no wish to face any more of Ellis' friends and shook his head quickly.

"I need to get back to my own lodgings, but I will see you on Saturday as we arranged."

Ellis looked as if he might object, but then drew a breath and managed a smile. "I owe you so much—it is but small recompense. Until Saturday."

The door closed and Gideon was pleased to hear the sound of bolts being driven home as he and Danny turned to retrace their steps to New Palace Yard and walk the short distance back to The Bell.

"Saturday?" Danny asked.

"On Saturday morning he has promised he will be able to allow me and my servant into the Paper Office in the Holbein Gate."

"That will please Philip," Danny said, sounding happy.

"What did you do to delay pursuit back in the tavern?"

Danny looked askance at the note of accusation.

"Nothing that sinister. I locked a door. Now, how about a game of Piquet before we get to bed?"

It was just about the last thing Gideon wanted to do, but he decided Danny had earned it. So he sat up late playing cards, then slept without dreams, to wake feeling as if he had forgotten something important. The feeling lingered as they went to break their fast and found Sir Philip Lord already awake. As Danny had predicted he was restored to himself and listened with interest to Gideon's account of the evening's events.

"Saturday?" he queried when Gideon finished.

"It has to be Saturday," Gideon explained. "That is the next day that a friend of Ellis is working there and will be able to let us in."

Lord surveyed him for a moment then nodded.

"You have done better than I would have thought. Well done."

"I, of course, merely walked in Gideon's star-spangled wake," Danny said, grinning.

"The difference being," Lord told him, getting to his feet and brushing a few stray crumbs from his coat, "I expect you to do better than I think you will—you always do."

"It seems to me Gideon does too," Danny observed, winking at Gideon as he got up.

Lord considered him.

"That remains to be shown. Although the signs are indeed promising so far. But come, Sir Theophilus is an impatient man and I think we should return to Mortlake."

THE ALCHEMIST'S PLOT

Gideon opened his mouth to point out that Sir Theophilus might not be a welcome visitor, except Danny forestalled him by speaking first.

"All of us?" Danny asked.

"Did you have other plans?"

"Perhaps. Someone needs to find Mags and I am not without resources as to who might be able to tell me where he has wound up."

"Your guild?"

"It was never a guild," Danny said, his tone one of patient explanation. "It also no longer exists as a single body, but the Company of Maisters of the Science of Defence still has a presence, if not a very visible one and I am counted a provost in its ranks. If you will grant me leave to do so, I will go and find out what I may. If Mags is in London, you can be sure it will be known."

Lord nodded. "An excellent notion, except I need your company today. If Gideon is accorded leave to undertake an investigation, someone will need to be with him."

Gideon saw the look that passed between the two men.

"What if," he said quickly, his tone drawing the gazes of both his companions. "What if instead of the boorish and insensitive Sir Theophilus returning to Mortlake to demand a tapestry be made forthwith, I go instead. I take my trusty armed servant, Tom, and see if Jannekin de Maecht would indeed like me to investigate?"

Lord looked at him for a moment and then smiled and gave a brief laugh.

"Danny, I think you are right. Exceeding expectations seems to be a trait you indeed share with Gideon."

Danny grinned then and slapped Gideon on the back.

"Welcome to the ranks of those who are seen to fail even when they succeed because they don't succeed well enough to suit the whims of Sir Philip Lord. Talking of which," he reached into his coat and pulled out a folded sheet unfolding it as he put it on the table, "Michael and Gabriel."

Gideon recognised the face of Gabriel as the man who Ellis had argued with and not someone he had seen before that occasion.

But the face of Michael made him draw a sharp breath. Lord looked at him.

"You know that man?" he sounded surprised, which suggested that he, too, had recognised the face.

"Sir Gilbert Brandon, he was someone my father knew well. He saw fighting in the German Wars, for Sir Horace Vere and then Count Mansfeld. His wife's family are one of the leading lights of the Hostmen cartel of Newcastle. But I haven't seen him since my father died."

"Hostmen," Lord echoed. "I wonder if he in any way influenced why it was you who received the invitation to go to Newcastle last year. If we have a chance to chat with Sir Gilbert, we must ask him."

"If he and Ruskin are the kind of men who are amongst the more senior in the Covenant, they seem not to be that great and powerful," Danny said. "More just wealthy and aspiring."

"That is because these men are just the servants of the Covenant, led on with promises of future high status—and often true believers in the insanity of it. The great ones always hide their faces behind masks so that they will not suffer if anything goes awry." Then Lord looked suddenly thoughtful. "Though one does have to wonder if any of the truly great are still committed. The Covenant is perhaps like a goose that has been beheaded, but its body still runs on."

"That might make it less dangerous at least," Danny observed.

"Or more," Lord said. "Do not underestimate the ferocity of those who seek power and feel it ebbing away between their fingers."

Gideon thought of Sir Bartholomew Coupland and Sir Richard Tempest, the two men he had met who he knew belonged to the Covenant.

"And their ruthlessness," he said.

"Indeed so," Lord agreed. "But now, gentlemen, we have work to do to thwart them."

Danny left them to set off into the London streets alone. Gideon took a wherry with a transformed Philip Lord clad as a servant, his

THE ALCHEMIST'S PLOT

face pocked, hair straggling and black and no longer with a paunch about the stomach.

They reached Mortlake a little earlier than they had on the previous day and this time it was Gideon who led the way up from the river to the main road and past the houses to the tapestry works. It all seemed undisturbed and as it had the day before, except of course when he reached the door there was no Jan Engles coming out. Instead, when he knocked, the door was answered by a tall thin man with a stoop who said that *mevrouw* de Maecht could be found at the limner's house, a couple of houses along, where she was visiting with *mevrouw* Cleyn. He seemed uncurious about why Gideon might want to speak to Jannekin de Maecht and as soon as he had offered that direction, closed the door again.

"I have the feeling," Lord murmured, "that the tapestry works is not working today. Perhaps we will find the limner is limnering."

The limner's house was a neat modern residence. Patently the house of a man of some means and Gideon was to learn that Francis Cleyn, the limner, was indeed such. He had received a regular pension of one hundred pounds a year from the king for his work, which must have placed him well above the earnings of even the best of the weavers. But then his task was to design and create magical pictures that would be recreated in silk and wool for wealthy clients.

Approaching the house, Gideon could hear someone playing the lute in one of the upstairs rooms, picking out a tune in the manner of the unskilled. And there were sounds of children laughing from somewhere within. It seemed a much less sombre place than the tapestry works by more than just its appearance. It struck Gideon that if the limner was indeed at his easel, he was a man who had little care if other distractions were going on around him, But then he realised he was mistaken to think that the art would be done in this house at all. There was no doubt a room set aside for him next door in the tapestry works so the whole process could take place under one roof—from initial designs through to the final woven item. He looked back at the long building and thought of the weaving hall. It was indeed an impressive manufactory and whoever had conceived of bringing the people and the process all under one roof was a man of some vision.

Lord stood behind him as they reached the door and Gideon knocked. At first, it seemed as if no one had heard and he had reached to knock for a second time just as the door opened.

The woman—no, the girl who opened it had a mass of brown curls tamed into fashionable ringlets. From her dress, she was no servant and from her age, a daughter of the house. Gideon swept off his hat in a brief bow.

"I apologise for disturbing you, but my name is Gideon Lennox, I am a lawyer, and I was hoping that *mevrouw* de Maecht might be willing to see me."

The girl, who Gideon decided must be in her mid-teens, studied him with as much surprise as if he had said he was an acrobat.

"Oh, a lawyer," she echoed. Behind her loomed the figure of a man who clearly was a servant and as if realising her time to do so was shrinking, she stepped aside with a welcoming gesture. "Then you must come in, Mr Lennox. I shall see if Mrs de Maecht will see you. Simon here will see your man is offered some refreshment in the kitchen."

From what Gideon could tell from his expression, Simon was wishing very much that he had reached the door first and prevented the importuning of a guest. But he grunted assent and took Lord off through the house in one direction whilst the girl led Gideon in another. At least it meant that Lord might be able to discover any servants' gossip whilst Gideon spoke to Jannekin de Maecht.

Gideon had expected to be shown into an empty room to wait, but when the girl opened the door into a private parlour, it was already occupied by two women. There was something in the glint the girl had in her eye that told Gideon she knew she was breaking polite convention and delighted in doing so.

"Mama," she said stepping into the room without waiting to be invited. "This is Mr Lennox, a lawyer who wishes to speak with Mrs de Maecht."

"Penelope!" The speaker had to be the girl's mother, sharing the same hair and eyes. She rose to her feet, her expression

THE ALCHEMIST'S PLOT

scandalised. But the other woman, who was indeed Jannekin de Maecht, put a hand out to touch her companion's arm.

"Peace be, Sarah," she said. "The girl has spirit. And I do wish to speak to Mr Lennox if you would be kind enough to allow it. Alone."

Gideon realised then that Jannekin was also related to the other two women.

Penelope's mother, who Gideon assumed must be Sarah Cleyn, drew herself up in silent disapproval and then with gaze lowered swept from the room, taking the girl with her, and letting the door smack shut behind her.

"I apologise, Mr Lennox, we are all fraught." Jannekin's voice had a soft lift and rounding to it that the Dutch seemed to bring to English. "Please come and sit with me. I promise you my tears have all been shed and you need not fear to be embarrassed by such."

"And I promise you I wouldn't be," Gideon assured her, stepping into his lawyer's role with an ease that surprised him. "It is understandable you would be distressed at such a time and if you wish me to leave now or at any point, please say."

Jannekin studied him with her forget-me-not gaze.

"It is strange, is it not, that it is the young like Penelope and the old such as myself who seem to care the least for convention? It seems those in the middle must be governed by it at all times. I think perhaps the young find it daring to flout, to challenge, but the old..." she smiled at Gideon as he sat in the chair she indicated, the one abandoned by Sarah Cleyn, "The old have learned to discern when convention has a purpose and when it is an obstacle. And, of course, we dare to say so and act accordingly."

"Convention has its purpose," Gideon said, wondering where this was leading. "Without it, we would often not know what to do or say."

"And wouldn't that be a marvellous thing sometimes?" She must have seen Gideon's discomfiture because she relented at once. "But you, of course, belong to the middle years and so we shall keep to convention as much as is possible under the circumstances."

"I shall be guided by you," Gideon assured her.

"Then let us get straight to the heart of this," Jannekin de Maecht said. "My brother and my cousin's son have both been murdered. Yet somehow both have been made to seem as if they took their own lives. You said you would be willing to help show that wasn't so. But I must tell you I'm not a wealthy woman. We live amid silk and gold, of course, but we are not owners of that. We borrow it from the wealthy to create their tapestries. So, if I cannot pay you much, are you still willing?"

Gideon nodded.

"I don't need to ask for any payment from you. Sir Theophilus is my employer, and he has agreed that I should do this. He understands very well that until this matter is cleared up it will be difficult to have his tapestry woven."

She seemed to relax a little at that as if she hadn't been sure of him until then.

"Of course," she said, "and that is how it should be." Then she released a sigh. "But I must confess that despite my conviction in this matter, I have no notion how to show it is so."

"That is my part," Gideon assured her. "Your part is to answer my questions, even if you find them strange, and to enable me to access wherever I may need to go in the tapestry works. I have a feeling that your husband might not be willing—"

"My husband is my concern," she said. "I will make sure you can go when and where you will."

That was exactly what he hoped to achieve.

"Thank you." he said, meaning it, then continued in the role he had cast himself. "You are so sure neither man who died was despairing, unhappy or in the frame of mind of self-hate?"

"Of course not. Gerhard was his usual cheerful self and Jan was very happy. He was in love."

Gideon recalled encountering Jan coming out of the tapestry works.

"Why might he have had reason to steal a bookstand?"

"A bookst...?" Jannekin de Maecht lifted a hand and clapped it to her knee. "He wished to sell it, of course. My Phillips is a parsimonious man at the best of times, and these are not the best of times. He would keep the better furniture to sell himself. I can only think Jan had gone back into that accursed room to take something from it to sell instead knowing no one would go in there and it would be some time before anything from there was noticed to be missing."

"What did he need the money for?"

"What do the young ever need money for? He had in mind to buy a lute."

"A lute?"

"That is what I said. And I thought it is we older ones who are supposed to be hard of hearing."

"But why—?"

"As a gift. I told you Jan was in love. It makes his death so cruel." For a moment her soft blue eyes filled with moisture, then she blinked. "Ah, the smoke in here."

Gideon looked at the blameless hearth and gave Jannekin de Maecht a few moments to compose herself.

"You are a good man, Mr Lennox," she said after a short while. "I have met some lawyers in my time, and most are not as kind. Do you have more questions?"

Feeling a fraud, Gideon avoided her gaze. He was here to exploit her grief so they could search the house. Then he knew he couldn't do that and live with himself. He was far from her conviction that the deaths were murders, but he would apply himself to the task of uncovering what had happened so he could at least show her the truth.

"I do have questions," he admitted. "However, they can wait for another time."

She lifted a hand.

"Please. You must ask them."

Gideon decided to start with the easiest and most obvious.

"You must all know each other well, living and working in the same place?"

"We do. It is as if we are one big family." The thought brought a smile to her face. "When the tapestry works were set up twenty-three years ago, some came from France, some from the Spanish Netherlands and some from the United Provinces, although they tried to stop us. We even received special dispensation to worship according to our faith. Sir Francis Crane was a good man. He paid us all well. Of course, our children often chose to wed and before long everyone was related to everyone else by marriage if not by blood. It was a good life. Then Sir Francis died. His brother had no head for the business. He sold the works to the king and the king told us we had to shift for ourselves as he wouldn't pay us." She sighed again, this time with an edge of frustration. "Even so we would have done well. Many wealthy patrons wished for our work, but then this war came, and no one wants to buy tapestries. Now we are broken. Some have left to go back home, others are talking about it. But for most of us, this is our home now so we turn our hands to what we may."

It was a sad story, but one which Gideon knew was being repeated in small ways across the country as the war disrupted trade and ruined businesses that needed peace to prosper.

"Is there anyone you can think of who might ill wish your brother and Jan Engles?"

Jannekin de Maecht shook her head at once. "I have thought over that very question many times and no, there is no one. Oh, some in the tapestry works have feuds with each other. God be thanked, none have yet come to blows, but Gerhard was always a content man and Jan was the soul of cheerfulness and joy. They were neither of them men to argue, unlike my Phillips, of course."

"And, I have to ask, for no one said at the time, but did Jan Engles die as your brother died?"

"On the high loom? Yes. But no one else will. My husband has had the thing broken up now and burned. He has also removed the lock from the door of the room so no one else can perish in there."

Which wasn't very helpful for Gideon who would very much have liked to see the exact circumstances of the deaths so he could better judge what had occurred.

A tap on the parlour door announced the return of Sarah Cleyn.

"We will be having dinner shortly, is Mr Lennox to stay?" Her tone made it very clear what she wished the answer to be.

Gideon got to his feet. "I wouldn't think to do so. I shall go."

Sarah Cleyn granted him a smile then.

THE ALCHEMIST'S PLOT

"I shall show you—"

"I shall show Mr Lennox out, of course," Jannekin de Maecht said. "As soon as we have finished our conversation."

Gideon wavered.

"We are to have dinner in less than half an hour," Sarah Cleyn protested.

"Then I will show him out on my way to dinner," Jannekin de Maecht assured her.

Left with no choice, Sarah Cleyn left the room and closed the door behind her.

"You see, Mr Lennox," Jannekin said, her light blue eyes dancing now with mischief, making her look very like Penelope Cleyn, "the old can bend convention and those who are trapped in its embrace have no choice but to bend too, of course."

Gideon sat down again as defeated as Sarah Cleyn had been.

"There's not much more to ask anyway," he said, trying to stifle the acute embarrassment he felt at being caught between the wills of the two women. "Is there anyone you couldn't speak for in the household, anyone who is not of your family?"

"Oh yes," Jannekin's face tightened again. "We used to have some very reliable servants who would keep the works clean and do much more besides, but with the way things went, we had to let them all go. Now we just have that slattern, Hester Lovegood. She is more about giving herself graces than cleaning well, but she is all we can afford."

Hester Lovegood. Why was he not surprised at that choice of name?

"Does she live in?" Gideon asked.

"She has a room at the west end of the works. She has little pay because she has full board here."

"Who employed her?"

"My husband, of course. She came with a letter of reference from someone in London, which he said was very reassuring."

"You don't know who the reference was from?"

"No. Is it important?"

Gideon shook his head. He was already sure she worked for the Covenant and the chances were any letter of reference would be falsified.

"Not really," he said., "One final question, can you arrange for me to have access to the tapestry works? I am not sure your husband will be—"

"Phillips will be content to allow it, I promise you. But it might take me a short time to convince him of that." Jannekin smiled and got to her feet, patting her skirts down as she did so. "I think I shall show you out now, Mr Lennox. This afternoon around three, I shall be at home. My parlour window is beside the door. I shall keep an eye out for you."

THE ALCHEMIST'S PLOT

Chapter Nine

A short time later Gideon and Sir Philip Lord were in the same private room they had occupied before in The Queen's Head on the Barnes Elms road, enjoying a meal of broiled mutton in claret sauce.

"That," Lord said, refilling his cup with a claret that was of a decidedly finer quality than the one used in the sauce, "was an interesting morning."

"You learned something from the servants?"

"Servant. Singular," Lord corrected. "The man you met, Simon, was not the most garrulous individual. I heard him utter less than a dozen words. However, his wife—who does the cooking—was a veritable waterfall of words, a torrent of talking, a stream of speech that seldom stemmed. All I needed to do was direct the flow by asking pertinent questions or make a mild observation at the right moment."

"What did you learn?"

"Firstly, no decent thinking English woman—or man—would set foot in the old sorcerer's house. It is haunted by his evil spirit and the demons he summoned there. Which is, you understand, the sole reason they had to bring in Dutch weavers to live and work there once it was bought cheap for the purpose. So it is, in Goodwife Shaw's well-informed and considered opinion, not surprising that there have now been two self-killings there in as many weeks. She is more surprised such never happened before."

"The house has a reputation then?"

"It has an eldritch and sinister one with some locals. Bessie Shaw had tales of lights and sounds, apparitions and phantasms from her childhood, almost all of which went away when the Dutch weavers moved in. Which makes Goodwife Shaw wonder why. She is not so keen on the foreigners with their own ways of worship, though she is generous spirited enough to grant that they have been good and godly neighbours in the community overall."

"But she works for a foreigner," Gideon pointed out, wiping the last of the sauce from his plate with a piece of bread.

"Bessie Shaw is quick to point out, her master attends the local church and is no longer foreign as the king gave him letters of denization. He is allowed to vote and own land like any natural-born Englishman and that makes him English enough for anyone." As he spoke, Lord's voice shifted to match the tones of the cook.

Gideon laughed then shook his head. There was little to laugh at in all this.

"Does she have an opinion on Hester Lovegood?"

"Goodwife Shaw has many and strong opinions on Hester Lovegood, who is, you must understand, a kind and most pious woman sent to the weavers in their hour of need. The hard work she does in that big old place and her not receiving more than a groat a week on top of her keep. The woman is close to beatitude if you will believe Bessie Shaw."

That made Gideon grimace, recalling the accounts he had been given of the devout and compassionate Mistress Goody who he knew for a fact had been torturing the women in her care.

"She's good at acting that part," he said, hearing the bitter note in his own tone. "I suppose there is little doubt she is working for the Covenant?"

"I suspect so."

"And whether she saw me or not, she will have heard the name Lennox mentioned and she will know it."

Lord nodded. "Which is why you are not going to be alone in that building."

"I wonder," Gideon said, the idea coming to him as he spoke, "if hers is the hand behind these deaths."

Lord frowned at him.

"You think they were murders, despite the evidence to the contrary? The inquest on Gerhard Spijker brought in a verdict of suicide." He looked thoughtful. "The inquest for Jan Engles is to be held here tomorrow afternoon. Perhaps you should attend."

"Not if it means missing an opportunity to search the house as, presumably, the weavers will be attending it."

Lord inclined his head.

THE ALCHEMIST'S PLOT

"A good point. What did you learn from *mevrouw* de Maecht?"

Gideon went over what he had talked about with Jannekin and the cold hostility he had felt from Sarah Cleyn.

"I suspect she is being protective. Her husband, Franz, is a step up from the weavers even though he is of their community. In fact," Lord added, reflecting, "I think Sir Theophilus might well visit and ask for a sitting tomorrow." He pulled his watch from its pocket and studied it. "Three o'clock did she say? Then we have time to see what we can learn about the affairs of the tapestry works from the local people." He hid the watch away again, an item that the servant he was pretending to be would certainly not be able to afford. "I will stay here in the tavern and see if I can find someone talkative in the common room. You could visit the church. Speak with the minister if he is about. Such are a good source of local knowledge."

Gideon felt a stirring of unease. "You think it safe for us to separate?"

Lord considered.

"I think it unlikely we have been remarked yet, although I could be mistaken. Certainly, no one followed us here. Be vigilant, but I think it should be safe enough."

In the end, Lord stepped outside, as Gideon left the inn so as to watch and ensure that there was indeed no one taking any interest. Since he wasn't called back, Gideon kept walking the short distance from The Queen's Head to the lychgate.

The Church of St Mary the Virgin was opposite the tapestry works. It had a sturdy tower crowned with a cupola and belonged to the last century. As Gideon walked into the quiet of the small graveyard, it struck him forcefully that Gerhard Spijker's death being ruled as suicide meant his body wouldn't be committed here or in any church. Instead, he would face burial in unconsecrated ground, in an unmarked spot that even his family might never know.

Justices with a more modern and compassionate understanding might choose to return a verdict of *non compos mentis* instead. If deemed insane, and surely no one sane could commit such an act, then the suicide could still receive the grace of the Church. But

Gerhard had been given the harshest fate. If it was indeed murder Gideon knew he must not allow that to stand. He would be saving the family untold grief and perhaps the soul of Gerhard himself from harm, though Gideon struggled with the notion of God rejecting someone falsely accused of a crime and therefore not correctly buried.

Distracted by such thoughts, he nearly missed the slight figure walking towards the church and stepping through the door. Brown curls escaped from beneath a lappet cap, marking her a possible member of the Cleyn family. Gideon quietly followed the young woman inside.

The church was plain within, with white walls and the stark ribs of the beams supporting the roof above. Very modern and not at all like the old churches that had once been Catholic. Some local dignitaries had been preserved in marble busts upon the walls and names chiselled into flags on the floor.

Gideon realised this must be the final resting place of John Dee. For some reason, that thought lifted the hairs on his forearms. If Sir Philip Lord had been born in the tapestry works, it would have been just before the death of John Dee and when it was still his house.

The woman was kneeling in prayer, head bowed and body shaking as if she was sobbing. His instinct was to retreat and leave her to her evident grief, but his resolution to clear the two weavers from the crime of suicide was stronger.

"Mistress Cleyn?"

The woman looked up at him with anguished eyes the same soft blue colour as Jannekin de Maecht's. Her tear-streaked face was an older iteration of Penelope Cleyn.

"Yes. I'm Magdalen Cleyn. Who—who are you?"

"I am a lawyer, Gideon Lennox, and Mrs de Maecht has trusted me to look into the deaths of Gerhard Spijker and Jan Engles." The woman's eyes widened at the mention of the names as Gideon thought how to express his intention without mentioning the calamitous words 'suicide' or 'murder'. "Mrs de Maecht is sure they were both slain by other than their own hands."

THE ALCHEMIST'S PLOT

There was a sudden look of hope in the blue gaze that met his own.

"And you, Mr Lennox, is that what you think too?"

Gideon hesitated. What did he think? Before he had spoken to Jannekin de Maecht he had been confident that these were suicides, but somewhere in the conversation that certitude had failed. He nodded.

"I believe Mrs de Maecht is right and I want to help prevent a great wrong being done to both men."

"We're not even supposed to mourn," the woman said, staring at her hands as if troubled that they committed some crime. "Jan and I—" Then she looked at Gideon, frowning. "No one knew. It was just between us. He said we had to wait, that it was a bad time to talk of marriage." Her eyes filled with tears again and she blinked them away.

"Mrs de Maecht knows how it was," Gideon said, wanting to give this woman a safe harbour for her grief. "She told me Jan was in love. It's the reason she's convinced he was harmed by another."

The young woman's eyes widened in surprise then her expression softened into relief.

Gideon spoke gently. "Is there anything you can think of to help me understand what happened to Jan?"

Fresh tears appeared, wiped quickly away as Magdalen Cleyn shook her head. "No one would have wanted to hurt Jan. He was such a good man."

"Yesterday I came with Sir Theophilus Bassington to enquire about having a tapestry woven. Jan was trying to take a book stand from the house to sell it. Mrs de Maecht said it was to purchase a lute."

For the first time, a smile transformed the woman's face.

"He had promised me a new lute for my birthday." The smile faded. "I wish I could think of something that might help you, but I cannot. Please, Mr Lennox, if you can show it was not…" Her voice and strength failed her, and the tears flowed again.

"I will do my best," he promised.

He left her praying and walked from the church only to step back quickly into the concealing shelter of the church porch.

Emerging from the main door of the tapestry works opposite was the unmistakable figure of Hester Lovegood. She was carrying a basket and set off at a brisk pace along the road.

Gideon's first impulse was to follow her until he realised the presence of the basket probably meant she was just going to purchase some more bread. She was still in sight when a man crossed the road from The Queen's Head and, turning too quickly, collided with her, sending the basket flying.

Gideon was grinning to himself at Hester Lovegood's evident discomfiture, but then his heart started hammering in his chest. He recognised the man and had seen him last dressed as a coachman, using horses to trample a man to death.

It was too far away to hear what they said but seemed little more than the apology and recrimination such an encounter might merit. However, when the man rescued the basket and restored it, Gideon was sure he had reached inside it as he did so. Keeping still and, he hoped, invisible, Gideon sheltered in the shadows of the church porch. But neither Hester Lovegood nor the ex-coachman so much as glanced towards the church. The man was headed towards the river steps and Hester Lovegood, basket on her arm, walked away along the street.

Sure what he had witnessed was the passing on of some message or report from Hester Lovegood to the Covenant, Gideon had to make a decision. Should he follow the man himself, or should he hurry back to the inn and fetch Lord first?

The sensible side of him said that the latter was what he should do. He already knew the man to be a ruthless killer. But the problem with taking that most sensible path was that if there was, by chance, a wherry already waiting on the foreshore, the coachman could be on it and away before Gideon could fetch Lord and the two of them get to the river steps. If he went directly, he could reach the river ahead of the man.

The decision seemed to make itself and he hurried across the churchyard, and along the road towards the river. He stopped the moment the crossing came into sight. There was indeed a wherry at the shore. Without thinking of the consequences, Gideon broke

THE ALCHEMIST'S PLOT

into a run and clambered into the wherry, pushing a coin at its owner.

"I'm in a hurry, please go right away."

The wherryman was clearly not a man to be ruffled and had his mouth open to protest, but the coin was enough, and he pushed out into the river. The coachman turned the corner and started running to the foreshore. He shouted for the boat to come back then caught sight of Gideon and glared. A moment later and having realised as Gideon had that there was no other boat in sight, the coachman turned and hurried back the way he had come, lost to sight behind the houses.

"Can you land me on the bank there?" Gideon pointed to a place beside a willow tree where there was a cut through past the tapestry works and which he was sure led to the road. "If you do and you keep going down the river there's another angel in it for you."

The wherryman still looked doubtful, so Gideon produced the promised angel.

"It's a bet I have with my friend back there," he said, mustering a grin. "A game we have on. I just ask you to take a customer from the next landing, not Mortlake, and this is yours."

The expression on the wherryman's face said exactly what he thought of young gentlemen who played such games, but he gave a dour nod and took the coin before pulling close to the bank so Gideon could alight.

Now it was a matter of luck. He just had to get to the inn and tell Lord. Pleased that the boatman seemed content to continue on downriver, Gideon broke into a run. The path he was on cut beside the tapestry works on one side and the wall of the house next to it, creating a brick-sided alleyway as it reached the road.

Which was where his luck ran out.

The coachman had made better time than Gideon had thought he might and was passing the entrance of the alley when Gideon was still a few paces away. Gideon froze, hoping the man wouldn't see him and would walk by, but something must have caught the coachman's attention because he glanced along the alley and their eyes met.

Gideon was reaching for his sword, but the coachman had already changed direction and closed the distance, grabbing his arm before he could finish freeing it. Gideon kicked out hard and spun away from his attacker in the narrow space he missed his footing.

That saved him.

The knife cut air where his throat would have been. Gideon tried to recover his balance and grab at the arm that held the knife, but it wasn't there anymore. They were as close as if in an embrace and the breath of the coachman filled Gideon's nostrils, the scent of onions and ale. Gideon saw the brief movement begin, that was all the man would need to plunge the knife into his stomach. He tried to bring up his arm to catch it, knowing even as he did so that he was too late and too slow.

Then the man was pulled away from him and hurled back against the wall, his head hitting it with a sickening crack.

"Good God Gideon, I said to be vigilant." Sir Philip Lord pulled the coachman up, stared at him for a moment then let him fall. "Pity," he said. Then, "At least you had the sense to get murdered in a place away from public view. Let's get him in the river before anyone notices. There's a stand of trees and a convenient willow that I can see."

They managed to move the dead coachman held between, arms over shoulders as if he were a drunk. But there was no one to see and they made the promised trees unregarded by the continuing bustle on the street at the far end of the alley.

"Who was he and what did you do to upset him?" Lord asked as they put the body down, shielded from both river and land by the willow's dense woody mass of branches which were ridged with unopened leaf buds.

"He was the man who drove the coach that was set to abduct Ellis and then trampled one of his own people so Danny and I couldn't take him alive."

"Covenant then?"

Gideon nodded, the reaction to violence and its aftermath taking the heat from his body and leaving him shivering in uncontrollable

THE ALCHEMIST'S PLOT

bursts. He sat on the dry ground at the base of the tree and leaned against the trunk.

"He was passed something by Hester Lovegood in the street and would have been on a boat and gone if I had done nothing."

Lord started searching the man.

"I will commend your courage," he said, "whilst questioning your good sense. There is nothing in this that is worth you dying for." He pulled a folded paper from inside the dead man's coat. "And it would have been my fault if you had."

"It's not just about you," Gideon said, examining his scraped hand. "Two men were killed in the tapestry works because of this. That would have happened whether you and I were here today or not."

Lord held up the paper which was covered with several rows of random letters.

"One for Danny I think," he said, then refolded it and slid it into his coat. "You are right, of course. Some local people are convinced that it was the house itself that killed the men—John Dee, they say, performed alchemy and summoned demons there."

"I met the woman Jan Engles had hoped to wed," Gideon told him. "She is a daughter of Frantz and Sarah Cleyn, I suspect their eldest. Jannekin de Maecht told me Jan had wanted to find something he could sell to buy a lute. Mistress Cleyn told me he had promised her a new lute for her birthday." Gideon tried to stop the shaking, furious with himself that he showed such weakness. "I promised her I would find out the truth about his death."

"Let us hope this ciphered sheet can be broken and will tell us more." Lord crouched beside Gideon and studied him for a few moments. "You are sure you took no injury? You look very pale."

"No. I am alright," he insisted. "We need to deal with this," he gestured to the dead man, "and then keep my appointment with *mevrouw* de Maecht. There is little time. They have already condemned Gerhard Spijker to a nameless and unconsecrated grave. I wouldn't see Jan Engles also thus disposed of and the inquest is, you said, tomorrow afternoon."

Lord straightened up shaking his head. "You're determined, I see that. Then we will do what is needed here and return to the inn and take a room for the night so we can see this through. You need a drink, I think and right now, so do I."

"What about Danny?"

"He will wait for us if he has even finished his own task."

It took a little time to dispose of the body in the river, weighed with heavy stones so it would remain undiscovered for a time. Fortunately, the bank below the willow tree was steep and once they had rolled it into the water, the body vanished.

"It buys us a few days, perhaps, before the Covenant find out what happened to him and realise that whatever information is in that note is likely no longer secret," Lord said.

By the time they got back to the inn they had managed to brush off most signs of the encounter and Gideon was no longer shaking. He sat in the private room, absorbing the warmth of the fire and sipping on a cup of aquavitae whilst Lord arranged what was needed in his name. Then, with Gideon somewhat restored, they left the inn for the tapestry works a little bit after the appointed time.

Jannekin de Maecht was as good as her word, and no sooner had they approached the door than she was there to open it herself.

"My husband knows you are here and will show you upstairs to the room you need to see," she told him, her gaze moved to Lord. "Your servant—"

"I will keep Thomas with me," Gideon said and something of understanding seemed to touch her lips and sadden the soft blue of her eyes.

"Of course," she said. "That would be wise." There were footsteps in the passageway behind her. "And here he is now. Phillips? You will show this man the room, please?"

De Maecht gave a resigned nod, gesturing to the stairs and Gideon had to wonder how his wife had persuaded him to cooperate with what she wanted.

"This way, if you will, Mr Lennox."

He led the way upstairs, past the door to the weaving hall and onto the upper gallery. This had three chambers to the side. It was the furthest room of the three he took them to—a now empty room. Dominated on one side by an impressive fireplace, which included

THE ALCHEMIST'S PLOT

a frame across the mantle with rondels of the Tudor rose, a design which was carried on around the panelled room with the roses painted in red and white.

Gideon felt the hairs on the back of his neck prickle as he saw the central design above the hearth. It, too, was decorated with a circular rose, red outer petals, white inner and an embossed golden centre. But the whole was painted as if pinned on the breast of a black eagle, wings and tail feathers spreading out from the sides of the rose and below, its proud beaked head, crowned and surmounting the rose.

He could feel the stillness in Sir Philip Lord beside him and knew that he was having a similar moment of chilling memory. They had both seen an identical design on a ceiling in one of the secret rooms in Howe Hall. If they needed any further proof to link the two this was it.

ELEANOR SWIFT-HOOK

Chapter Ten

London.

Danny knew it meant something different to those who grew up here than to men like himself—men who came here as youths because of what London was. To men like himself, it would always be a place to make the pulse beat faster, a place where the very cobbles seemed to shimmer with promise. A place where vibrancy and excitement gave life to the veins and made everything that was dull and tawdry, shine brightly.

Having travelled over much of Europe and around the Mediterranean in the last ten of his thirty-odd years, Danny still loved London over anywhere else. But he would never choose to live there again.

Part of the love was grown in absence. Part of the joy was in rediscovery, and a huge part of the delight was in knowing this was the place to which he had given the dreams of his youth. Every street ambushed him with memory: there the tavern he had won his first angel at cards and there the shop he purchased the first hat he chose for himself. Some were less pleasing like the alley where he had been beaten up on his second day in the city. Back then he had walked the streets as prey—naive, innocent and hopeful. Now he stalked them as a predator—experienced, skilled and knowing. Knowing too much, perhaps.

Hanging Sword Alley ran behind Water Lane and never quite made it to Fleet Street. Its strange name came from the sign of a sword which once hung out over the alley where there was a fencing school. There had been one there for over a hundred years as far as Danny was aware. One end of the alley was a set of steps, so narrow that to pass someone on them you had to turn sideways, and the other end was The Crown. Between the two was a stretch of open gutter, lined with cobbles and flanked on either side by old houses, three or four stories high, where entire families lived in one room and thought themselves lucky to do so. In places it was

THE ALCHEMIST'S PLOT

so narrow Danny could hold his arms out to either side and press his palms flat on the walls.

Once it had been Whitefriars after the Carmelite monastery that had occupied this ground. But even after the monastery was gone the place kept its right of sanctuary and had been granted freedoms that amounted to self-rule. So here had come those seeking to escape justice, debtors, fraudsters and worse.

Today they called this place Alsatia. Some wit had come back from devastated, war-torn Alsace and seen the state of these tenements and alleys between the prisons of the Gatehouse and the Bridewell and named it after that ravaged province. The name had stuck, testament both to the conditions in the place and the fact that there were many men there who had served in the armies and returned home to England with little or nothing to show for it except perhaps a missing limb. Even those who lived here and hadn't been abroad to fight, knew the names of the battles, the sieges and the great commanders. The boys in the streets could recite them better than their alphabet. The gossip of foreign wars and old soldiers was the gossip of Alsatia. And now they had a war at home to talk of too.

If you were a citizen of average means you would look wealthy here. Having no wish to draw attention to himself, Danny wore his servant's garb and had a grey knitted bonnet crushed over his hair and an old soldier's coat in faded mulberry with darker marks that suggested blood stains to Danny's expert eye. The coat covered most of his sword, which went some way to concealing its worth. It would be irritating if he had to keep drawing it to defend his right to keep it.

The Crown sat in a tiny courtyard, and it was moot whether its front was on Fleet Street or its back. Either way, it was the most prosperous-looking building on the alley. Sitting like a guardian crouched at the gates of hell, the crown on the sign was a depiction of the coin, not the headwear. It was the closest most of those who lived in the tangle of streets and alleys behind it ever got to see such a thing.

He had expected to be able to slip in unnoticed but was doomed to disappointment.

"Danny!"

"Oh my God, look who it isn't?"

"By all that's holy, what is *he* doing in here?"

"Fallen on hard times, Danny?"

It was as if he had just walked in after a week away, not close to a decade. He was slapped on the back and bought drinks. Someone pulled him into a card game and when he won, he slipped half a crown to the hostess to buy drinks for everyone there. Then he lowered his voice.

"And a word, if you can, I have news you need to hear."

Jude Rider, the hostess of The Crown, leased the tavern as her mother had before her and her grandmother before that although there was no daughter to take over from her. But Danny thought, perhaps a niece who might one day. Her dark complexion and braided hair, now showing traces of grey, spoke of her father who had grown up under an African sky. She took Danny's coin and then gave him a hard look. "It's Matt?"

Matt. Matthew Rider. Captain Matthew Rider, though he had held higher ranks in his time. The man who had been Philip's mentor and friend, and Danny's too.

He nodded, hating that he had to do this, but knowing no one else could or would. Matt had grown up here. This was the only home he'd ever known except an army camp. Jude served the drinks and then drew him into her kitchen, ignoring the bawdy calls that followed them there. The Crown was a tavern, not an ordinary, but you could still buy a meal as long as you were happy with pottage.

She surveyed him with her knowing dark gaze.

"Matt's dead, isn't he?"

"I should have written," Danny said. "But..." There was no 'but'. He should have written. It wasn't as if she couldn't read.

"No. You did right," she told him, placing a hand on his arm. "I knew the last time he was here that he'd never be back one way or another. He was my brother. I just knew." She stepped away from Danny and sighed, moving to turn her back and stir the large cauldron seething in the hearth. "How did it happen?"

THE ALCHEMIST'S PLOT

And that was when it got almost too hard. He didn't want to say, but she had to know.

"He was murdered, Jude. Poisoned when he was just recovering from a knifing."

Her whole body stiffened, and her head lowered.

Danny had been glad she had her back to him. She wouldn't want him to see her shock, to see her pain at the knowledge that her brother hadn't died a soldier's death of the kind she had always thought he must but been destroyed in a coward's act.

It was a full minute before she was able to turn and face him. The longest of minutes in which he stood, bleakly, in the comfortable warmth, hearing the sound of happy voices from the common room and with the familiar smells of pottage, malt, ale, and smoke from the fire.

When she turned, she was composed, and her dark gaze searched his face.

"There is worse." It wasn't a question.

"The man who killed him convinced Máire and Liam that he was their friend, and another's hand was responsible." Swallowing hard Danny finished what needed to be said. "He took Máire as his woman and Liam to be like a son. They went with him. Only Brighid saw through the act and stayed." Danny knew his words were lacerating Jude's very soul.

"And where are they now?"

"They went back to Máire's people," he said, giving the words conviction. "Ireland somewhere."

That was what he had heard from some who had left Mags and it was what he had told Philip. He hoped it was true. But he had also heard a breath of rumour about an Irish woman and her son being hanged for stealing, and her two young daughters being taken in by a godly family to raise them as true Protestants. It was only a rumour and he kept it to himself.

"You were wise not to write," Jude said. "So, this man still lives. Why is that?" The taut anger and challenge in her voice made him feel shame.

"Because of who he is," Danny admitted. "You will know of him. Many in Alsatia know and admire him."

"The Schiavono." Her assumption was rigid. As if it were a known fact.

That struck Danny hard, like a physical blow that winded him. But then Judith Rider had never met Philip and Danny had long since realised Matt preferred it that way. He had always kept her apart from his work. Rightly so too for her safety. Danny only knew her because he had known Jude before he met Matt.

"No. It wasn't the Schiavono," he said. "It was Mags."

That made her eyes widen. The implications ran through his mind with the rapid-fire calculation of a mathematical equation.

"Christ," he said. "What have you heard?"

"Someone was here. Weeks ago. He told everyone the Schiavono had killed Matt. I didn't know what to believe."

Danny drew a breath. He had to remember these people knew the ruthless reputation. They didn't know the man who held it.

"Who was saying that?"

She shook her head.

"He was a soldier, home to join the army here. Came in one night with tales to tell. I can see if any remember his name."

Danny shook his head. "I'm sure a man sent with such tales has names to fit every occasion. Did he say why Matt was killed? That must have been a clever story as everyone who knew Matt knew he was a man the Schiavono trusted."

Jude pulled her shoulders into a hunched shrug.

"He didn't need to give a reason. Why do such men kill one another? You'd know better than I. He got drunk, perhaps? Or Matt said the wrong thing at the wrong time?" She shook her head. "You say he was killed by Mags. What's the difference? Why would Mags want Matt dead?"

"Because Mags wanted Matt's place."

Which made no sense to Jude, as he could see. How to explain that Mags had been humbling himself so he could rise? What could the battle for power between two such men as Philip and Mags ever mean to her? How could he begin to explain it and the consequences that flowed from it? He didn't even try. Instead, he spoke words Jude would understand—words all of Alsatia could understand. Words of vengeance.

THE ALCHEMIST'S PLOT

"I came here because Mags is somewhere in London, and I am going to find him and make him pay for what he did to Matt."

"Your word on it?"

"I swear to God, I'm here to kill the man who killed Matt."

She studied his face for a moment longer then gave a brief nod. "I believe you. And you'll want my help."

He nodded. She might not understand his world, but she wasn't a fool.

"If anyone has word of where Mags can be found..."

"I'll ask about." Wiping her hands on the apron she wore, Jude pushed a straying braid back under her coif. "Not much happens that news of it won't come to The Crown.'

"Have a care when you do so."

"I always do," she said, picking up a wooden bowl and putting a ladle full in from the cauldron. "You'd best have something to eat." She set it on the old wooden table, with a battered pewter spoon. She gestured to the loaf that sat beside it. "Help yourself to bread."

Then she turned to the door and would have gone, but Danny called her back.

"Jude." He reached into his coat and pulled out the purse he had put there. "This was Matt's. I can't give it to Máire, and Brighid is well looked after—there's someone she has her eye on, one of the Schiavono's officers, a good man. I think Matt would have wanted you to have it."

Paying a debt. The coin was his own. The debt for himself and Philip.

Jude frowned and took the purse, then feeling its weight opened it, tipping the coins onto the table and the sparkle of gold caught like dust motes in the air. She stared at the money and then looked up at Danny, her eyes wide.

"This is too much." She picked up a unite and held it cupped in her hands as if it were a priceless gem. "There must be twenty pounds here. Now, what am I supposed to do with that?"

Have a better life. What the hell else was money for?

Danny gestured about them. "You could use it to do this place up."

At least that made her smile. She scooped the coins back into the purse and pushed it out of sight into her bodice.

"You eat," she said, more firmly than before. Then she was gone back through the door. The food would be good, if far from the finest and he was tempted. But perhaps later. He still needed to visit one more place in Hanging Sword Alley to pay a very different kind of debt.

He left The Crown by the back door and wasn't too surprised to find that two men barred his path. He knew neither, but they both seemed to know him.

Sadly for them, they didn't know him well enough.

There were no words, but blades spoke, and his spoke with the sharpest and most cutting tones. Perhaps they thought being two on one they would find the task easy. Danny sidestepped the first clumsy thrust and used a solid kick with the sole of his boot to dissuade the second attacker whilst he downed the first. He even pondered the notion of letting them both go but knew if he did then word of his weakness would bring more of the same.

So he drove his sword home and turned to slice at the second man, carving his ear away from his skull as cleanly as a surgeon. Then he brought the point to his ambusher's throat.

"I'm going to let you live," he said when the man began burbling words. "I don't know who you are, and I don't care, but be sure to tell any others who might think to try me, that Danny Bristow spared you to warn others not to do as you and your friend tried to do."

Then he pressed the severed ear into the man's hand before letting him go. The man ran off and vanished into the depths of Alsatia, clutching at the side of his head.

And this was the civilised end of the place.

Danny stooped to wipe his blade on the dead man's coat. It was Alsatia. A dead body left in an alley was not uncommon. Sooner or later his friends would come and carry him off.

He put his sword away and walked along the alley to where the eponymous hanging sword had once hung. It had been a painted wooden blade, or so Danny had heard, although time had long since rotted it away. But the name survived and the place it had

THE ALCHEMIST'S PLOT

marked was still there. The door was one of the more solid in the area, metal strapped, but it opened easily enough. The trick was that the weights would swing and make the bell ring upstairs. Danny had done that, and he was proud it still worked.

Knowing his arrival wasn't going to be any secret, he ran lightly up the stairs. The room was as wide as the house and about twice as long as it was wide. In the middle of the wooden floor was a large painted circle and the panelled walls were decorated with dusty framed sketches of men with puffed breeches and ruffs in the various basic postures of fencing.

At the far end three young men, stripped to shirts and breeches, were standing in imitation of one of the poses on the wall and trying to look as if they knew how to hold their swords. To the side of the three youngsters, two of whom at least Danny was sure were still in their mid-teens, stood a man wearing a sleeveless leather jerkin over his shirt. He was tall, half a head over Danny, and straight as a scouring stick. His long grey hair was pulled back from his face and bound with a leather thong. He held his sword as if it grew from his hand.

He glanced at Danny, taking him in with a single look. Danny wondered how he would feel about what he saw. But there was no trace of reaction. Not even a flicker of expression. Then his attention was back on the three students. Correcting their posture and putting them through the most basic of moves. It was their first or second class.

The clock on the wall whirred and chimed and there was a look of relief on the faces of the youngsters as they were dismissed. Two waited by the door, one frowning at Danny in his poor attire, as the third stopped to pay for his tuition. Then the door closed behind them, and their voices and footsteps could be heard going downstairs.

Danny stayed where he was, a pace or so to the side of the door. He had lived this moment in imagination a few too many times and the reality of it wasn't as he'd thought it would be.

"You came back then?" Even today after over twenty-five years lived in London and being a naturalised Englishman who once trained a prince, he still had a Venetian accent.

"I said I would." Danny gestured to the room. "You're still here."

This was the place he had come to when he had discovered he could be taken on by a master in weapons training as an apprentice if he fought for his place. He had fought and won, beating all the others who tried, and this was the man he had been apprenticed to as a result.

Venturo di Zorzi.

"I said I would be, Daniele." He frowned. "Why would you doubt me? Did I ever lie to you?"

And there it was. The inevitable accusation. But Danny wouldn't have come here if his promise had been a lie.

When he didn't answer, di Zorzi came a pace closer.

"Your room is still here if you wish to stay."

That was low. He was no apprentice.

"I'm not staying," Danny said. "I need to find a man."

"One who is hunting you too?"

"It seems very possible, but I don't know for sure."

Master di Zorzi smiled, and his sword vanished into its scabbard. He strode over and embraced Danny in the way the English did, showing none of his professional Venetian reserve.

"You were always popular with everyone. Even those you defeated. It is something any man could envy. I heard you sold your soul to gunpowder."

Danny moved his hand so his coat was pushed back from the hilt of his sword.

"That's not the whole story."

Di Zorzi's eyes widened. "Let me see."

With great reluctance, Danny drew his blade and offered it hilt first. He felt naked. But a promise was a promise. Di Zorzi took the sword and touched a finger to wipe away a trace of blood. "You have not forgotten how to use it, I see."

In his imagination of this meeting, Danny had seen himself having to prove that and bring the man who he'd never defeated to admit he'd been bested by his own pupil. But that man had been ten years younger. Faced with the reality Danny found he had no stomach for such a match. He would take the loss of his sword. It had been pledged and it was little enough in payment for what this man had taught him. The knowledge that had kept him alive the last ten years—ten years of life he wouldn't have had without that teaching.

"I could never forget," he said.

"You forget other things though." Di Zorzi's face seemed to darken, and he looked at the sword in his hand lifting it to study the workmanship of the basket-weave hilt.

"No. I don't," Danny said carefully. "That's why I'm here."

"I thought you were here hunting a man?"

"I came to London to hunt a man. I went to The Crown to find news of him. I came here—" Danny wondered why it was so hard to say. He knew that even three months ago, had chance brought him here, it would have been easy. But that was before he knew Christobel even existed. Before his life had any real value. Before he had realised the real value of this blade. "I came *here* because I promised that I would."

"It was a promise made a long time ago. Some might think that makes it less binding."

Dear God! Did the man not want him to be here? Didn't want him to have come to fulfil his promise? Didn't want to take the one thing Danny had that made him the man di Zorzi had trained him to be?

Danny screwed up his nose, hoping to show what he thought of the notion. "I am not that sort of man."

Venturo di Zorzi laughed as if Danny had made the best joke in the world.

"You have the expression of a man facing the gallows, Daniele—the gallows. I'm not a hangman. Why come to me as if you expect me to berate you? I will not hold you to the words you spoke when you were little more than a boy. I never intended to do so. All I wanted to know was whether you ever would become a man who would live up to his word and his responsibilities, a man I can be proud to say I trained. I knew if I made you take that vow that, were you not become such a man, you would never return. And that would be no loss to me as it would mean you were not a man I could ever wish to know."

With a simple fluid motion, he moved his grip on the sword and offered it, pommel first, back to Danny.

"Take it. Keep it. It is a better blade than I ever thought you would win, and I suspect it came to you through friendship as much as through fighting. Swords like that one, do not find their home by violence alone." That had always been his way, to talk of swords as if they were living things. "You can redeem your pledge another way. Promise me instead that you will take on an apprentice. I would not have my best student fail to pass on such skill to another. It would be a travesty of my life's work."

Danny felt his whole being petrify. As if he'd become a granite statue of himself. His hand paralysed, fingers just short of touching the hilt. The image of a young man stark in his mind, branded there by blood. Then his hand moved and fell back to his side, and he was able to breathe and speak again.

"No," he said. "You keep the sword."

Di Zorzi studied his face for a moment, then nodded.

"Very well, I will," he said. "When you come to me with an apprentice one day, you may redeem it."

Danny shook his head. His hand was shaking slightly, wanting to curl back around the familiar grip, wanting to reclaim what was his own. "That will not happen."

Then he made a stiff bow, of the kind an apprentice owed to his master. He had done what he came for and before he could give in to the basest part of his nature, he strode to the door.

"Daniele, take this."

He turned to see di Zorzi holding out his own blade, the one he'd been using to demonstrate to the class when Danny walked in.

Danny drew a breath, the anger and anguish inside him fighting like cats in a sack, but he pushed them both away. "I don't—"

"I have no need for this one as it seems I have a much finer one now. Take it."

Pride grappled with reason and fired by the heat of his emotion, pride was winning. But he'd forgotten di Zorzi had once known him better than he'd known himself. Now the Venetian smiled and gave a brisk nod before Danny could respond.

THE ALCHEMIST'S PLOT

"I will be in The Crown in an hour. If you are there, we can play piquet for it."

Pride bowed its head and Danny found his face relaxing enough to respond with a smile of his own. "I'll be there."

Then he closed the door behind him and ran down the stairs and into the streets of Alsatia.

ELEANOR SWIFT-HOOK

Chapter Eleven

Gideon was frustrated and perplexed.

This was the room where the murders had occurred and for them to have been murders despite the locked door, there had to be some kind of secret passageway hidden in the walls such as he and Sir Philip Lord had found in Howe Hall. The problem being there was no such secret passageway. Or at least none that they could locate.

Having persuaded Phillips de Maecht to leave them be, Gideon and Lord went over the entire room, studying the panels, feeling around each of the roses for any hint of a concealed lever and even stepping into the empty hearth and looking up the chimney. There was no indication of any way to open a hidden door, no clues to be had in any of the most obvious designs or features in the room. Each rose was identical to the one beside it as far as he could tell with red outer petals, white inner and a yellow centre. The wood panels themselves seemed to be flush against the wall with no obvious way to move them unless with tools designed for the task.

It was beginning to turn to twilight when Lord slid down the wall and sat, long legs outstretched on the floor, leaning back against one of the panels. "Either we are missing something, or we are completely mistaken," he said.

Gideon ran his fingers around the edges of the central boss on the fireplace, hoping against hope that he'd missed something the previous times he had done the same thing. It seemed a strange thing to have the bar running above the hearth with its roses and the plaque, and the most obvious place to conceal a secret lever. But, as before, there was nothing there and the heraldic device itself was firm and unyielding.

"Unless the deaths were in fact suicides, there has to be another way into this room. What about the window?"

Lord pushed himself to his feet again and went over to the window, peering out.

THE ALCHEMIST'S PLOT

"It might be possible to climb along the outside wall to the next room, but it would also be very obvious if anyone were to do so as these windows overlook the road."

Gideon sighed.

"So not the window then."

"Not the window, the fireplace, the panels," he stamped on the floorboards, "or the floor. What are we missing here, Gideon?"

"I wish I knew."

Lord sighed and stretched.

"I think we should abandon this search for today."

It was hard not to agree, but it was harder still to give up.

"Tomorrow afternoon Jan Engles could be declared *felo de se* and denied the right to have a decent Christian burial as a suicide. I am not happy to just abandon this. Besides, we know there must be something here. The Covenant have one of their own here—Hester Lovegood."

"Unless," Lord said, "she is here as you suggested because this is a place they could be certain I will visit at some point."

Gideon felt his frustration bubble up.

"Perhaps we should ask her then?"

Lord looked at him sharply.

"You know you could be right. She might be venal." His expression shifted and became thoughtful. "Except this is a matter of murder and if she is involved in it then she will hardly be willing to condemn herself even for gold and we lack the ability here to employ any more coercively persuasive approach."

Coercively persuasive.

Gideon suppressed a shudder. He had seen how persuasive Lord could be using torture. It was a grim thought. But the unavoidable fact remained that they needed to do something. Hester Lovegood would know Gideon was there and that would change things.

"Perhaps if she thought I was here alone and vulnerable, she might make some attempt…" He broke off. It could be more than an attempt. Whoever she was, Hester Lovegood was a cold-blooded killer. "My concern is if she feels herself to be in any danger she will do what she did in Pethridge and disappear again."

"I think as long as she has no notion that I am here she will stay," Lord said. "She may even see you as a possible lead to me and if so—" He stopped talking abruptly. "Anyway, we have done what we can here for today. We should go."

Gideon led the way downstairs to find Phillips de Maecht waiting for him by the weaving hall.

"Did you find anything, *meneer* Lennox?"

Gideon shook his head. "Nothing so far, I regret, and it is getting too dark to continue to search, so with your kind permission I will return in the morning to continue."

"You mean to come back?" de Maecht just managed to keep the appalled tone from his voice, but its presence was clear.

"I do indeed," Gideon assured him. "I shall be staying at The Queen's Head tonight." Then to soften the impact he added, "Sir Theophilus has also asked me to begin the preliminaries regarding the matter of his tapestry. I will speak to you about that as well."

Which served to mollify the tapissier enough that he bade Gideon a cordial good night.

The Queen's Head kept a good supper table and at Sir Philip Lord's insistence, they were to eat in the common room.

"You are going to express a strong interest in anything to do with Dr John Dee," Lord explained in the privacy of their bed chamber. He pulled out the servant's truckle provided and prodded the mattress experimentally. "He was, as he admitted in his own words, renowned as *a companion of the hellhounds, a caller and a conjuror of wicked and damned spirits.* He was astrologer and councillor to Elizabeth, the very queen whose head adorns this hostelry. He was also accused and arrested for seeking to murder, by magical means, her half-sister—my putative great and maybe more grand-mother. I am sure there must be many tales that those who live here will know or have heard from parent or grandparent."

"And do you believe he conjured spirits?" Gideon asked.

"What I believe is not important," Lord said, straightening up. "What is clear is he believed that he did."

THE ALCHEMIST'S PLOT

They went down to the common room, where Gideon applied his skill in conversation bringing the talk around to the topic of John Dee.

It wasn't difficult as the recent deaths of the two tapissiers seemed to bring back many memories about the previous inhabitant of the house. There were plenty who were keen to speak about Dee casting horoscopes and strange lights seen by night. Rumours he had been conjuring spirits or practising alchemy and making lead into gold in his laboratory. Most spoke of him with wary respect, some as a baneful influence. But a few Gideon talked to, mostly the older people, seemed to have a very different view. They remembered Dee as a benefactor and spoke of him with high regard and even affection.

One in particular, who introduced himself as Richard West, seemed happy to share what he knew. He spoke of Dee as a stately old man, a good Christian, kind to his neighbours and given to study. West was an older man and someone of more substance.

"He was my neighbour, you see," West explained. "I own the houses on both sides of what is now the tapestry works and live in the one next door and downriver. Of course, Dr Dee was a very old man when I was still little more than a boy, but I remember him as kind enough. The wild stories told about him were made by the ignorant and foolish. You see, Dr Dee was a real scholar, the kind who loved learning for its own sake. And he was generous too. Before his library was spoiled, he made it open to all who wished to study there. Mortlake had some fine and famous visitors at the time because it was the best library in all Europe. But that was before my time, of course."

Gideon, a lover of books, thought of the tapestry works and wondered how many it could have once contained.

"What happened to the library?"

"When Dr Dee was away on his travels, he left his wife's brother to look after the house. Thieves broke in and stole some of the rarest books and messed the rest up. Many survived, but when he got back and found what had happened it took the heart from him. He had been so proud of the library."

ELEANOR SWIFT-HOOK

"What was done with the remains of it when he died? Did it go to his children?" Then realising he had no idea, Gideon added: "Did he have any children?"

"Oh, he had children. Some outlived him even. His eldest son, Arthur, was in Muscovy as physician to the tsar himself. He came back to England a few years ago when his wife died, and the king took him on for a time. Last I heard he was in Norwich, but he must be an old man now. Another son, Rowland, he became a vintner, I think, and his daughters..." West screwed up his face in thought. "Katherine married a Welshman if I recall. The younger one was a pretty thing. She had a strange name, slips my mind what it was, but I don't know what happened to her."

"And it was Arthur who had the library?"

Gideon's heart sank at the thought. Norwich was a long way.

West took a sip of the wine Gideon had bought for him and nodded his appreciation of it, before setting it back on the table.

"No. Not at all. There was a sale a couple of years after Dr Dee died. Katherine organised it just before they left Mortlake. Furniture, books and so forth. I bought some items myself. The man who took all Dr Dee's remaining things after that was Sir Robert Cotton. He came here and turned the place over. He was even digging in the grounds. I could see him doing it from my window. If there were any books or papers left, he had them away. They'll be somewhere in his library today. Sir Thomas, his son, still keeps it."

Gideon felt a sudden pulse of excitement. He knew the Cotton library and had visited it before. They had walked past it several times since arriving in London. It was in a street near Westminster Hall. Like Dee's library, Cotton had made it available to scholars and he had the finest imaginable collection of ancient manuscripts in it. Was it possible that what they sought had been bundled up with other papers and placed there?

He put the idea to Philip Lord when they retired to their room.

"It is possible," Lord agreed. "But not probable. Cotton was a studious man, an antiquary. He would have been through the papers and if he had found such—" He broke off. "If he had found such, the Covenant would have been exposed and destroyed whilst

THE ALCHEMIST'S PLOT

I was still a young child. I would either have been killed or imprisoned as a clear threat to the state." He spoke of it so dispassionately that Gideon shivered.

"Unless he kept them secret."

Lord inclined his head in tacit acceptance of the possibility.

"If we find nothing here, we could look there." He agreed, making no move to prepare for bed, instead staring out of the window which overlooked the road.

"We should get some sleep," Gideon suggested. He was sitting on the bed and had begun working his boots off.

"You may if you wish," Lord said. "I have other plans." He strode over to the door. "I would like to see Mortlake by night. It could be enlightening."

Gideon wondered what on earth they could see by night which wasn't better seen—and safer so—by day.

"And this is the real reason you wished us to stay here tonight?"

Lord considered, hand on the door latch. *"Nolo contendere."*

"You do know this is more the sort of behaviour I would expect from Danny?" Gideon protested, pushing his foot back into the boot.

"And where do you think the estimable Mr Bristow gained his taste for such things?" Lord asked, his eyes catching the candlelight and gleaming with a feral light. "Before he met me Danny was a mild-mannered child who attended church three times on Sundays and spent his days in charitable good works and his nights in peaceful slumber. Besides, as I recall, it was you who decided to walk the streets of Paris in the yoke, buckets and hoop of a water seller. Next to that, my suggestion of a moonlit stroll is very tame."

Gideon sighed. He was never going to be allowed to live down that incident. "May I at least ask the why and where for this outing?"

"The where is the tapestry works and the why…" Lord trailed off. "A soldier's instinct, perhaps."

He opened the door and Gideon followed him out, then led the way downstairs. It wasn't yet late, and the common room still had several local people sitting there as well as a handful of guests staying there. Richard West nodded to Gideon as they passed through and stepped out into the cool night of early spring.

The moon gave only the slightest assistance as they walked by the churchyard. Lord stopped. There were lights dimly visible in some of the residential rooms of the tapestry works.

"What are we looking for?" Gideon asked, keeping his voice to the same low tone Lord was using.

"I will tell you when I see it," was all the reply he received. "Let us look at the back of the works."

Gideon recalled the grounds behind the building. He had no wish at all to go there in the dark, but Lord was already moving. They took the same alley between the houses and the tapestry works where Gideon had been attacked. But once free of the walls of the outbuildings, the way down to the river was open. The river itself flowed dark, with ripples silvered to beauty by the moon, whose face was reflected in the water. Lord stepped forward and was swallowed into shadows. Gideon followed, picking his way with care. The back of the house came into sight, some rooms with lights, one of which went out as they made their way across the grounds.

It was so dark that Gideon didn't realise Lord had stopped and nearly ran into him.

"What are you doing?" Gideon whispered.

"Counting windows," Lord said softly. "It seems I was mistaken."

Gideon suppressed his annoyance. "We could have counted windows better by day," he said tightly.

"We could," Lord conceded. "Then we could not have acted had my idea been proven to be correct." He stepped past Gideon, and they began the careful trek back to the path that led between the buildings and back onto the road. They walked in silence. Gideon might have shared the disappointment he felt emanating from Lord if he'd understood what they were looking for. Since Lord hadn't troubled to explain, he felt irritation at both that silence and the fact he had been dragged out to tiptoe through the bushes in the dark of night for no good reason.

THE ALCHEMIST'S PLOT

They reached the road, which was now deserted as the honest residents of Mortlake settled themselves to sleep. Crossing over to the churchyard, Lord turned and looked back. Gideon kept walking. It wasn't a warm night and he had damp legs and cold feet from the undergrowth they had pushed through.

Behind him, Lord gave a low laugh, which made him stop and look back.

"Perhaps we may yet uncover the mystery after all."

Gideon turned to follow Lord's gaze. Looking at the house, he saw there was a small light being carried through the weaving hall, illuminating the windows one by one. Someone was carrying a candle which they were shielding with one hand because the glow was so small and diffuse. At the far end of the weaving floor, it vanished then reappeared in the next window, the room at the end of the weaving hall. It stayed there a short time, then it went out.

Gideon waited for it to be lit again. Whoever was in that room would surely not remain there in the dark? But no gleam resumed, and a sudden conviction gripped him that what he had seen was no earthly light at all. He recalled the hauntings that the local residents had spoken of—strange lights that appeared and disappeared, floating figures, odd noises but no one was there... His flesh shivered and tried to push such notions from his mind. They were just superstitions, there was bound to be an explanation—

"There," Lord's voice was barely a breath, but it was a breath of pure excitement and vindication.

Gideon blinked.

The glow of light had appeared again but this time it was in the room they had been in earlier that day. The rose room.

"I was wrong, and you were right," Lord said softly.

Gideon watched the light moving around the room and then settling in one place, by the hearth he thought, although it was hard to be sure.

"I was right about what?"

"You were right to think it was a waste of time to count windows. I had thought there would be a secret chamber which was concealed in plain sight."

"With a *window*?" Gideon knew his disbelief must be obvious in his voice.

"For the room to be what I had assumed it to be, it would need a window." Then Lord placed a hand on his shoulder. "Come, we have seen what there is to be seen. Now we know where to look in the morning." He looked back at the house. "Of course, had I been with Danny we would be climbing the walls and catching whoever is with that light, but—"

"I can climb," Gideon said.

As a boy banished to his bedroom by his father, to reflect in silent prayer upon whatever sin he had committed, he had often made the dangerous climb from the window and back again. But he was far from sure he still had the same skill and agility.

"Silently?"

"Quietly, I am sure."

"The education of a lawyer includes elements about which I was previously unaware," Lord said, the amusement plain in his voice. "Besides, I doubt the tapissiers will do more than ask us to leave even if we are caught dangling from their windows."

Lord led the way from the path to the rear of the house, moving with silence and surety. In Lord's wake, Gideon felt clumsy. Foliage grasped at him as if determined to try and trip him. They reached the rear courtyard and moved like thieves in the shadows until they were under the window Danny had said could be opened.

"How good are you at acrobatics?" Lord's voice in his ear was softer than breath. He bent beside Gideon linking his gloved hands to indicate what he was offering. Gideon looked up at the window above. He was almost tall enough to touch the casement whilst standing on the ground. The lift from Lord would take him level with it. The problem would be trying to force it open from the outside, whilst holding on to the wall.

He felt the wall for possible toe and finger holds and found a small projecting brick. It wasn't in a very good place, but it would serve.

With help from Lord and the projecting brick, he reached the window and ran his fingers around the outside of the closed

THE ALCHEMIST'S PLOT

casement. He had just begun to prise it when a door opened on the other side of the courtyard. Lord dropped into a crouch to be deeper into the shadow, leaving Gideon like a spider on the wall, his body pressed close against the bricks, hoping his toes didn't slip from the slight projection that supported him and hoping even more that whoever it was who had decided to take a stroll in the night air would think again. Sweat beaded on his brow and the space between his shoulder blades prickled.

His fingers were slipping and knew that he was going to fall. Heart hammering in his chest, so loudly he was sure anyone nearby would hear it too, he prayed he could hold on. The sound of the house door closing came at the same moment as he lost his grip. Thankfully Lord, rising fast, caught him before he fell.

Getting his breath back, Gideon braced himself again and worked the fingers of one hand at the edge of the casement. This time he managed to persuade it to move enough so he could slide his fingers inside the frame to ease it open.

The room beyond yawned open into darkness. There was a little light from where the moon managed to reach slender fingers through the windows, turning the looms into hunched giants, waiting, silent in the gloom.

With help from Lord, below, Gideon pulled himself up and through the window, entering in a sprawl of limbs. A moment later Lord was beside him having somehow swarmed up the wall and slipped through the window in less time than it took Gideon to stand up and look around.

Touching Gideon's arm to say he should follow, Lord moved with the silence and grace of a stalking feline along the length of the room. Gideon, by contrast, managed to catch his foot in one of the looms and would have fallen full length had a strong arm not braced him. After that, they went more slowly and reached the door at the end of the weaving hall.

Lord paused and listened, then eased the door open. The whine of protest was slight, but in the silence of the tapestry works it sounded to Gideon as loud as the yowling of a cat.

"I think stealth is no longer such an issue," Lord said as he finished opening the door, his voice soft, but no longer a breath. "Speed may be, however."

Gideon had a brief impression of what was surely the artist's room with windows to the side and front of the building. These would offer good light by day and captured the full force of the moon, such as it was, on this night. Directly in the path of the moon's illumination was an open wall panel, but narrow so most men would have to turn sideways to enter.

Lord plunged into the darkness and up the stairs. Following, Gideon stepped out through the wall beside the deeply set window in the room with the roses where Gerhard and Jan had both died.

One mystery solved.

But the room was empty. As Gideon stepped into the room, he heard the sound of footsteps running down the main staircase and then a door opening and closing. The candle had been left burning on the mantle above the fireplace which looked as it had when they left it earlier. The door to the rest of the works was closed.

"Our bird has flown," Lord said. "We should too. If anyone heard and came to see, then we might be the ones accused."

He took the candle and led the way down the hidden staircase and through the bottom door before turning to examine it. Then he pushed it closed. As he did so there was a very slight sound of some mechanism moving followed by a solid click. Presumably using counterweights, the door upstairs somehow opened and closed with this one. It seemed an odd arrangement.

Gideon noticed shelves along the wall and recalling what he'd found at Howe, slid his fingers along the bottom of each in turn. Yes. There. The same concealed catch, invisible and recessed so no one could accidentally disturb it. Had he not already found such before by chance and so known where to look, he would never have suspected it might be there.

Lord looked at him as he straightened up again.

"We have the key to the door? Good, then we should go."

He blew out the candle and led the way back through the weaving room.

THE ALCHEMIST'S PLOT

There was an unpleasant moment when Gideon had to close the window to conceal their mode of entry and, slipping, nearly fell onto the flags of the courtyard below. Apart from that they made their escape without incident and walked quickly back to The Queen's Head, Gideon's mind clamouring with turbulent thoughts.

"I would be willing to place a large sum of money," Lord observed as they reached the inn, "that it was Hester Lovegood who we disturbed. The limner's room is kept locked when he is not using it and she would have the key."

But that was not the thought which kept Gideon from sleep. Instead, he was trying to think why there would need to be a secret stairway between the rose room and the artist's room.

Chapter Twelve

It should have been simple, but of course, it wasn't.

Gideon found himself caught up in a mix of frustration and guilt.

"No. We have to keep it secret for now," Lord said. They were dressing for the day in their inn room. Lord pushed the truckle back under the main bed with his foot as he spoke. Gideon had expected to take the truckle himself, but Lord had occupied it upon their return and bar shedding his sword and boots, slept as he was. "If you go to the inquest and speak of hidden passages you will make potential murderers of every man and woman in the tapestry works and they will not thank you for that. Not to mention I will lose my chance to investigate the house further."

"So Jan Engles will be condemned as a suicide and buried, who knows where?" The injustice of it was unspeakable. How could anyone not see that? Gideon pulled on his boot with force.

"Think, Gideon." Lord sounded just as frustrated. "The men are dead. Wherever they may be buried for a few days is hardly going to imperil their immortal souls. Their families will be heartbroken anyway and the last thing they need is to find themselves facing accusations of having killed the one they loved." He drew a breath and then his tone changed. The voice of reason. "It will only be a few days. Then we should have the answers—both for the bereaved and for myself—and those two falsely accused dead men will have justice and a proper burial. If we act too soon all that is placed at risk."

It was reasonable and sensible. Even though a part of Gideon wondered if Lord made it sound so and argued for delay because he cared more about the documents the house might contain than about any injustice to the two dead men.

"What do we do today?"

Lord crossed to the door and opened it. "First, I think a bite to eat might be in order."

Having secured the private room they had enjoyed before, Lord then went off in his role as a servant to arrange for something to

THE ALCHEMIST'S PLOT

eat. He returned having done so a few minutes later and with a written note addressed to Gideon. It was from Jannekin de Maecht and had been delivered first thing that morning. In it, she asked if Gideon would be kind enough to visit her at his earliest convenience.

Walking back to the tapestry works in full daylight seemed strange after the events of the previous evening. Gideon glanced up at the window of the room where two men had died and wondered again if it was indeed right that he should withhold from the inquest the true circumstances of Jan Engles' death.

The door stood open as they reached it, and they heard a heated argument within. Gideon recognised one voice as that of Jannekin de Maecht and the other as her husband, but he had no idea what they were saying as they were arguing in Dutch. He glanced at Lord.

"Husband and wife," Lord said softly, "have different ideas about whether or not we should be here today. I wonder who will prevail?"

Just as Gideon was thinking they should beat a retreat for politeness' sake, the argument finished. A moment later Jannekin herself appeared in the doorway.

"I do apologise, *meneer* Lennox, it is very kind of you to come to see me. My husband sees things in primary colours and clean lines." She smiled. "But his heart is always in the right place, of course."

"I can come back another time if it's not—" Gideon began, but Jannekin de Maecht shook her head ferociously.

"No. Come in. There is someone you must meet. Bring your servant too."

She turned away and walked towards the stairs before Gideon could say anything more, leaving him with little choice but to follow, whilst thoroughly misliking the idea that he was going against her husband's wishes.

Jannekin de Maecht led the way upstairs and into the weaving hall. One man was working at the single loom Gideon had noticed before was in use. The weaver glanced at them and Jannekin gave him a nod and a smile, which he returned before going back to his painstaking work. Gideon had heard that a skilled weaver might produce all of a yard of tapestry in a month. Seeing the weaving in progress, he could understand why the process was so slow.

The window they had used to enter the room was pushed slightly open, which troubled him as he was sure they had closed it on the way out. They continued through the room, stepping aside to avoid the huge looms and Gideon realised they were heading for the door at the far end—the door to the artist's workshop, the room with the entrance to the secret passageway.

Having tapped on the door, Jannekin pushed it open and stood aside. Gideon hesitated and she gestured with her arms as if shooing them like errant chickens.

By daylight, the artist's room was brilliantly lit. A table had been set to benefit from both windows, covered with pots of ink, pens, paper and partly worked sketches of horses' heads, armoured helms, or brawny elbows. A man was working there, and he looked up at them from over the rim of a pair of spectacles, then got to his feet and inclined his head in a polite bow. He wore clothes of fine quality wool, but simple and with a wide plain collar much as puritans favoured. Wavy grey hair was pushed back behind his ears and brushed the collar, framing a face that was broad and partly concealed by a well-combed beard, too long and wide to be fashionable. He was an old man, of an age with Phillips de Maecht and very probably even older. But the eyes that studied Gideon were bright, clear and intelligent.

"Frantz, this is *meneer* Gideon Lennox, the lawyer we spoke of, of course, and this is *meneer* Klein, Frantz Klein."

"Or Francis Cleyn for English tongues," the man suggested. He spoke with a marked German accent, very different from the softer Dutch one of the weavers. "It is good of you to come, Mr Lennox. *Mevrouw* de Maecht has spoken of you. She tells me you are committed to helping us somehow prove that poor Gerhard and Jan were murdered."

"If it can be done," Gideon said, hating that he had the means to show it and must not say.

"Then you have my thanks. We are a close and happy community here, despite the terrible pressures this war has set upon us. These deaths have come near to tearing us apart. Even husband and wife." He looked at Jannekin with a distinct frown, but only a brief one when she returned his gaze serenely. Gideon decided he wouldn't wish to thwart or cross Jannekin de Maecht.

"It has been a difficult time for us," she agreed. "But these are difficult times for many families. The Aldgates lost two sons to the war and Mary Cook lost both her brother and her husband. At least our young men are not required to fight."

"Those who remain," Cleyn said gently.

Jannekin sighed. "Of course. And now I have served my purpose, you will forgive me if I withdraw and leave you gentlemen to discuss such matters as are needful."

She turned and swept from the room, as stately as a queen. Gideon saw the brief lift of fond exasperation in Cleyn's expression before his gaze moved to settle on Gideon as the door closed.

"I am hoping you will be able to assist me with a small matter," he said. "I have been told that I am an observant man, and, indeed, I never forget a face. But there is more to a man than a face. I am not sure what it is. The artist in me says it is the soul which I strive to capture in portraiture, but I am not sure. What do you think, Mr Lennox?"

Gideon blinked and tried to unravel what the question was that he had been asked.

"I—I am not sure," he said, honestly. "I am not an artist though, so perhaps it is not something I could know."

"When I first came to England, twenty years ago now, I came at the invitation of the present king, who was then a prince. But he was not here to receive me. He had gone to Spain in search of a bride. Instead, it was King James, his father who made me welcome. He was keen to see my skill, so he graciously permitted me to make some sketches and from them a painting—a portrait of someone in his court. He approved the result to such a degree that he wrote to my then patron, King Christian in Denmark, asking for me to be permitted to come and work here at Mortlake." As Cleyn spoke he picked up the sketch he had been working on and held it up. "I always recalled the subject of that work. There was some quality about him which, young as he was, set him apart from the rest of those who the king had about him."

Gideon stared at the sketch and realised he must be gaping. The picture showed a young man, perhaps more a boy, with fine features, the naivety and arrogance of youth, but also intelligence and depth as if Cleyn had seen the potential for greatness even then.

It was a picture of Philip Lord.

Philip Lord as he must have been in his mid-teens.

Behind him, Lord laughed and then stepped forward to make a bow.

"I would not be so churlish as to deny you," he said, his voice warm.

Gideon could only think how disconcerting it must be to be confronted with the image of yourself, still a child, and knew a moment of gratitude that his family were not of the wealth or status to have ever afforded such a portrait of himself.

Cleyn inclined his head.

"I knew you when I saw you from the window yesterday, but it took me a while to realise who you were under that disguise. There is more to a man than just his appearance; that is something every good artist must learn."

"And you are a great artist," Lord said. "I have seen and admired your work in some of the finest houses and palaces of Europe."

That delighted Cleyn as his eyes lit up when he smiled.

"You are very kind," he said.

"No. I am honest," Lord insisted.

"I am glad to hear so," Cleyn said. "That means I might receive an honest answer when I ask you if it was you who came to visit this room last night?"

His words sent a frisson of cold through Gideon. He expected Lord to dissemble in his usual easy and effective manner. Instead, he saw with mounting horror and surprise that Lord nodded.

"Yes. And I was here before as Sir Theophilus Bassington, to commission a tapestry from de Maecht—you can reassure him that I still intend to do so."

Cleyn was smiling and nodding.

THE ALCHEMIST'S PLOT

"I will do so, although I will allow Phillips to believe that such reassurance has come from Mr Lennox, as I think he would struggle to understand the subterfuge."

"Thank you," Lord said. "I would be grateful if my identity could be kept just in your keeping. It could bring danger to others than just myself were it to be known I was here."

"An artist sees many secrets and I learned young to keep them close," Cleyn told them. "However, I do not have your name to share, even were I so minded. My memory for faces is impeccable, but I have never been so able to set names to them. If you prefer it to remain that way, I will respect your wish. Although I can give you my word that if you are willing to remind me of your name it will stay only with me."

Gideon was about to say that they were grateful for his discretion, but Lord was already speaking.

"Sir Philip Lord." He accompanied the words with a slight bow. "I am also known amongst fighting men as 'the Schiavono'."

Gideon's throat tightened in anxiety. He couldn't believe Lord was being so open with this man they had just met.

"Indeed so? That is a name I have heard spoken before." Cleyn's tone was edged with new respect. "Are you willing to tell me why you broke in by night?"

Lord put a hand on Gideon's shoulder.

"I think Mr Lennox can show you."

What the...?

What had happened to the need to keep it secret?

Lord smiled at him and gripped his shoulder, giving it a small shake at the same time.

"You have to trust sometimes."

It made no sense to Gideon that they should trust this man, but at the end of the day it was Lord's secret more than his own, and Lord was the one with the most to lose. Gideon moved to the shelves on the wall and reached to release the catch. There was a sound in the walls and the panel moved a little. Lord pulled it open.

"It is narrow and dark," he said, gesturing to the opening behind it, "It leads to the room where the two tapissiers died."

Cleyn was staring at the opening, a small frown of puzzlement on his face.

"This explains a lot," he said, turning on Lord. "We must tell the coroner. It will show it is murder."

Lord pushed the panel closed and the same noise rumbled in the wall briefly.

"It would also bring suspicion on everyone in the tapestry works, upon you and your family too. All of you would be questioned, even the children. Who knows where blame might be placed in the current mood of the world? If we find the one who did the deed first then you can take them, their confession and this proof to a justice."

Cleyn's frown deepened, and he nodded reluctantly. "It is a terrible thing to say, but I can see you are right. The thought we are harbouring a murderer here fills me with both concern and loathing. How did you even know this was in the walls here? Is there some plan of the house that shows it?"

"Not that I know," Lord told him. "I wasn't certain until last night. But there is another house that has similar secrets and this building was once owned by the man who had a connection there too."

It was a lot for Cleyn to take in. But then, how could it not be? It must be a shock to find a secret passage right next to his desk of twenty years. Who wouldn't be taken aback by such a discovery?

"But why would there be…?" Cleyn was looking at Lord, and although Lord's expression didn't alter, something passed between the two men, because Cleyn shook his head. "No. I can see that is not mine to ask and I'm not sure I would want to know anyway. Instead, I shall ask if there are more such?"

"That we don't know," Lord told him. "I would much appreciate the opportunity to find out."

Cleyn nodded. His demeanour had shifted from concern to consideration.

"It would be difficult to undertake such investigations with others in the house. Even at night."

"Our murderer," Lord said, "may well be under pressure to solve the puzzle."

THE ALCHEMIST'S PLOT

"They seek treasure?" Cleyn guessed.

"It is something personal to me," Lord assured him.

Cleyn frowned, then his expression cleared.

"Something that could be held over you, perhaps?"

"In the wrong hands, it could."

"And I take it you also know who the murderer might be?"

"I am not certain and even if I were it is not wise to make accusations until we are sure and have the proof of it too."

"And I am supposed to accept that?" Cleyn bristled. "To carry on here knowing one of my fellows is a killer? You ask a lot."

"I know I do," Lord agreed. "But were I to speak a name and be wrong it would do great harm. An innocent individual would be clouded with calumny and the real killer might flee."

Cleyn's lips pressed together.

"And if you stay silent and another is killed?"

"I don't think there is any possibility. The loom is gone and the room is no longer lockable." Lord's jaw tightened as he went on. "I wish to entrap our killer so that their guilt is not in question, but first I need to explore the house. To find what they seek so we may bait the trap."

The old man looked gravely troubled and shook his head a few times. Gideon thought Cleyn would insist on Lord speaking up or would refuse to help them and demand that they left.

"It appears to me that I have little choice but to trust you on that, as you have trusted me with the rest." Cleyn picked up the picture of the young Philip Lord and scribbled his initials on it then held it out. "You must have this. I wouldn't keep it here in case any see it who should not, and it is a crime to destroy a work of art, no matter how simple it might be."

Lord took the sheet and studied it, then rolled it carefully, before placing it in his coat.

"I thank you. It is a very great gift."

Wondering if despite Cleyn's supportive words they were still about to be dismissed, Gideon spoke up.

"Mr Cleyn, is there any way we could search the premises here without needing to worry about being disturbed?"

Cleyn shook his head, then lifted a hand. "Wait. There is one time each week when the building is deserted. Every Sunday all the tapissiers and their families attend the Dutch church in Austin Friars, and they are gone for much of the day."

"No one is left?" Gideon asked, wondering why Hester Lovegood had risked other times if she had that.

"Nowadays no one. All the servants are given the time off in Christian charity to attend their own church and the building is locked."

For a moment Gideon thought of the window. Then he thought how unlikely it would be that Hester Lovegood would have the strength or skill to get in that way.

"Then who holds the keys?"

Cleyn smiled. "One is kept by Phillips de Maecht, and I have the other. My family and I attend St. Mary's." he gestured in the direction of the church, "That means I am here if there is any problem and keep an eye on the building in their absence. It used to be different, when we had all the valuable materials and tapestries, then people would stay. But now there is nothing of real value. Besides, the town is busy here on Sundays with people coming to church."

"Then we have our opportunity," Lord said softly.

"I can attend the early service," Cleyn said. "I will tell my wife I have some things I need to look at on behalf of Sir Theophilus Bassington."

"This afternoon there is the inquest for Jan Engles," Gideon said. "Most of the people here will go to that?"

Cleyn nodded.

"Most of the men will, of course, but the women I think will stay away."

It wouldn't be the opportunity he had hoped it might be. Perhaps he should attend the inquest himself after all.

"We will be here on Sunday," Lord said. "Would it be better if Sir Theophilus came rather than servant Tom?"

Cleyn considered. "It would perhaps better explain why I am opening the works. If it was the one time Sir Theophilus had to visit. This preliminary meeting with Mr Lennox having established what is needed."

"Then that is what we shall do," Lord said.

Cleyn gave a slight bow. "Let me see you out." Then he remembered and smiled at Gideon. "Mr Lennox."

It was as they were walking through the weaving hall that Gideon noticed Hester Lovegood cleaning the windows. He kept his attention on Cleyn who was explaining the weaving process to him as they walked. So he wasn't prepared when she nearly bumped into him with a bucket of water. She bobbed a curtsey, and apologised, then went on to begin to clean the next window.

Once they were outside the tapestry works and had covered some of the distance back to the inn Lord looked at him.

"What did she give you?"

"A note, I think." Gideon opened his hand to reveal a folded slip of paper, white against the dark leather of his gloves.

"She certainly recognized you. She is probably wondering why you have said nothing."

Gideon unfolded the slip of paper. It was written in ink in handwriting that suggested the author wasn't someone well trained in shaping their letters.

St. Mary's. Two o'clock. Come alone.

He passed the note to Lord.

"That is the time the inquest is due to begin," Lord said thoughtfully.

He handed the note back to Gideon who pocketed it as they walked on.

"You think she means to try and harm me? That she might have men lying in wait for me if I go to meet her?"

Lord looked speculative. "I would be surprised. After all, she knows you are not here in Mortlake alone, even if she wants you to meet her on your own."

"Why would she want to meet with me?" Gideon shook his head, trying to think of possible reasons.

"There is an easy answer to that," Lord said.

Gideon frowned. "I can't see it."

Lord laughed. "I meant that you should go to the meeting and find out."

They discussed the details over dinner, but there remained little more to the plan than that Gideon would go to the church and Lord would ensure he was close enough to intervene if danger threatened from any quarter.

"I will go and take a look over the place first," Lord said. "I am sure she would expect you might send a servant to do that before committing yourself. But I have a feeling she just wishes to speak with you."

"But why? She is the one who killed those men."

"Perhaps to find out what you are doing in Mortlake?" Lord reached into his coat and produced the encrypted note and unfolded it. The lettering was the same as that on the message Gideon had been given. "I lack a mind that can break a cipher swiftly. But we can try if you would like."

Gideon looked at the letters and shook his head. He had spent enough time working on decoding and encoding known ciphers in recent months to realise it would take him longer than the time they had available to make any inroads.

"I envy Danny his ability for such things," Lord said, refolding the paper and putting it away. "He would solve it whilst winning a *partie* of piquet at the same time."

Gideon pushed his half-empty plate away. The coney pie was overcooked and nearly inedible.

"You seemed very sure that Cleyn can be trusted," he said.

Lord was frowning at his meal and looked up with a piece halfway to his mouth.

"He has no reason to betray me and every reason not to do so." He studied the unappetising morsel of food and then put it back on the plate. "Besides, we need his help if we are to get this done. I think any idea of further creeping around at night expecting to remain undetected is foolish."

"Hester Lovegood was doing so last night," Gideon pointed out.

"Hester Lovegood didn't need to break in and would have been able to explain her presence were she discovered."

THE ALCHEMIST'S PLOT

Which Gideon had to admit was a very good point.

Lord looked at his plate in disgust.

"I suspect the cook has been distracted by the upcoming event. Two inquests within a week must be something of a record for a place like Mortlake." He got to his feet and picked up his hat. "It is time I went. You make your way to the church for two o'clock and know that the Lord will be watching over you."

Gideon stayed where he was for a time, hearing the inn's common room fill as those attending the inquest began to assemble. He could picture the scene. There would be the coroner—of course—and the jury, along with any witnesses and half of Mortlake. From the sound of it most were already assembled. Hester Lovegood had chosen well the time when she might meet with Gideon and avoid anyone even noticing.

When he heard signs that the inquest was about to be called to order, he got up. The common room was so full that Gideon had to push his way towards the door. He exchanged a nod with Richard West, who was moving in the opposite direction having just arrived. When he approached the door, Lord was coming through it, adjusting his breeches as if he had stepped outside for a very obvious reason and smiled at one of the women serving, saying something which made her laugh.

"I've ordered the ale as you wanted, sir," Lord said in his servant's voice when he saw Gideon. He gestured to the retreating figure of the serving woman, "She said there's an empty table at the back if we're quick."

Completely confused, Gideon gave a terse nod and followed Lord to the unoccupied table. It was very much out of the way and offered no view of the proceedings to anyone sitting there, and with so many standing between, little chance to hear what was being said either.

The serving woman appeared almost at once as they sat and put down two mugs of ale on the table before vanishing again into the crowd.

Lord took a drink from his mug and then leaned forward over the table.

"Hester Lovegood was already sitting in the church when I got there," Lord said, his voice low. "She was dead. Stabbed."

THE ALCHEMIST'S PLOT

Chapter Thirteen

At Lord's insistence, they had stayed for the inquest.

This time, thankfully, the coroner seemed swayed to compassion and decided Jan Engles had taken his own life *non compos mentis*, his mind being affected by the death of Gerhard Spijker.

At least, Gideon thought, the Engles family and Mistress Cleyn would be spared the worst. It was just after the coroner departed in his coach that someone came running to say there had been another death.

No one suspected that Mr Gideon Lennox or his servant might have any involvement. The inn staff could swear both had been in their private room dining and then at the inquest for the afternoon. Indeed, it became obvious that no one had seen anything.

Gideon went with a group of gentlemen who hurried to the church, citing his legal training as a reason. With him was Richard West, who kept shaking his head and murmuring about how tragic it was. There were already others in the church, all local and all caught with morbid curiosity. None of them, as far as Gideon could tell, were from the tapestry works.

Whereas Lord had said she had been sitting when he found her, Hester Lovegood—for whatever her real name might be, that was the name she would perforce take into eternity—was now laid out upon the flagstone floor. Over the last year, Gideon had seen more violent death than he had any desire to ever witness. He told himself that this was just one more. The death of one he had known as an enemy. Someone who had falsely accused him of murder and would have felt no remorse had he hanged. Now she was dead—murdered—herself. There had to be something of divine justice in that. So why did he feel a sense of tragedy in seeing her dead?

She had been stabbed once, in the side of her chest, and if she had been sitting, the blow might have come from someone sitting beside her. Perhaps she had been meeting another before her assignation with himself. Someone suggested it was a vagrant who saw Mistress Lovegood go in alone and thought she might have something of value. She had no purse and a mark on one finger where a ring had been.

The vicar had found the body and he was beside himself and not just for the loss of a parishioner. He kept saying that the building would now need to be blessed, if not completely reconsecrated and how difficult that would be to arrange in short order.

Gideon left when it was clear he had learned all there was to be learned. He walked back towards the inn with Richard West, who seemed shocked into incredulity.

"I've lived all my life in Mortlake," he said as they went through the lychgate. "All my life. I have never known such as this. Someone killed in the church." He shook his head. "She was a servant in the tapestry works. Those poor people have known dire fortune in these recent days."

Gideon nodded. It was impossible to disagree. "I saw Mistress Lovegood today," he said, "She was cleaning the windows in the weaving hall." There was always that little jump of dissonance. To have seen someone alive and hale just a short time before—and then lifeless and dead. He shook his head trying to push the thought away.

"You were at the tapestry works?" West asked.

Gideon nodded. It was hardly a secret he had been there, and it might be a chance to establish a good reason for them to be there in the future. "Yes. I was speaking with the limner about creating a design for my employer, Sir Theophilus Bassington."

West looked interested.

"He might commission a tapestry or two, you think?"

"I am sure so. He is meeting with Mr Cleyn on Sunday to discuss the matter further."

"Sunday?" West looked startled and then frowned. "Not a day to be transacting business."

"I think no business will be transacted," Gideon assured him. "Sir Theophilus is a devout Christian and a very busy man on Parliament's account. It will be to consider the artistic requirements. I will arrange the business side of things separately."

THE ALCHEMIST'S PLOT

West nodded but still looked disapproving. He was clearly one who expected nothing but religious engagement on the Sabbath. It made Gideon bristle inwardly. He had spent too many Sundays shut, perforce, in his room with a Bible and the exhortation to consider his sins and pray. It was a shame West had such an attitude. Gideon had thought him a very reasonable and likeable man when they had been talking in the inn the previous evening, more so than many of the local people who were steeped in superstition.

As they reached the inn, West bid him a rather curt farewell and crossed the road. His house was the one on the other side of the alley cut-through where Gideon had been attacked. The inn was still full. People had delayed departing to express their opinions on the fresh outrage in Mortlake and what should be done about it. Lord had been talking with a group of servants waiting for their masters to decide to depart and excused himself from their company when Gideon returned.

"The tide is right if you are ready to leave, sir," Lord said as he joined Gideon. Then he dropped his voice to an undertone, "I think our answers are not going to be found here today."

Gideon nearly objected, confident if they stayed they would find out more. Whoever had killed Hester Lovegood could be the same person who had killed the two tapissiers. But then he recalled that they had to go back to Westminster. He had arranged to go with Ellis to the Paper Office in the Holbein Gate first thing the following morning. There was also the ciphered note that Danny could, he hoped, unravel for them.

They took a wherry back to London and were met midstream by armed men in a boat demanding they declare their identities and intentions. It turned out to be an exercise by some of the local trained bands. Used by now to dealing with such, Gideon told them what was needed, and they were allowed to proceed past the line of defences and into London. It was a salutary reminder, if one were needed, that whilst they were preoccupied with events in Mortlake, the wider world was still fighting a war.

As they reached the Westminster Steps, the first slender fingers of twilight brushed over the sky, gentling the blue and grey to a

157

softer shade and then pulling the darkness up from the horizon. Crossing New Palace Yard, Gideon pointed out the turn beside Westminster Hall leading to Parliament's house in what had once been St. Stephen's Chapel and the way to where the Cotton Library could be found.

"Perhaps," Lord said, "after we have finished raiding the Holbein Gate and digging through matters at Mortlake, we could go there and search for more papers." Then he laughed. "My life seems defined by what is written on scraps of parchment, vellum and paper scattered across London."

They crossed the road to The Bell and went inside only to discover that Danny hadn't returned.

Lord was unperturbed. "This is Danny, and we are in London, which he knows well. I have little doubt that he is occupied with his task. I'm sure he will appear later this evening and demand we all sit down to a game of *primovisto* so he can humble us yet again with his acumen."

"Before or after you ask him to break the cipher written by Hester Lovegood, deceased?"

Lord considered. "During?" he suggested, then laughed. "Probably after. It would act as an incentive if he knew he would have the chance to beat us at cards having done so."

And that made Gideon laugh.

But Danny didn't return that evening. They ate a brief supper without him before retiring to their separate rooms for the night.

Gideon woke early, the sounds of city life outside his window bringing a strange feeling of comfort. The familiar cries of the streets and the rattle of wheels, the clip of hooves on cobbles and the shouts and calls. He lay in bed for a time just absorbing them and wondering if he would ever be able to become a part of this again. Sometimes it felt as if the experiences and actions of the last few months had severed him from it completely and for good.

Danny hadn't returned overnight, and Lord—still servant-clad—remained unconcerned.

"He knew we had plans for this morning which wouldn't involve him," Lord said as they broke their fast on fresh bread and some of yesterday's beef broth.

THE ALCHEMIST'S PLOT

"What if he is in trouble?" Gideon asked

"Danny is more likely to be the one causing trouble for others than getting into it himself," Lord said. "But were that the case I'm not sure how we would find him quickly enough to redeem him from it." He finished eating and got up. "If he is not returned by the time we are, perhaps we will see what we can find out about where he might be."

The Holbein Gate earned its name because it was said to have been designed by the artist Hans Holbein and Gideon had to admit whoever had designed it had created something completely unique.

Like other gates, it was a rectangular building on three floors with an arched passageway beneath which allowed the passage of horses and coaches. There were footways on either side through the supporting octagonal towers. Above the arch was a beautiful oriel window and the floor above that had a regular window with six lights. The towers, too, were buttressed with windows, creating an impression of light and grace. And both sides of the gate had a facing chequerboard pattern of flint and stone, which gave the whole its very distinctive appearance. There were also stone carvings mounted on the tower, the one above the arch showing the royal arms supported by two shield-bearing griffons. Around the base of the windows on the octagonal towers were more royal symbols, including a Tudor rose. In the crisp March sunshine, the Holbein Gate seemed to glitter as if made from jet and pearl.

"Pretty thing, isn't it?" Lord murmured. "A jewelled casket containing treasures beyond price."

"I suppose that is a good way to describe state secrets," Gideon agreed. He was on edge as he knew well the level of security they could expect to have to pass through to be allowed access to the Paper Office. This wasn't a library of public documents like the Records office in the Tower, this was the king's—and now no doubt parliament's—repository of papers on matters of the gravest import.

Except, when they approached the gate, the only challenger was Ellis Ruskin, in company with a burly armed man.

"This is Martin," Ellis said. "Your other servant Adam recommended I asked at one of the fencing schools for someone to hire, someone who I could be sure was not partisan to any faction."

"I would have thought most of the fighting men would have been persuaded into the army," Gideon said, looking more closely at the man.

"They leave me alone, sir," Martin said and lifted an arm which had lost its hand. "But I can still use a sword fairly."

"Have you had any problems since we last met?" Gideon asked Ellis, who shook his head.

"I sent a letter to my father as you suggested, and he replied saying he had no idea what I might be referring to and assuring me if I wished to distance myself from his affairs, he would respect that."

It seemed a little too easy to Gideon, but he was pleased that Ellis seemed safe enough for the present. In his company, they were allowed into the gate and up the tight winding spiral, past the lavish apartments on the floor over the arch, to the rooms above which were being used by clerks and scribes.

"What was it, in particular, you were looking for?" Ellis asked.

There was no way around telling him. He would need to request access to the specific document store.

"I need to access the documents taken from the house of Sir Edward Coke shortly before his death. They would have been lodged here by Sir Francis Windebank, nine years ago in the September of Thirty-four."

Ellis seemed unconcerned about the nature of the request and having had a brief word with the man who seemed to be overseeing the ongoing work, beckoned Gideon to follow him.

"Your man will have to stay here with Martin," he said, "but you are to be allowed in with me."

Gideon glanced at Lord but could see no trace of the intense frustration that he must be feeling. Lord made a brief bow in acknowledgement as the door was unlocked and Gideon allowed through.

THE ALCHEMIST'S PLOT

The room Gideon was taken to was full of papers. Some were stored in dated bags and boxes on shelves, and some held by strings with a label to identify their contents. They were ordered by topic and context first, then by date and Gideon knew from previous experience of asking to access a document here that unless the enquirer could be very precise it was hard for the archivists to locate any specific one.

But this time it wasn't a single item that Gideon sought, it was an entire collection. Even so, as the archivist walked along shelves and pulled out boxes, shuffling through the contents and frowning.

"It was before my time," he explained. Which wasn't very surprising as he was a contemporary of Gideon and Ellis, so couldn't have been working there for more than two or three years or so at most. "It is most odd there is nothing like that with other of the late Sir Edward's documents. Who did you say would have lodged it?"

"Sir Francis Windebank," Gideon repeated, a dread rising within him that the Covenant might have already seen the danger and managed to arrange the removal of any relevant or incriminating information.

"Here it is." The archivist pulled a bag from behind a document box. It brought a cloud of dust with it and an examination of the seal showed, to Gideon's relief, that it hadn't been disturbed since the year it had been deposited. The archivist hefted the bag onto a table and removed the seal. "There you go. If something gets put in here it tends to stay put." The archivist had an unfortunate braying laugh which he gave way to. Gideon laughed politely and Ellis thanked his friend, who left them saying he'd make sure they had left before he locked up for the day.

More confident than before, Gideon opened the heavy canvas and pulled out some of what was within. There were notes, strings, ledgers and loosely bound deeds and documents. It was going to be a long task to look through it all, far longer than just the few hours he had today. The thought wasn't a good one, but he tried to reassure himself that it should be easy to dismiss the irrelevant papers and narrow his search down to a much smaller selection which would require more detailed perusal.

"Can I help you with whatever you are looking for?" Ellis asked. He picked up one of the bundles. "These all seem to be in Latin, contracts and deeds at a guess."

It was tempting and Gideon found himself trying to weigh up the risk against the immense benefit of having a second, skilled and educated, pair of eyes to work through the mound of documents with him. Then inspiration struck.

"I am not entirely sure what I am looking for," he said, which wasn't even untrue. "I will know when I find it. However, it will be from twenty-three or maybe twenty-four. You can discard anything before those years or after them."

Ellis nodded and began leafing through the bundle he held.

"This is all from before then," he said and set it aside.

It was a good way to begin winnowing the chaff and Gideon started in from his side of the table using the same simple guideline. Within a little over an hour, they had managed to reduce the original mountain to a small hillock and Ellis was packing the unwanted documents back in the bag whilst Gideon started looking through what they had found that related to the time when Sir Philip Lord had been turned into a traitor.

He had no idea what he was looking for. There wouldn't be a confession, *I, Sir Edward Coke, do declare that I fabricated evidence to convict Philip Lord...* The thought made him smile. If only. No, it would be something subtle, something small, something easy to conceal, if indeed there were any traces to be found.

Whatever was done would have to have involved a payment of some kind. He reached for the financial ledger for the year March to March. Then ignored anything before October because that had been the month Buckingham had returned from Spain and found the white haired fourteen-year-old, Philip Lord in close company with King James and observed the boy as a threat to his position.

Buckingham would have gone to a man who would relish the chance to secure his favour, a man who at that time wasn't in royal favour and might be very willing to undertake such work. A man who not only knew the law but created it, Sir Edward Coke. Perhaps they had met in Whitehall Palace or at Theobalds, under the very nose of the monarch they intended to hoodwink. That he had secured some favour was shown in the fact that plans to dispatch him to Ireland at the time had been stopped by the then Prince Charles. But however it was done it would involve some financial transaction at some point, and Coke, being a scrupulous man, would have kept a record of that in his accounts.

There.

He found it.

A reference to a payment from 'my Lord of Buckingham' for the sum of five hundred pounds. There was no reason given but the date in November of the year was surely too much of a coincidence. There were then a series of disbursements following all labelled 'for expenses arising in the matter pursued on behalf of my Lord of Buckingham'. These began almost immediately and went on until August of the following year.

On its own, of course, it meant nothing. It proved nothing. After all this time it could have been payment for any number of things. But to Gideon, it meant that there was indeed something to look for now in the papers and he could narrow down the date.

"You have something?" Ellis asked as Gideon closed the ledger.

He nodded.

"Not what I am after but a strong indication that what I am after exists to be found."

Invigorated by the discovery Gideon commissioned Ellis to help him search for anything from that time a month before and a few months after. They spent another couple of hours going through the small pile of possible documents several times in detail, and whilst Gideon learned altogether too much about Coke's domestic affairs at that time, there was nothing.

It was beyond frustrating to have found one small piece of evidence and yet no more. Gideon wondered if he should try and remove the ledger, but he doubted Ellis would be a willing conspirator. Besides, without any other references, there was nothing to say that is what the amount referred to. It could have been for any purpose. A family matter even, after all, Coke had been father-in-law to Buckingham's mentally unstable brother Viscount Purbeck.

ELEANOR SWIFT-HOOK

While they were restoring the documents to the box they had come from, he found the note scrawled by Sir Francis Windebank himself, reporting how he and his men had searched the entire house for documents '*excepting we refrained from disturbing the chamber of Sir Edward, who was on his death bed, at the insistence of Lady Purbeck, his daughter who remained at his side until his death*'.

Gideon felt a slight pulse of interest. If there had been any incriminating documents perhaps Coke would have kept them close, perhaps they had been in his bed chamber. But if so then Lady Purbeck would probably have seen them destroyed to protect her father's good name. Sighing at the futility of it all, Gideon closed the box.

A few minutes later and well into the afternoon, he and Sir Philip Lord were walking away from the Holbein Tower, Gideon having thanked the archivist and Ellis. He ensured Ellis intended to keep Martin in his employ for the foreseeable future and to keep himself well away from entanglements suggested by his father. Without revealing too much it was the best Gideon could do to ensure his safety.

"It is not easy, is it?" Lord observed. "When you can see the crouching gargoyle that lurks in the shadows ready to pounce but can do nothing substantive to prevent it."

Gideon glanced at him sharply, wondering if he was that easy to read.

Lord gave him a smile in return. "Martin is a good man. He will keep Ellis safe."

"If Ellis listens to his advice on such things," Gideon said. "I'm not sure he will if he thinks it stands in the path of advancing his ideals."

"You have done all you can."

Aside from taking Ellis into his confidence, a choice that wasn't his to make, that was true.

"I take it," Lord said after they had walked halfway back to The Bell in silence, "that there was no grand epiphany?"

Gideon shook his head.

THE ALCHEMIST'S PLOT

"There was a single large financial transaction which then had some disbursements to unlisted individuals over the next nine months. It was at the right time and suggests a campaign of the sort that might be needed to fabricate the evidence against you. But whether it is even related..." He trailed off and shrugged. "There was nothing that was solid proof," he admitted.

Lord looked away. The disappointment must bite hard. Lord had spent his adult life hoping to find the evidence that would free him from the taint of treason. Gideon half-expected that Lord would lash out with his frustration and accuse Gideon of not trying hard enough.

"That is a shame," was all he said.

"I looked through it all. There was nothing," Gideon felt compelled to defend himself despite there being no accusation.

Lord bowed his head briefly as they walked.

"I am sure you did. You are also far better qualified than I to understand and identify the significance of what was there. If you found nothing, then I am confident there was nothing to be found." He lifted his head and met Gideon's gaze. "I trust you."

For some reason, Gideon felt as if a weight had been lifted from his shoulders.

"There was one thing," he said. "But it might be nothing. Windebank included a short report of his actions and he said he had searched every room in the house except the chamber where Sir Edward lay dying under the care of his daughter."

Lord's head went up and his brow furrowed slightly.

"Lady Frances Purbeck?"

"You know her?"

"Kate was friends with her once." Lord frowned. "Did you know her father kidnapped her and beat her until she agreed to wed John Villiers?" he shook his head and Gideon wondered if he was thinking of another woman who had been kidnapped and forced into marriage. "When the fact she was having an affair came out—hard to hide as she had a child—Buckingham would have had her accused of witchcraft as well as adultery if he had been able to have his way. Kate was a good friend to her when most shunned her."

They reached The Bell and Lord opened the door for Gideon, their roles as master and servant requiring it.

"I'm sorry I found nothing," Gideon said quietly.

"But you tried," Lord said, "and as Kate is so fond of telling me, it changes nothing that matters."

They ate an early supper having missed dinner completely.

Danny didn't appear and Gideon could tell that it was beginning to disquiet Lord. He kept glancing at the door as if expecting it to open.

"You said we would do what we could to try and find Danny if he wasn't back by now," Gideon said.

Lord shook his head.

"I did," he admitted. "On reflection, I still think it's too soon. The kind of places Danny might be, even asking after him could place him in danger. I am sure he will come back when he is ready. Until then we will have to manage without him."

Lord sounded confident but Gideon was no longer sure that he meant it.

THE ALCHEMIST'S PLOT

Chapter Fourteen

The steady dripping was wearing on Danny's nerves.

He'd lost track of time. It was completely dark in the underground room, and he'd been unconscious when he'd been thrown in. It could have been a few hours or over a day. The only good thing about his present position was that he'd not had any bones broken—yet.

Although that was chance more than anything from the way things had happened.

He'd gone to pay his debts to the past. To Venturo di Zorzi, his old sword master and to Jude Rider at The Crown. It had been playing piquet in The Crown that evening with Master di Zorzi he'd heard tell that a man part swathed in bandages had been seen crossing the river to Southwark some weeks before in company with someone known to those in Alsatia. Turk Nelson. Turk was one of the men Mags had stolen from Philip and kept close.

Danny had history on the south bank too.

Parliament had closed down most of the entertainment there, the theatres and bear baiting, and Holland's Leaguer, where Beth Holland had once held court in her castle. Instead, he'd gone to The Cock, its name betraying its real purpose. There he'd learned from a whore named Lucy where to find Turk Nelson.

It had been his bad luck that as he was breaking into the house to ask Turk a few quiet questions, Mags had shown up with his men. Of course Danny fought, but there were too many against him. He heard Mags shout an order that he shouldn't be killed. He took two of them down before they disarmed him and a third was going to be nursing a broken arm. But by then he wasn't in too good a state himself. Turk had taken some pleasure in avenging with his fists the men Danny had downed.

"I was sure I'd run into you sometime." Mags, half his face a ruined mess of puckered flesh and one hand a useless claw, sat on his horse as Danny was held face down in the filth of the stableyard. "And you know what I'm going to do with you,

ELEANOR SWIFT-HOOK

Danny? I'm going to do to you what you did to me, but I'll be finishing the job. Slowly mind, but we'll get there. Starting with your feet and hands, I'm going to roast you alive, a little bit at a time. You've a day or two, first though. A day or two to think about it before I can give you the attention you deserve. There are some people I know who'd like to ask you a few questions first. Questions about something you stole and the company you've been keeping."

They'd beaten him unconscious then and he'd come back to himself in the dark, aching and stiff from both pain and cold. At least he was unbound, but that meant there was going to be no way out. He was hungry, but that wasn't hard to ignore. He'd had long practice at it in the past. The dripping was fresh water that tasted clean, so he'd not be parched.

It wasn't so easy exploring the limits of his confinement with his hands, but lacking the use of his eyes due to the complete lack of light, that was all he had left. By feeling his way around the walls and pacing across and across, he managed to map out the shape and size of the place so he could picture it in his mind. The only exit, he decided, would have to be a trapdoor in the ceiling. But the ceiling was beyond his reach even at full stretch, so he had no way of confirming that. He was also sure that whatever this building was, it wasn't well used because there was very little noise from above.

Sometimes he heard feet walking overhead and once he heard voices and a burst of laughter, but too muffled for Danny to be sure what they said. The fact there was so little activity gave him some hope that if he could find a way to access the trap, he might be able to escape unless it was bolted or locked. But he was too bruised and stiff as yet to be confident in performing the kind of athletics that might enable him to get up the wall. Even then, unless by chance the trap was close to the edge of the room, he would have very little chance of being able to reach it.

That left him only one other option.

Waiting until they came to get him out.

He slept again.

THE ALCHEMIST'S PLOT

The sound of the trap being lifted woke him. Brilliant light came streaming in from above in the middle of the room. It revealed that the ceiling of his prison was no more than a few inches beyond the reach of his fingers at full extent. It also revealed his chances of breaking out of this cellar room were negligible.

There was a rattle, and someone pushed a ladder down into the cellar.

"You can come up."

Danny didn't know the voice. He gripped the ladder and climbed up. Anything had to be better than being shut in that pit.

He emerged blinking in the glare of muted daylight. There were three men awaiting him. Two armed men, soldiers or ex-soldiers by the look of them, and the third a gentleman. The room he emerged into from the floor gave away little about its location. It was plain walled and empty of any furniture, with a high window through which he could see only a tree branch and another wall.

"Come with me," the gentleman said, nose wrinkling at the stench Danny knew he must be radiating. The man was in his late forties or early fifties but had a hard edge to him that told Danny he wasn't the kind to be relaxing by his hearth enjoying the fruits of his labour. He took no time to introduce himself, so Danny didn't trouble to ask.

Instead, he considered his chances with the two soldiers and caught a look from one challenging him to do so. He rebuffed with an attempted grin, difficult because of the bruising on his face, before following the gentleman from the room and along a passageway.

The room he was taken to betrayed that this was nowhere near the squalid tenements of the Manor of the Maze. It was an elegant dining room with carefully chosen furniture including an impressive oak table with matching chairs and a large hearth. Broad and high windows of extensive and expensive glass gave him a view over a green sward dotted with ornamental shrubs and then the river with London beyond. There was even a private jetty with a wherry moored, ready to take the house owner or his guests wherever they might like to go.

Three more men were waiting in the room. Two he knew already having met them in Yorkshire at the house of Sir Richard Tempest. The third was older, with narrow eyes, sagging jowls and a heavy body. He was the only one of the three sitting down, and the high-backed unfurnished chair had been moved away from the table where its fellows were set so he could sit with his colleagues. He had an old-fashioned close-fitting cap, a cane in one hand and the look of a man much given to ponderous thought and reading.

These must be the Archangels of the Covenant. Michael and Gabriel were the two he had met before. The other two would be Oriel and Raphael.

Smiling at his own cleverness, Danny made a point of bowing, albeit stiffly, to the group, managing not to wince as he straightened from it. He realised then that Mags might be deprived of his entertainment. Danny Bristow had something to trade, after all.

"Gentlemen, you have the advantage of me," he said, pleased he could talk reasonably clearly, and it didn't hurt too much. "And in more ways than one."

It wasn't what any of them had been expecting, but the man he knew as Michael was the quickest to recover.

"We do indeed, Lieutenant Bristow, and I would advise you not to lose sight of that fact."

"I assure you I am very aware of it, sir," Danny told him. "How may I be of further service to you?"

The man who had been with the soldiers crossed over to the large man and whispered something in his ear, to which he nodded, jowls wobbling.

"It is good to learn you are willing to cooperate," the large man said. His voice was deep and seemed to begin somewhere in his round belly and emerge from his mouth only once it had echoed around his stomach a few times. "It would be much better for you if that is indeed the case."

Danny wondered if he was supposed to feel intimidated.

"I'm very happy to do whatever I may to assist you, gentlemen. I believe I already made that clear when we met before."

THE ALCHEMIST'S PLOT

Gabriel lifted a hand in dismissal. "You haven't kept to what we asked of you."

As he stepped forward, Danny was instantly seized by the two soldiers behind him. He didn't attempt to resist their grip and at a gesture from Michael, they released him again.

"I would disagree with you, sir. I've had no opportunity, until now, to present myself to you to report on my progress. I wasn't given any instruction on how to contact you should I need to do so. But I have been working hard on your account, as you asked me to."

"You were not asked to attempt the murder of the mercenary commander Graf von Elsterkrallen," Gabriel snapped.

"No, sir," Danny agreed. "But you did ask me to ensure the safety of Sir Nicholas Tempest. However, the graf might choose to tell the tale, he was set on killing Sir Nicholas and I acted in Sir Nicholas's defence."

His words brought an awkward silence. He could imagine how he must appear to them, filthy, stinking, his hair matted, his clothes fit to be burned, bruises purpling his face. But he held himself as he would for a military drill, body erect, shoulders set. He had no intention of letting them see how much it cost him to do so or to know the price of ignoring the pounding ache in his head and the dull throb that seemed to emanate from every part of his anatomy.

"You deciphered the message?" that was from Michael.

"Yes, sir. As I am sure you knew I would."

"And you didn't think anything of it?"

Danny met his gaze. "I assumed that what I read there was by way of a test for Sir Nicholas and a fair warning to me that I should kill the graf if he looked at all as if he might harm Sir Nicholas." He managed a tight smile.

"This is not important," the large man rumbled, but he didn't deny Danny's words. "Whatever games you were playing with the Tempest boy, what matters is the girl. You took the girl, Bristow. Why, and where is she?"

Danny knew his face wouldn't betray him, which was as well because he was struggling to control the force of emotion their words had evoked. But the muscles across his bruised body tightened at being reminded these bastards had such an interest in Christobel. She had no idea of the role they played in her life but she had been their pawn as much as Philip had. What made him sick to his soul was knowing their sole interest in her was as a broodmare. The fools would never see that she had more intelligence, fire and spirit than any of them—than any woman he had ever met.

"My instructions from you, sir, were to ensure the safety of Sir Nicholas and to obey what he asked of me." He schooled his voice to be cold, impartial and professional. "The two were not always easy to reconcile."

"Make yourself clear, man. We do not need riddles," Michael snapped. "Taking the girl wasn't anything you were ordered to do by ourselves or by Sir Nicholas."

"Sir Nicholas required that I bring his wife to him in York. I went to Howe Hall at his command to collect her. Having taken her into my custody I realised that if I carried out Sir Nicholas' command it would lead to his death. His wife was set on murdering him—or failing that killing herself, or both. By my assessment of her and her capabilities and determination, it was clear to me she was more than able to do so. The one way I could see to both keep her and Sir Nicholas safe was to remove her to a place she would no longer feel under threat until the matter could be reconciled."

That led to a stony silence. But something in the quality of it told Danny he had touched a nerve. There was no doubt in their expressions, more a cold acquiescence and even, perhaps, a grudging admission that he had done what was needed. They just didn't like it.

"Where is she?" Michael demanded.

There was no point in not saying. If their influence reached there, they would find out sooner or later and she was very safe with Kate and under the ultimate protection of the princes and the king himself.

"In Oxford. In the care of a woman of my acquaintance there. She is quite safe, and she is not compromised."

THE ALCHEMIST'S PLOT

Something about the silence that followed and the lack of another question told him that he had simply confirmed what they already knew. It had been another test.

"But you didn't return to Sir Nicholas," the large man said.

"At that point, I couldn't." Danny took a breath. This was where he would either fly or fall. "I was prevented from returning by Sir Philip Lord."

There were indrawn breaths and glances between the four.

"Sir Philip Lord?" Gabriel echoed. "The man you said you had fallen out with?"

"Yes. Although I was keen to convince him I was reconciled. Had I not he would have either had me killed or imprisoned. He is a full colonel of his own regiment and has the ear of Prince Rupert and the king himself."

"So," the large man said, "Lord has the girl?"

"No. As I said, sir, she is in the care of a woman I know." It was no lie. Kate wasn't Philip and Philip wasn't in Oxford anyway. "She will be kept safely until I go to collect her."

That led to another cold silence. Danny looked between the large man and Michael who was standing beside him.

"You are no fool, lieutenant. You know very well your life is in the balance here. The graf wishes revenge for what you did to him and, as I see it, you have taken actions that place our endeavours in high jeopardy."

Danny drew breath. It was getting harder to marshal the words he needed. Harder to deliver them with the confident ring required. Harder simply to stand there.

"You placed upon me a responsibility that I have tried to uphold to the very best of my ability. You asked me to ensure Sir Nicholas be kept alive, and he is."

"No thanks to you," Michael muttered.

"I regret that you are misinformed, sir. I left men loyal to myself with him to carry out your orders," Danny said. "Since Sir Nicholas himself commanded me away from him to fetch his wife from Weardale, I ensured your orders would be carried out ongoing by those I could trust to do so. Skilled as I am, it is beyond my competence to be in two places at once."

"Don't be impertinent," the large man growled.

"My apologies," Danny said and shaped a bow. It had to be a shallow one as the pain was too marked. But he could feel their uncertainty growing. They had begun this sure they were dealing with a traitor, now they were questioning that assumption. All he had to do was nudge them along that road a little further. If he could. The trouble was he was nearing the end of his endurance. His body was complaining more loudly by the moment and his thoughts were beginning to drift from their focus.

"If, as you claim, Sir Philip Lord refused to allow you to return to York, how is it you come to be here in London?"

That was one he had already prepared for. Of course, if they knew how he had come to London or he had been observed or linked with the man who attacked those who tried to abduct Gideon's friend Ellis...

"I know London well," he said. "I was an apprentice here in my youth. I also have a passing acquaintance with military architecture. Lord sent me to find out what I could of the state of preparedness of the defences and fortifications here in anticipation of an attack by the king."

The man who had collected him from his prison and so far, not contributed much at all to the conversation stiffened visibly at that. A man committed to Parliament as well as the Covenant then.

"And when given your liberty," Gabriel observed, frowning, "you came to London instead of seeking to rejoin Sir Nicholas?"

"I had no choice," Danny lied. "I was smuggled in on a boat, not allowed to go where I willed."

"And you intended to complete the task you were set by Lord?"

"No. I had learned Ma—the graf was still alive and in London. As I saw it, as long as he lived, he represented the biggest threat to the life of Sir Nicholas as well as to myself. He lays claim to the title that Sir Nicholas holds." He sighed and spread his hands. It was a little theatrical, but they didn't seem to notice. "If I hadn't been attempting to carry out my promise to you, I wouldn't now be in this predicament."

There was a short silence in which all four faces before him remained stone.

THE ALCHEMIST'S PLOT

"And what," the large man asked, "were you planning to do with Sir Nicholas' wife?"

Oh God, what a question. Just the thought made his whole body feel warm and something within him, something tender and protective, broke out like the bud on a fruit tree, coming into full leaf. It was as if he were steel to her lodestone, a force as powerful and as natural, drawing him to her from the moment she had met his gaze with her strong trust and defiance.

I will go with you, she said. And it was done.

He realised his mind was beginning to wander and it took more effort than he liked to pull it back.

"I'd planned to ensure Lady Christobel was kept safe until I could either return her to her husband, having warned him of the danger she represented or until I could make contact with you and appraise you of the situation." He gave a helpless shrug and his shoulders protested. "I had to take action in the moment, but I had no way to inform you that I had done so. I am used to acting on my initiative at need—and accepting the consequences of doing so. I assure you the outcome would have been much worse for all concerned if I hadn't taken action as I did."

There was another silence.

He wondered then if he had said enough—or too much. For a moment it was as if there was the pressure of a huge wave around the edges of his mind, an ocean of panic and uncertainty. *You've screwed it up again Danny, sometimes you're too damn clever for your own good.* He drew a breath and held himself together with the discipline of the duellist and the composure of the cardplayer. No one had ever said it was easy, but it was possible. Just.

"I wonder if you are a loyal man or merely a brave one." Michael might have been seeing into his mind. Danny shivered. It was becoming harder to hold things at bay. He was tired and weak and—

"I think it is possible to be both," he said, hoping with new desperation that this wouldn't go on much longer. He had no wish to collapse on the floor before these people. "I gave you my commitment and I have worked to the best of my ability to carry it out."

"The girl," he heard the large man murmur. "We need to get the girl back."

Michael looked as if he was about to say something to that, then he frowned and shook his head instead. "You have given us much to consider Lieutenant Bristow. Much that we need to discuss amongst ourselves."

They were going to put him back in that hole again. His whole being revolted against it, and it took every ounce of his willpower not to try for his freedom. The two men behind him believed him acquiescent now. They wouldn't be prepared. But he was too weak and knew it. Even if he could deal with the men set to guard him, three of the four who were questioning him wore swords.

Instead, he bowed his head. He had endured worse. He could endure this.

The man who had collected him from the cellar had moved to the door, no doubt to escort him back and now spoke. "Since we might need to have further dealings with the lieutenant, I for one would appreciate it if we could arrange for him to be less—less noisome."

Danny looked up and saw the large man nod agreement.

"Indeed so. See to it that he has a change of clothes and some water to wash in."

His body had begun shivering. Danny had to clench his jaw closed to avoid his teeth chattering. He executed another stiff bow at the group of men, then turned and followed his escort from the room.

He was taken back along the same passageway and had a brief terror that he was, after all, to be discarded back into the oubliette. But just before they reached the door to the room where it lay, his guide opened a door to one side and stood back so he could enter.

"Please respect, lieutenant, that you are a guest here," the man said, his tone admonishing. "Then we will have no need to treat you as if you were a prisoner."

Danny managed a final brief bow and the room he stepped into swam about him as the door was closed and bolted. He had to put out a hand to steady himself against the wall and fight back a sudden and intense nausea, drawing slow breaths to settle his body. It must have been a good five minutes before he was able to overcome his weakness and look at his surroundings.

The room was bleak but compared to what he had been treated to before it appeared palatial. There was a low bed with a hessian straw-stuffed mattress on it, a small table with a candle stub and a chair. No hearth, but a window. Above head height and barred, but a window bringing blessed light into the room, albeit the light of afternoon.

Using the last of his strength, Danny gripped the bars and pulled himself up to look out. It was much the same view as he had seen through the big windows. There was the broad swath of grass with a few clumps of trees and some ornamental bushes. Between and beyond them he could see the river, the jetty with its wherry and now with a view of London on the far side. It seemed he was still in Southwark.

Letting go of the bars he dropped down and turned, sliding down the wall as his legs protested at supporting his weight. For a short time, he just stayed where he was, back to the wall, sitting on the floor. He was still sitting there when the door opened and the promised water to wash, and some clean clothes arrived.

Shaking as he did so, he managed to clean the worst of the filth from his face, hands and hair and encase his body in blissfully clean linen. He had just finished doing up the buttons on the old-fashioned doublet with fingers that seemed not to belong to him anymore when they came to take his dirty things and bring food and drink.

Danny didn't even remember eating, though he was sure that he must have. He only recalled collapsing on the bed and having just enough wit left to pull the blanket up over himself.

Then he slept again.

ELEANOR SWIFT-HOOK

Chapter Fifteen

Returning to Mortlake early on Sunday morning with the peal of bells across London summoning the faithful to church, Gideon realised it had been three weeks since he had last been to church and he missed attending worship. He made a promise to himself and God that he would do so next week. Sir Philip Lord seemed to need little spiritual comfort if any, but with a lifetime of faith behind him, Gideon felt the lack.

There was a light rain to accompany them on the Thames and the sky was overcast with just the occasional glimpse of sunshine.

In his persona as Sir Theophilus Bassington once more, Lord was pontificating on any and every topic that occurred to him. This wherryman was of the loquacious variety who was willing to be engaged in a battle of opinions regarding everything from the price of coal—which was much too high and the sooner Parliament took Newcastle the better as he saw it, to the weather—it was going to be a damp summer and a bad harvest.

A bad harvest was a given, Gideon thought if the war went on much longer. There would be too few fields planted and too few men to bring in the harvest when it came.

It was a depressing thought.

He recalled listening to the much-repeated received wisdom that the war would be over by Christmas. Well, it was now March and, from the recalcitrance and bitterness that he had witnessed on both sides, it didn't seem likely to Gideon that it would be over by the next Christmas either. He wondered if it would be like the German wars, never-ending, ripping the very fabric of society and country apart and leaving a desolate wasteland in its wake.

By the time they reached Mortlake, the rain had stopped, and the sun was making a more determined effort to banish the clouds. It helped lift Gideon's morbid mood a little.

Cleyn stepped out of his front door as they reached it.

"I am glad you were able to make it here today, Sir Theophilus, *Herr* Lennox." Cleyn accompanied their names with appropriate bows, a deep inclination of his shoulders for Lord and a brief dip of the head for Gideon.

He led the way to the tapestry works and unlocked the door, relocking it behind them.

"I kept an eye out for you and saw when you stepped ashore. I have a good view of the river landing from my room," Cleyn explained. "I am glad you came. After what happened on Friday, I wasn't sure that you would."

"We heard your servant was killed," Lord said. "Has there been any progress in finding out who was responsible? This time no one can try to claim it as suicide."

Cleyn shook his head and looked very sober. He led the way up to the weaving hall before he replied as if he needed light and air to be able to speak of such things.

"Killing someone in a church is a terrible thing to do. But no one saw anything. Everyone was either at home or in The Queen's Head for the inquest. Jannekin said that Hester was supposed to be working, so what she was even doing in the church remains a complete mystery."

"Can we see her room here?" Gideon asked. "There might be something amongst her things which could provide a clue to her death."

Cleyn frowned.

"There was a search made and nothing found except her clothes and a couple of books. The women have packed all her possessions, but we have no notion of where her family might be. I gave her letter of reference to the constable in the hope they might be able to find some relative we can give her things to—that and the pay she was owed, little as it was."

"I would consider it a kindness if you would allow Mr Lennox to look," Lord said, his tone emollient. "We are sure she was not killed by chance, whatever might be the conclusion of the inquest."

Reluctant and, Gideon decided, half-convinced that their interest was more morbid than seeking information, Cleyn took them back down the staircase, through a pleasantly furnished parlour and then to a room with a locked door at the back of the house. It was close to where Lord and Gideon had been when breaking in and once Cleyn had the door open Gideon could see that the one window indeed looked out over the courtyard.

It was a small and very empty room, containing a low roped bedstead with a wool-stuffed bed and some blankets. A wooden chest was in one corner and a small table in another. Lord stooped to examine the fireplace which hadn't yet been swept out. There was a bundle placed on the bed, wrapped in a blanket and tied with a black ribbon. The sight of that made Gideon wonder anew if anyone would be mourning the loss of Hester Lovegood.

He opened the bundle and found it contained a few clothes, of the number, type and quality one might expect a female servant to own. Two books had been wrapped in the clothes.

One was a battered copy of *The Countess of Pembroke's Arcadia* by Sir Philip Sidney; the second sent a chill through Gideon as he saw the image on the first page. *Monas Hieroglyphica, Johannis Dee, Londinensis, Ad Maximilianusum, Dei Gratia Romanorum, Bohemiae et Hungarie Regem Sapientissimum...* Without being able to help himself he opened it. His subsequent stillness must have summoned Lord to his side.

"How apposite," Lord said and started reading at the place Gideon had opened to. "*Oh, Maximilian! May God, through this mystagogy, make you or some other scion of the House of Austria the most powerful of all when the time comes for me to remain tranquil in Christ, in order that the honour of His redoubtable name may be restored within the abominable and intolerable shadows hovering above the Earth. And now for fear that I myself should say too much I shall immediately return to the burden of my task...* A man of many mysteries and secrets was Dr Dee and, as we see there, one not averse to making grand promises to powerful people to persuade them into his plans."

He took the book from Gideon's nerveless fingers and closed it. Picking up the *Arcadia* as well, he turned to Cleyn.

"May we borrow these? I will return them."

From his expression, Gideon thought Cleyn might refuse, and Lord must have thought so too because he smiled and tapped the books.

THE ALCHEMIST'S PLOT

"I will be back again to finalise the details of the tapestry commission. I promise you that whatever else might be of artifice or illusion about my visits here, my intention to purchase a tapestry is not."

After which, Cleyn couldn't be happier to loan the books and Gideon took possession of them.

"You have seen all you wish to here?" Cleyn asked. Gideon retied the bundle of clothes with care, took a last look around and nodded. It seemed Hester Lovegood had left nothing more. If she had any substantive possessions or property, it was elsewhere.

Cleyn relocked the door behind them.

"Her death has been another shock," he said sadly.

"It must be making things very difficult for those belonging to the tapestry works, with the local community," Gideon said. He knew from personal experience that it took little for those who were seen as different, by language, dress, habits or beliefs to be viewed with hostility by those around them. Having the tapissiers seen as a source of strange troubles might be enough to tip local feelings against them.

Cleyn smiled at him.

"We have lived here long enough to have made many friends. Although some voices might mutter things, more speak with sympathy for our troubles." He gestured around them. "Most blame this house for what has happened, not those in it. But I thank you for your concern on our behalf." Then he rubbed his hands together. "Now, with that unpleasantness behind us, where did you want to start this exploration?" He was clearly excited at the idea of unearthing whatever mysteries the house might hold.

Lord must have noticed his mood because he inclined his head and smiled. "I think that hidden stairway would seem obvious unless you have any other suggestions? Are there any odd things in the building that you have noticed that you think might be connected with what we have found?"

Cleyn considered.

"If there were to be any room in the tapestry works which might be said to hold a mystery, it would be the rose room—the room where Gerhard and Jan both died."

"We already searched that room very thoroughly," Gideon admitted.

"We also failed to notice the existence of the door to the staircase," Lord said. "If we have missed that perhaps we missed something else in there."

Gideon shook his head. Why would there be more than one secret in that room? Why would—? Then he had an inspiration. "Do you recall counting windows? Looking for a room that wasn't there?"

Lord looked at him, a faint frown creasing his brow then smoothing in understanding.

"You believe the rose room was the one previously hidden?" He turned to Cleyn. "Mr Lennox here is right. It would make sense if that had once been a room with no other access than the secret staircase before. Perhaps it was discovered and made into a regular room when the tapestry works were established. It would only have taken the addition of a door after all."

Cleyn looked thoughtful.

"I wasn't here at the time this was first established," he said. "I joined the works some five years after it first opened its doors, but I have heard no tales of such a thing, and I am sure it would have been something the local people would have been very excited about had it been known."

Lord gestured that Cleyn should lead the way. "Let's go and see if there is anything there that can enlighten us."

The door to the rose room was much like all the others and no clue in the frame might suggest it was newer than the others. But then it might have been moved from elsewhere in the house. Inside the room, though, Gideon's theory began to seem more likely. On closer examination, it was clear that the panels and the roses must have been in place before the door was put through them. Whoever had fitted it had made a good attempt to line the frame up, but it still sliced through the panelling in a way that wouldn't have happened had the panels been set around the door.

"You were correct," Lord said, smiling at Gideon, "and now I am sure you will have a theory as to why it was done?"

THE ALCHEMIST'S PLOT

Gideon crossed over to the place where the panels concealed the stairs down, his fingers searching for, but finding no recess or means of opening it. He thought then of the rooms in Howe Hall that could only be opened from one side and then shuddered, recalling what Lord had said of how those rooms had been used.

"I think I might have," he said. "This must have been done by Dr Dee himself, or those he trusted. It exposed a room that from the decoration we can be sure was of some great significance. But why would he do that, unless he had to?"

Lord said nothing, waiting. Behind him, Cleyn cleared his throat.

"Perhaps because he knew this would be discovered anyway if anyone else took over the house?"

Gideon nodded.

"Exactly so. To leave this room concealed would be to suggest to anyone who came into the building that there was a secret here."

"You think Dee exposed it as it was pointless hiding it?" Lord suggested.

"Yes," Gideon agreed. "But I think there was another reason."

Now both Cleyn and Lord were waiting for him to speak.

He began talking through his thoughts, running his hand over the panel that hid the staircase as he did so. "If I were Dr Dee and I had this house with its secrets, I would look at what was going to be revealed whether I wished it to be or not and I would, with regret, open the door onto that. But, by doing so might I not also hide something less obvious? If I left a secret chamber that was uncovered, it would encourage someone to keep looking, to assume that where there was one secret there might be another. Whereas, if there was no secret room found in the first place, why would anyone think to look?"

Lord was nodding now. "So Dr Dee wanted to hide something somewhere else in the house by exposing the rose room."

"I'm not so sure it's somewhere else."

Lord looked at him then. "You mean the staircase?" he surmised. "You think it conceals something more?"

"I think it has to be that. Otherwise, it would have been wiser to open that staircase when the rose room was opened. Or as it is so narrow and no longer serves any purpose, why not remove it altogether? By leaving it there it risks discovery."

"I don't see why," Cleyn protested. "I have worked right beside it for twenty years on and off and had no notion it was there."

"But someone did," Gideon pointed out. Although it was of course possible that the Covenant had known about it all along.

"More to the point," Lord said, "we have searched the rose room and the only sign of anything secret there is the staircase." Then he shook his head. "But the fact that the room was left with its telling symbolism intact, to me suggests it is still key to this mystery."

"A Tudor rose on an eagle," Cleyn observed. "That is a strange thing to see."

"It is," Lord agreed. Then he looked at Gideon. "If you think the stairs were left for a reason, we should be using the time we have to search them."

"I will go and open the door then," Gideon said. "We have yet to observe it being opened from this room. Perhaps there is some clue in that?"

"I shall watch closely in case there is," Lord assured him.

"Then I had better come with you, Mr Lennox," Cleyn said. "My room below is locked."

Gideon led the way back down the stairs and through the weaving hall. Cleyn was about to unlock the door to the artist's room when Gideon heard a sound from outside. Footsteps on the flagstones outside. He put a hand on Cleyn's shoulder to draw his attention as it was clear the old man had heard nothing. Standing in the small courtyard, beside one of the outbuildings and frowning up at them was Richard West. In one hand he held an iron crow and his other rested on his sword.

Cleyn made a tutting noise. "That man is the most irritating of neighbours." Then he pushed open the same window that Gideon and Lord had used to access the house by night. "Can I help you, Mr West?"

West stopped frowning and his expression changed to one of relief.

THE ALCHEMIST'S PLOT

"I was just passing and thought I heard people in the building. I know that the works are always closed up on a Sunday and feared thieves were trying to break in, Mr Cleyn. I thought I should do my neighbourly duty and make sure all was secure here. I was about to summon my servants, so I am glad to see you there."

"Well as you can see everything is as it should be," Cleyn said, his tone tart. "I am here discussing something with Sir Theophilus Bassington, not that it is any of your business. Though I do find myself wondering what you were planning on doing with that?" He pointed to the metal bar in West's hand.

West lifted the iron crow and looked at it almost as if surprised it should be in his grip.

"Oh, that was in case there were thieves in the building and I needed to force my way in to deal with them," he explained.

Cleyn sighed. "That was most thoughtful of you," he said, but the sarcasm was either ignored or wasted on West who just nodded.

"I'm glad there was nothing sinister going on," he said. "I bid you good day, Mr Cleyn," his gaze shifted to Gideon. "And to you, Mr Lennox."

West strode off and disappeared around the wall of the house, no doubt taking the alley cut-through back to his own house. Cleyn closed the window shaking his head.

"That man has been a bane as long as I've been here. He seemed to have some kind of land dispute with the previous owner. Phillips de Maecht told me that he had heard when the tapestry works were first purchased to be such, West nearly prevented the sale as he claimed he owned the land here. He has been trying to press that claim in the courts, I understand, on and off, but with royal patronage, we had no problem. Though with how things are now, who can tell?"

"Is there any basis to his claim?" Gideon asked.

"I think not. He owns some of the houses on either side, but I have not seen anything to suggest he ever had any claim to this land between them." He sighed. "Still, it was good of him to look out for us if he thought we were being robbed."

Gideon agreed that it was. Privately he thought that West was being overcareful. After all, Gideon had told him that he and Sir Theophilus would be visiting. Though to be fair to the man, knowing the works would be closed, he had probably assumed they would meet in the limner's own house.

Cleyn went back to the door of the artist's room and unlocked it. Inside it smelt of treated canvas, oils and something metallic, all caught up in the charcoal smell from the hearth.

"It amazes me," Cleyn said, as Gideon felt for the catch. "I had no idea there were such secrets in this place. I had always thought the tales told by the locals were just that—tales."

"Well if they are tales of supernatural happenings, they are likely still just tales," Gideon said, as the panel clicked open. "These might be concealed things, but they are very much of human make."

"And ingenuity," Cleyn agreed. "It would be fascinating to see how all this has been contrived."

Gideon pulled the panel open to reveal the narrow stair and Cleyn peered up.

"I would like to try it," he said, "but perhaps after you."

Gideon turned his body to slip into the narrow entrance. He realised then that whereas it was easy enough for him, a corpulent man would struggle to make it up these stairs. He was a little surprised to find that the door at the top hadn't been pulled fully open by Lord but was still just unlatched. He could see a chain which must be attached to weights, running down the side of the door, whoever had made this must have the skill of a clockmaker only on a much larger scale.

He pushed the panel open and stepped out into the rose room, aware of Cleyn's tread on the steps behind him and noticed that the stairs themselves made no sound. Philip Lord had his back to them studying the hearth area.

Cleyn stepped out from the concealed stairway and looked around as if seeing the room for the first time. "Truly amazing," he murmured.

THE ALCHEMIST'S PLOT

"This perhaps explains much," Lord said, turning. "Do you recall, Gideon, how we saw the light in this room and the candle was left here?" He touched the mantelpiece above the hearth.

"You think that was significant?" Gideon asked.

"I think it was very much so. I did wonder why our explorer was in this room when we had already searched it so thoroughly. It also explains why someone was able to take both Gerhard Spijker and Jan Engles by surprise."

"What does?"

"When you opened the door downstairs, whilst there was no doubt a sound as the panel here is released at the top of the staircase, the main distraction for someone in the room would be the sound and movement around the hearth."

Gideon looked at the hearth and could see no difference between it now and earlier.

"I'm not sure…"

"I will demonstrate," Lord said. "Then there will be no need to try and explain."

Stepping lightly between Cleyn and Gideon, Lord vanished down the narrow stairs in the wall. A few moments later the panel door swung shut as if of its own volition, accompanied by a very slight sound from deep within the walls. Much quieter than, but not unlike, a mill wheel turning.

A few moments later there was a distinct metallic chime from the hearth, much louder than the other sounds. Gideon looked and the central boss of the coat of arms on the bar over the mantlepiece rotated in its setting as the entire bar seemed to shift very slightly to the left.

For anyone in the room, it would have been impossible to miss, and Gideon was drawn irresistibly to examine the hearth, just as the two murdered men must have been before him. A sword point made him freeze.

"And it would have been that simple," Lord said, restoring his sword.

Gideon breathed again.

"It would," he agreed. "Although I believe the murderer must have used a ligature so that it would be easier to make it appear as if the two victims had indeed hung themselves. The only question being how he could then get them on the loom."

"That wouldn't have been too much of a problem," Cleyn said, his voice tight, and Gideon chastised himself. It was easy to forget that they were speaking of the doing to death of men Cleyn had known well. "Neither Gerhard nor Jan were big men, nor were either of them that heavy and the loom, as I can show you on the ones in the weaving hall, was firmly attached to the rafters you see in the ceiling and had pulleys to lift the threads, designed to take weight as they need to hold both the tension and the tapestry. A man of both reasonable strength and ingenuity would have had little problem adapting it to the task and if…" His voice failed him with emotion, and he swallowed hard. "Perhaps if you would be kind enough to excuse me a few moments, gentlemen. I shall be in my room below."

He didn't wait for any reply and as he turned away Gideon caught a glimpse of his eyes which held sudden, unshed tears. He went out through the usual door of the room and his footsteps receded then could be heard on the main staircase.

Lord shook his head. "Perhaps you could be a little less vivid in your description next time, Gideon?"

And that was when Gideon realised that the reason Lord had used his sword to make the demonstration was to keep such images as Gideon himself had then conjured, as far away as possible from the mind of Francis Cleyn. It always took him by surprise that a man as hard as Lord could be had such awareness of his impact on those around him. Chastised, Gideon bowed his head in acknowledgement.

"I was thoughtless," he agreed. "It was because I was so distracted by what happened. I saw something move in the mantlepiece."

"If you hadn't seen them move, would you have noticed now that they had?"

"No more than I did the night before last when we were here."

Lord walked over to study the hearth, frowning at the subtle shift that had occurred.

THE ALCHEMIST'S PLOT

"Whoever has designed all this had great skill," he said. "It is as if the whole house is a giant clockwork device. But then even in his youth Dr Dee was renowned for his mechanical contrivances."

"Perhaps the easiest way to unlock its secrets would be to tear it apart," Gideon suggested.

Lord shook his head.

"If I had been a man going to such extremes as these to hide something, then I think I might have ensured that should someone try exactly that approach, whatever it was I sought to conceal would be destroyed."

That was an uncomfortable thought.

"Do we have enough time today to find it?"

"I have no idea." Lord was staring at the ceiling which was plastered and beamed like the others. After a few moments of silence, he spoke softly, as if to himself. "I think it is most probable that I was born in this room."

Gideon felt awkward. An intimate moment he shouldn't witness. Lord kept his inner thoughts and feelings well concealed under an armoured carapace. Then Gideon realised he was wrong. This was the ultimate statement of Sir Philip Lord's trust in him. Gideon had no idea what to say.

Lord crossed to the window and looked out his thoughts unguessable, his expression distant. Then his lips became a tight line, and he shook his head.

"Things without all remedy should be without regard: what's done is done." He turned back to the fireplace, his attitude business-like. "Can you see anything apart from the fact it moved slightly? Has something we've missed before been exposed or revealed?"

Gideon shook his head.

"Nothing obvious, but then if there were anything obvious I am sure our murderer would have remarked it and not still have been searching for it the night before last."

"And last night too, for all we know," Lord said speculatively.

Gideon looked at him sharply.

"You think it is someone in the tapestry works after all?"

"It is not so much I think it is, as I can see no other alternative. Whoever it was left the light and fled down the stairs when they heard us."

"They could have left through a door."

"The doors are all locked and bolted at night. The only way in or out was the window we used."

"Unless whoever it was had a key?"

"It would still have left the door unbolted and we would have heard the sound of it, I am sure. I believe it was Hester Lovegood as she would have slipped back to her room unregarded."

There was an idea lurking at the back of Gideon's mind, but it wasn't ready to step into the full arena of his thoughts, so he let it be, confident it would emerge in time.

"We should see if we can spot something they missed," he said, running his fingers over the roses on their rail above the hearth. "Whoever it might have been."

THE ALCHEMIST'S PLOT

Chapter Sixteen

Danny woke up feeling as if he had been nailed to the bed. Movement was painful, his limbs were stiff as wood, and one eye was swollen enough to narrow his vision. He was grateful he had no looking glass as he had no wish to see what he might look like.

Having stirred with the first sounds of activity in the building, he used such time as he had before being disturbed, to finish eating the food there was left from the evening before—frumenty so cold and solid it could be cut into slices and used as a trencher—and making himself as presentable as possible with the very limited resources he had to hand. Then, with a swordmaster's training, he set to stretching and easing his muscles so he could move without seeming like a marionette.

When the door was unlocked, an hour or so after he had awoken, he felt almost human and ready to face whatever might come. He had expected it would be one of the Covenant men. It wasn't.

"Danny," Mags' voice had an almost affectionate lilt to it and his devastated face pulled up on the undamaged side into something close to a smile. "I hear you've been telling lies to the gentlemen here. That's not very clever of you."

He had come in with the same two men who had escorted Danny on the previous day. A good sign as they weren't his men. Mags was well dressed, in matching doublet and breeches in a blue damask and a cassaque that was of a quality crimson wool, lined with watchet dyed silk. Despite his finery, Mags looked monstrous and Danny wondered which of them appeared uglier at the moment—and which of them would be the most able in a fight. Although Mags wore a sword, he also held a cane and seemed to be needing that to help himself walk.

"I didn't tell any lies," Danny said. "I told the gentlemen here that you had tried to kill Sir Nicholas Tempest and that as I had orders to keep him alive that meant I had to try and kill you. Mind you, as you are now, I don't think even Sir Nicholas would find you much of a challenge, so perhaps my work was done better than I had hoped."

Mags spat.

"You think you can cozen them? The people here aren't such fools as you seem to think them. I'll have my chance to make you pay for what you've done to me."

Danny rubbed at his ear.

"Did you come to see me here for any particular reason? Or just so that I could admire your seven-heddle satin and that fine Norfolk worsted?"

Mags laughed a forced ratcheting sound.

"You can take the boy out of the drapers' guild, but you can't take the drapers' guild out of the boy." Mags smirked. "I've been finding out about you. More than you'd like me to."

"Mercers' guild," Danny corrected, keeping his tone to the long practised even patience that he found served well when he was frustrated or angry. "If you want to impress me you need to get your facts right."

Mags wanted to intimidate, but Danny had no intention of being intimidated. Besides, by turning Danny over to the custody of the Covenant, Mags had given up the ability to threaten convincingly. Nothing now would happen without their consent and Danny was growing more hopeful that he might have persuaded them of his value.

"Oh, I'm not here to impress you, Danny. I'll save that for someone worthwhile, not ungrateful shit like you. I don't know why you turned on me. I took you on when his high and mightiness Sir Philip Lord threw you aside for daring to disagree with him, I offered you the chance to be my second in an army that would king-make in this infantile war. We could have taken England and served it on a plate to whoever offered the best. But you turned on me like the low snake you are and in doing so you brought yourself down too."

It was an interesting interpretation of how events had fallen out, but Danny saw no reason to challenge it. If Mags was talking to him other ears would be listening in, directly or indirectly, and it was those he spoke to.

THE ALCHEMIST'S PLOT

"The difference is," he said, "I met these gentlemen who are our present hosts—the men you are working for too now. They showed me where our interests best lay. They showed me that there was already a plan in place to serve the needs of the nation and leave us—you and me both—very well off indeed. I was the one who was to bring that to you. The best offer of your life. And the good thing was I was still carrying out your orders to keep with your cousin, Sir Nicholas and keep him safe because that was the same I was being asked to do by these gentlemen too."

Mags made a scoffing noise and then laughed.

"That brat—"

"You held him in no small esteem once," Danny countered. "He told me how you saved him from an ambush by the Schiavono's men. Not once but twice. But that was when you were hoping you might be recognised by him as a true Tempest, wasn't it? He thought it was because you were blood kin—that you cared about the notion of family." Danny shook his head. He was sure of his ground now. "It's sad because then you offered *him* to be a part of the kingmaking so he could gain higher rank and then you could get something lesser and be granted Howe. If you recall, I was the one running between you at the time so I could see it."

"And after?" Mags was sneering, his disbelief obvious. "I got orders you deciphered for me so kindly, saying to kill him. Or was that your invention?"

"You know as well as I do the orders were to do so if he'd failed the test they set, which was me. I made sure he passed it. But you were set on killing him." Danny frowned and shook his head "What had changed then? What happened to 'family is everything'?"

"You'll have met Sir Nicholas?" Mags gave a bitter laugh. "I tried hard for the boy but despite it all, he couldn't see what I was offering. He was a stupid, arrogant little—"

"He was," Danny agreed. "He is. But that wasn't why you decided to sell him to Parliament after I kept him alive that night. You could have got him free from Selby and seen him home. Instead, you made your play for his title and tried to hang him. Did you mention that to our friends here? Your little bit of private enterprise?"

Mags' face, already hideous from the disfiguring burns, distorted further with anger.

"You have no notion of what you are saying. It was nothing like that at all."

"You say so." Danny shrugged. Then an idea occurred to him. "You do know that Sir Nicholas is married to Sir Philip Lord's sister?" He had no evidence Christobel was that, but from the care the Covenant were taking around her, he could see no other possibility.

Mags couldn't hide his shock. He believed it. Perhaps he knew it was too big a thing to lie about.

"Maybe," Danny said quietly, "you should be thinking more about what you have to offer to our hosts here and a bit less about how much you hate me right now."

Mags hawked and spat at Danny's feet.

"You think you have it all figured out, don't you Danny? Well, I won't be the man to disillusion you." Then he went back to the door, pausing before he went through it. "I've not forgotten what I promised to do to you. This just means that we'll both have to be a little more patient before it happens is all."

Before it had the edge of menace, now Danny heard empty bluster. He could, of course, be wrong. But he had a feeling that he'd just been tested by his captors, and he could hope he'd not been found wanting. It made him wonder how much respective value he and Mags might each have to the Covenant.

Before their last encounter, he would have said that Mags had a much higher value. He was a famous or at least infamous, mercenary commander whose name could be used to draw soldiers and recruits. Having Mags fighting under your banner would be one of the best recruiting tools there was. Added to that he was no slouch on the battlefield and had a good head for reconnaissance and logistics, he always had.

But now that reputation had been soiled. Word would have spread that he was a changed and disfigured man. That he'd been bested. Beaten. Destroyed. It was even possible they might hear

THE ALCHEMIST'S PLOT

whispered the name of Danny Bristow, though he doubted it. Danny had never been one to seek renown—or infamy. His reputation stood in very different circles from those inhabited by the kind of men Mags' name might be expected to draw.

The door opened again about half an hour after Mags had left, by which time Danny had persuaded his body over the worst of its immobility.

"Your presence is required, lieutenant." This time it was Gabriel who came with the armed guard to escort him, the golden blond curls immaculate and as before he favoured black head to foot, but not the black of a professional man. Danny wondered if it was a religious statement, an affectation or if he was in mourning.

They went to the same room as before, but this time the furniture had all been pushed to one side. The table was hard against the wall where the windows showed views over the grounds and an overcast sky allowed the occasional glimpse of sunshine. The chairs that had been arranged around the table were now pushed under it or put at the far end of the room, to where Danny was being escorted. Seeing that, Danny had a sudden premonition, and his heart sank.

The large man, who had been the only one sitting before, was seated on one of those chairs and on a second beside him sat Mags. Michael and the fourth of the Covenant men stood with them. Behind Mags' chair, Danny was surprised to see Turk, who was wearing a smug-looking smile and had his arms folded over his chest. The presence of Mags and Turk made Danny's skin prickle, especially as they seemed to be sitting in a place of power. The bruising on his ribs became more painful as his chest tightened at that thought.

When they were about three yards from the group, Gabriel put out an arm to indicate Danny should stop. He went to stand beside Michael, leaving Danny alone with his escort. Ignoring Mags and Turk, Danny made a polite bow to the Covenant men.

"How may I be of service, gentlemen?" He was wondering very much what this was about and trying to keep alert for any possible opportunity or advantage.

"That is the point at issue here," the large, seated man said, his fingers curling over the cane he held. Mags had lost his cane somewhere as it wasn't in evidence at all. "We are not sure. You might be surplus to our requirements."

It was so theatrical, Danny almost expected a chorus to appear from behind a curtain and start addressing an invisible audience somewhere behind him. But then he had seen that these Covenant men seemed to enjoy the high drama of their calling. What was it Philip had suggested? That the head, the real power and leadership had either gone or was so far removed from the front lines of this conspiracy that it was just going through the motions. Men desperately grasping the last shreds of power, even as those shreds were evaporating like mist from between their fingers as they did so. No wonder they needed to bolster themselves with theatre and ritual.

That didn't make them any less dangerous, of course, if anything it would make them more so—desperate men always were.

And there was also the possibility Philip was wrong and that these were men very much in control. With the disruption of war and the fragmentation of power through Parliament's many factions, the Covenant might have seen its chance and taken it. For all he knew these men were in all truth the powerful kingmakers they presented themselves to be.

Neither notion offered much comfort.

Danny drew a steadying breath. He reminded himself of something di Zorzi had taught him in his apprentice days— you can only be intimidated by another if you allow it to happen. Intimidation is something you do to yourself.

"What might help you, good gentlemen, come to some decision?" he asked, pleased to hear his voice sounding level and confident. Although he was sure they had already decided his fate. The smirk on Mags' face, visible despite the ruined flesh, said as much.

Michael answered. "We would benefit from a display of your prowess."

The premonition had been correct.

Danny thought for a moment.

THE ALCHEMIST'S PLOT

"If you wish. I could draw you up a scheme for the fortification of London. From what I've seen so far there is room for improvement. Or I could demonstrate the method I've recently devised for calculating the amount of powder left in a barrel. Or perhaps you would appreciate some guidance on improving the security of your ciphers?"

He had the satisfaction of seeing their expressions shift as he spoke. But despite that, he knew there would be no diverting them. It was something primal. He knew it well and despised it more. Even the most educated and high-minded men seemed blinkered by it.

"You are a man with many facets, Lieutenant Bristow," the large man said. "You have a truly universal intellect. That is much to be admired."

"Thank you," Danny said. "Though it might surprise you how little it is. If it is something more practical you wish of me, I could go to Oxford and redeem Lady Tempest. That would be the best proof of my commitment and fidelity that I could offer you."

The smile on Michael's face sent a cold chill down Danny's spine.

"No need to trouble yourself. We have people in Oxford. As I told you when we met, we have people everywhere. Our influence may be greater here in London, but don't doubt that we have loyal men with the king also."

It wasn't often Danny knew the kind of hate that made him wish to kill. Mags had earned it a dozen times over, but now he hated these men with the same fierce venom. Relaxing his shoulders, he let out a breath.

"That's a relief then. I was wondering how I might explain my battered appearance if I needed to travel there."

"You could," Gabriel said, "tell people you went under the hooves and wheels of a coach and horses."

Christ! Had they recognised him after all?

"That's a good suggestion, sir," he said, keeping what he hoped was a guileless note in his voice. "It might earn me more sympathy than the truth."

And that was when Danny wished very badly that he could play cards with these men because their demeanour betrayed them. Perhaps they had a description from the coachman. They hadn't been certain before and now they were even less so. He kept his expression as bland as his injuries permitted. If they brought the coachman in to identify him... But then why wasn't he here, since his evidence was crucial to them?

"What, then, was it that you wished me to do?" he asked.

"They want to see you fight, Danny," Mags said, and the side of his face that was still working, grinned broadly.

Premonition fulfilled. Could it get any cheaper and more predictable? Had these men no imagination? Even Mags had come up with a more creative, if more unpleasant, way to end his life.

"Why?" he asked, and the question was genuine.

That surprised them. It was almost as if they expected him to leap at the chance to wave a sword around and draw blood for no good reason at all.

Michael cleared his throat.

"It seems we have a matter of honour to resolve here. After that is dealt with... Well, after that, we will see."

Danny fought the nearly irresistible impulse to laugh. He had never yet seen a duel fought for honour. For pride, conceit, for hatred of the other party, for arrogance and base material gain, all those he had seen lead to a duel. Honour had very little to do with it and even less to do with the outcome. All knew God favoured the righteous. So, by definition, the righteous were those with the best weapons, the greatest skill and the most strength.

He bowed his head in what hopefully appeared to be respectful acceptance, as one was supposed to when challenged to a duel. It gave him the moment he needed to collect himself from what would surely be seen as inappropriate laughter. Then he lifted his head, his gaze direct and unflinching. It was a farce. He'd played it all before. He knew the lines.

"I am, sirs, of course, at your disposal," he said, then added: "Whose honour have I slighted? It can't be the graf because as we all know he has none to slight."

"Why you—"

THE ALCHEMIST'S PLOT

Mags sprung to his feet and was waved back down by the large man sitting beside him.

"The graf thinks otherwise," Michael said. "As the offended party, that means he is entitled to claim against you."

Danny made the best flourish he could muster towards Mags, wishing his body wasn't quite so sore. "I am more than happy to enter any litigation that—"

"Grow up, Danny," Mags snarled. "This is the real world. These people know the meaning of honour, they know the meaning of true nobility—of bloodlines that make it so—and they know the difference between a graf and a merchant who plays at being a soldier."

It was a situation in which Danny knew words would be wasted. These men, for whatever reasons of their own—and he suspected it was nothing more than the love of a good fight—had decided he should fight Mags. He had to wonder what their gain from it would be. Did they really think Mags could win? Or might they even be willing to risk Danny winning? If so, then perhaps there was a way out after all. Perhaps he could bind them with the chains of their own 'honour'.

Michael was speaking again.

"As the Graf von Elsterkrallen is badly injured, it has been agreed that Edward Nelson will fight in his stead."

Danny let the idea go again. There was no intention of them taking any risk at all that he might win. In his present state, Turk would be his match.

"I am injured also. Am I permitted to name a champion?" he asked instead.

"If there were any here willing, then it could be considered," the large man said, his tone magnanimous.

So that was a no then. Danny turned to the two men behind him.

"Would either of you be willing? Turk's not that good with a sword. Last time I saw him use one he nearly cut his leg open on a low parry."

The men were not looking at him, although one had to smother a grin at his words. They were looking behind him to those who paid their wages and Danny knew what response they would get there. Both shook their heads.

He turned back to the four men.

"Perhaps one of you good gentlemen would be prepared to…? No?" He let the breath puff from his cheeks in a theatrical manner. "Very well, let's get it over with." And his words, for once, reflected his true feelings. "What are we fighting with spears? Halberds? Axes? That might do some damage to the furnishings. Or are we being conventional and using swords?" As he spoke, keeping his tone light and irreverent, he was calculating distances and angles in his head. He had a plan and had he been in full health and fitness he would have been confident he could achieve it. But the big unknown in the equation was his own body. Would it be able to do what he was going to ask of it whilst in such a poor condition?

"We have our rituals," Michael said as if he was speaking of a religious rite. Well for all Danny knew it might be such to these people. Was it a blood sacrifice even? He had learned enough from Philip's attitude to religion to be very sure that whatever these people practised and proselytised, it wasn't any usual form of Christianity.

It was the fourth Covenant man, the man who spoke the least, who walked to the long chest set against one wall and opened a panel on the side of it. Danny couldn't see what he was doing, but a few moments later there was a clunk and whirring sound, such as a big clock might make before striking the hour. The lid of the chest split along its centre line and opened itself, allowing a platform within to rise to the level where the lid had been. Upon the platform was set a beautiful box of polished ebony, a good yard and a half long and perhaps two feet wide.

On the lid had been inlaid two symbols, each picked out in jewels and precious metals. One Danny had seen before on things to do with the Covenant—the *Monas Hieroglyphica*. But the other was new to him, it was a black splayed eagle wearing a crown and on its breast was pinned a simple rose with red and white petals and a golden centre.

THE ALCHEMIST'S PLOT

It was a beautifully crafted box and Danny had to admire its workmanship and the cleverness of the clockwork which had revealed it from the bigger chest. But then the box was opened, and he completely forgot it.

The two swords that sat within laid so the point of each was at the hilt of the other, took his breath. They were magnificent weapons. Even without touching one, he knew it would equal or excel the quality of the sword he had lost to di Zorzi. But what sent a small chill through him was the realisation that he had seen another which, aside from the wear and usage it had seen, would match these. That was the sword he had Gideon wore, a blade he had said he came by on the battlefield in the shadow of Edgehill.

The good news was that with such a sword in his hands, Danny became more sure he could do what needed doing. Because although Turk was a lethal fighter, he was someone who had learned his skills from the streets and the battlefield. A hatchet man who relied on brute force and speed. He had never learned to use a sword properly. With another weapon, any of those Danny had suggested or even—God forbid—with pistols, Turk might have stood a chance. But no matter his condition, as long as Danny could stand on his own two feet and bear the weight of a sword on his wrist, he could still win against such a man.

We have our rituals, Michael had said. The man who had opened the cabinet made a bow towards it as if it were a reliquary and then stepped back to stand beside the chairs. Once he was there, the large man heaved himself to his feet to stand by the sword table, supported by a cane. Michael moved to stand beside him holding a Bible.

Danny noticed the ritual had points in common with the form of words used for a trial by combat which he had himself overseen more than once to settle disputes amongst mercenaries. At various points, he and Turk were expected to place their hands on the Bible and repeat something. But he paid little attention to what was said, his focus was on what would follow. He didn't care about grandiose claims to truth and justice any more than Mags, who watched it all from his chair with a lopsided smirk. It was all a stage play, a sham—hollow and meaningless.

Then, they were allowed to pick up the swords. Danny needed to do no more than that to know all he had to about the blade. It wasn't as perfectly matched to him as his own—his *old* schiavona, but it was the third-best blade he had ever held. Philip's sword, of course, being something else again.

Turk had picked the other up and was cutting at the air with it experimentally, then made a couple of lunges and wore a big grin. Danny noticed the looks of tight disapproval on the faces of the Covenant men. No doubt they wanted this to be a sombre event, full of the gravitas they had established in their sombre ritual and Turk was busy ruining that for them. It was hard to muster even a mote of sympathy.

"Let's to it," he said because his principles required him to give a warning. If they wanted blood on the floor, he would provide it. He and Turk were standing side by side, a pace between them and with Michael and the large man two paces before them, Michael still holding the Bible in both his hands.

"Gentlemen," the large man started talking," if you would—"

But Danny was done with the words. He had a plan, and he had a purpose.

Turk still had his mouth open in protest when Danny turned hard on the spot and took him in the chest with the sword. He captured Turk's sword in his empty hand and cut down with it onto Michael, who was still reacting and threw up the Bible to catch the blow. Of course, the sword went through the book, but it was deflected, doing little real damage. Not wanting to delay more, because the two men who had been his guard had started to move now, Danny planted a hard kick which put the large man on the ground, his head cracked as it hit the floor.

Mags was on his feet and stepped forwards drawing his sword, seeming less crippled than before. This was the hard bit. The bit Danny dreaded because his body was already protesting, and the pain was weakening and slowing. But if any of this was to count, he had to try. He hurled the sword in his right hand away and heard a satisfying crash of glass as one of the windows behind the table suffered from its impact.

THE ALCHEMIST'S PLOT

Gabriel and the other Covenant man had drawn their swords as Danny reached Mags, but it was Mags who, blocking Danny's cut, shouted, "No! Leave him. He's mine."

Perhaps Mags had seen what the others had not, that the only thing keeping Danny on his feet and moving was sheer willpower. Injured or not, Mags was his match now and knew it.

As if by some primal instinct that this wasn't their fight, the other men in the room drew back. Gabriel and his quiet colleague had gone to help Michael with the large man who was already stirring, groaning and trying to sit up. Danny marked the fact and kept his full attention on Mags.

"You thought you broke me, did you, lad?" Mags pushed into an attack and Danny had to give ground. It was painful to move his arms, painful to command his feet to dance in the needed steps and painful to draw the air he needed to sustain the effort into his lungs. His entire body was bruised, and no movement could be as it should.

Whatever injury Mags had taken, it hadn't been as severe as he had made out. His movements were swift and lethal, pushing Danny closely. So closely that his breath, bearing the smell of onion and wine caught in Danny's nostrils.

"I hope you enjoyed your dinner," Danny said, disengaging and giving more ground along the length of the room to do so. "It was your last."

Mags closed the space between them as he spoke, and Danny's sentence was punctuated by the clash of steel. With any other blade, he would have lacked the strength to lift it again and again as Mags beat him down.

He was pushed to one knee. It should have been easy for Mags, but Danny didn't do what other men would have done, he waited, vulnerable, as the sword came in then caught the blade on his sword and turned it on the hilt, so it was Mags who took a cut to his arm and Danny regained his feet.

But the cost of the move was high. Every pore on his skin oozed sweat, his heart pounded, protesting the punishment. He knew he was almost out of time and if he made another slip like that one it would be his last—ever.

By that point, they were beside the table that had been set hard against the windowed wall. There were also chairs...

As he parried a low cut, Danny hooked a chair leg with his foot, pulling it out right in front of Mags, who stumbled onto it. That was all Danny needed. The moment the probing blade was down he sliced hard. Mags saw the danger too late, and his sword was only half raised to block when it fell from his fingers. The sword Danny held, bit true and a fountain of blood spurted from Mags' neck. There was no time for relief or satisfaction, no time for vindication or victory. Just the solid knowledge that Mags was dead.

The job was done.

Danny didn't even try to recover the weapon and he used the fallen chair as a step. A moment later he was on the table, through the broken window and rolling forward landing heavily on the wet grass. Beyond thought and beyond feeling, he snatched up the sword he had thrown out to prepare his escape and started running—stumbling—as fast as his body would allow him towards the river. There, as he had seen on the previous day, was the small wherry moored to the private jetty that belonged to the house.

His feet pounded the damp planks no longer feeling as if they belonged to his body and he fell rather than climbed into the boat. Somehow, he managed to locate and slice through the rope that tethered it to shore. He could hear the sounds of pursuit. But by then he was spent, and it was almost too much to use an oar to push the wherry out into the river's flow. That done he slipped to lie in the bottom of the little boat, feeling the rain gentle on his face and lacking the strength to move anymore.

"That was for you, Matt," he murmured. "For you, for Máire, Liam, Nessa..."

It seemed to matter.

Then nothing did.

THE ALCHEMIST'S PLOT

Chapter Seventeen

"Well, that was a complete waste of our time and effort," Gideon said, knowing he must sound sullen and not caring that he did so.

They were waiting on the river foreshore for a wherry to take them back to the Westminster Steps, but this far out and on a Sunday…?

Gideon was in a bad mood. They had found nothing more in the rose room and still didn't understand how the movement of the mantle decoration connected with the open door to the staircase. There had been brief excitement when Gideon discovered that the roses on the mantle could be rotated when the panel to the secret staircase was open and not when it was closed. But since turning them did nothing, they were forced to conclude it was a loosening caused by the shift in position unlocking the roses from being pressed hard to the bar behind.

Their time in the room had been as frustrating as before and a thorough examination of the staircase had revealed nothing further either. It was as if they had advanced one pace in the mystery only to find they were in truth no closer to solving it than they had been.

"It wasn't a complete waste." Lord was looking pensive, he had the *Monas Hieroglyphica* in his hands and was studying a diagram in it. "We learned a lot about how complex the house is, what not to do in the rose room—not to mention some interesting details about the late Hester Lovegood too. There were ashes of curled papers in the hearth in her room. She had been burning something incriminating, I think. And I am hopeful that one of these two books might be of assistance in solving the cipher. I am sure Danny will be delighted we retrieved them if so."

Except they still had no idea where Danny might be. And that was just one more issue to resolve. He was feeling despondent. Everything they had come to London to achieve they were failing with. He kept thinking that he had to be missing something obvious, something that if he could just bring it into focus would reconcile all the disparate pieces of information they had gathered and explain everything that was going on in the tapestry works.

Except, of course, it could never be so simple. There could be no one thing that could unravel the mystery of the house and explain the—

Then he remembered.

"The Cotton Library," Gideon said. He knew the excitement must be edging his voice because Lord looked up quickly. "We were going to try and get in there to see what papers Cotton had found at the house before it became a tapestry works. Rumour has it that he dug something up from the garden that contained a cache of documents by Dee, documents Dee thought too dangerous to keep in the house, or so Richard West told me."

Lord was looking interested now.

"Dee putting papers in a hole in the ground? Around here?" He shook his head. "That sounds unlikely to me. Unless they were in a lead coffin they would be destroyed by the damp in no time. Perhaps, if such documents do exist and are not a figment of popular imagination like so much else to do with Dr Dee and his house, Sir Robert found a way into a secret room there and claimed he had dug them up to put others off the scent." He closed the book and put it away in his coat. "However, I'm not sure we can walk into the library and demand access to some papers that Sir Robert may or may not have found, which may or may not have been in a hole in the ground in Mortlake—and may or may not have been put into the library collection, even if they do exist."

All of which was both true and depressing.

The wherry which eventually took them back to Westminster arrived with some of those from the tapestry works aboard, returning from attending the Dutch church at Austen Friars. Lord was quiet in the boat on the way back and Gideon found himself caught up in his thoughts too much to want conversation. He knew they needed access to the Cotton Library which was in the Cotton family's ageing mansion, but he could think of no excuse or deceit he could use to get that.

The twilight was beginning to sprinkle with stars and Gideon watched the brightest for a while, his thoughts coasting. Then, as

THE ALCHEMIST'S PLOT

he noticed a new star had winked into appearance, the germ of an idea began in his mind. Perhaps there was a way he could get into the library... just perhaps...

It was late dusk by the time they reached the Westminster Steps and took the now familiar route across the New Palace Yard and back to The Bell. With the coming of nightfall, the street bustle of London was giving way to indoor activity. People gathered in taverns—there being no more theatres or other such public entertainments. But even those seemed much less frequented than they had been before the war. It was as if the people of the city felt a need to creep indoors in their own homes for safety and bar the door against some unknown doom that lay in the future.

When Gideon walked into The Bell, Danny was sitting at a corner table in the common room playing cards with two other men. He was wearing a stained and worn yellow doublet slashed with red and black, and a dark red hat, the brim low over his face so that Gideon only recognised that it was Danny by the unmistakable unruly hair, bursting from beneath the hat. That, and the pile of coin he had accrued on the table before him.

Then Danny looked up and Gideon winced. His face, in the flicker of candlelight, was grotesque. A mass of bruises and a variety of colours from deep purple, through reds and blues to some small edges of yellow.

"I shall be in my room," Lord said in his best Sir Theophilus voice, clapping a hand on Gideon's shoulder as he pushed past, indicating that he expected Gideon to bring Danny. Gideon headed for the table as he heard Lord capture a passing server to order food and drink to be sent to his room.

By the time he reached the table at the back of the common room, Danny had freed himself from his coterie of card players and collected his money. He pushed himself to his feet, the stiffness and effort in his every movement made it clear to do so cost him pain. Even so, he managed a brief bow and a grimace that Gideon thought was approximating a grin.

"You will never know how hard it was to persuade Bill Austen to let me in here in this state," he said. "I managed to convince him I'd fallen amongst thieves."

"Bill Austen?" Gideon was lost.

"He is our host here at The Bell, the big man who you see shouting at the staff. And I'm not sure whether he objected more to my battered face or the offensive outfit. But the kind ladies of The Cock in Southwark had nothing else and by the time the watermen had me ashore my old clothes were not fit for use."

"The Cock in Southwark?"

Danny nodded and stifled a yawn which ended in a wince. "Forgive me. I shouldn't be so tired. I've been sleeping most of the day and I came here by coach, not an hour since, my head in the lap of a delightful young lady called Lucy."

"Lucy?"

"You're turning into a parrot. Yes. Lucy."

Gideon bit back on the questions he had, shook his head and led the way up the stairs.

Lord, still clad in his Sir Theophilus disguise, paunch and all, stepped towards Danny as they entered the room and Gideon closed the door behind them.

"Good God, what—? Then he stood still and broke off at something in Danny's expression.

Danny himself had stopped just a couple of paces inside from the door and with an effort that made him flinch visibly drew himself up to a soldier's parade stance.

"Lieutenant Colonel Bristow reporting my success in achieving your orders, sir." He completed the statement with a very stiff military bow.

Lord drew a breath.

"Mags is dead." It was not a question.

"Yes, sir," Danny said, then his body sagged.

Lord moved with a speed that made Gideon start, catching Danny as he staggered and both supporting and guiding him to the one furnished chair which sat by the hearth.

"You are a damn fool, Danny," Lord said, but there were acres of concern and almost no condemnation in his voice.

"What? For killing Mags?"

"No. For trying to stand up too long."

That made Danny laugh at least.

THE ALCHEMIST'S PLOT

"I met two more of your Covenant angels as well, I will draw pictures for you if you get me the means to do so."

Lord shook his head. "It can wait until you have eaten and rested at least. Besides, there is a more pressing task I would have you apply yourself to." He reached into his coat and produced the ciphered note.

Danny took it, unfolded the page and then his eyes gleamed visibly, despite the fatigue and the damage to his face. He glanced up at Lord. "Is this all?"

Lord produced the two books.

"These might be what you need as well."

Danny nodded then closed his eyes.

"How urgent is it?"

Lord took the paper from his nerveless fingers and slipped it into one of the books and set them on a small table in the corner of the room.

"Not so urgent that you can't eat and sleep."

Though Gideon had a feeling that was said more because Lord knew there was no alternative. It was obvious that Danny was spent. Whatever he had gone through to bring about the death of Mags, it had been achieved at a high personal cost.

"You have a new sword," Lord observed and glancing down Gideon realised with a shock Danny had an unfamiliar blade at his thigh, not the one he had worn as long as Gideon had known him, the one which he had lent to Gideon to fight a duel for his life when they had been at Wrathby the previous autumn.

"I do," Danny agreed.

Before Lord could ask more, the expected food arrived, together with a large jug of wine and a small decanter of aquavitae. Once the door was closed behind the servers, Lord poured a generous amount of the aquavitae into a cup for Danny, whose hand, Gideon couldn't help but notice, shook as he took it.

"Is there more we need to know?" Lord asked.

Danny downed half the cup in a single gulp then nodded.

"I suspect we won't be safe here for long. In brief, I killed Mags and escaped the Covenant. The watermen who rescued me from the river were paid for their silence and I am very sure the ladies of The Cock who took me in will say nothing, but the Covenant will be looking for me and they may have called upon the forces of Parliament to assist them."

Lord frowned. "Then tomorrow we will leave here. I had a mind to go to Mortlake once you were back anyway." He paused and Gideon opened his mouth to object, but Lord held up a hand. "I do remember we have one more task here yet. We will visit the Cotton establishment and somehow get to view their Library."

"Two more tasks then," Danny said. "I still need to speak to James Wemyss."

"You're in no fit state," Lord said.

"Then you'll have to go for me. I am sure if anyone can persuade him to move to Oxford you can and if he refuses, you have enough basic knowledge and the wit to get what we need from him." Danny gave his painful grin. Then raising his cup as if in a toast to Lord, he drained it. "So that is agreed. You two can go to your tasks and I will sit here, out of sight and out of mind, solve your cipher and draw portraits. Then we can take the horses over on the ferry and ride to Mortlake."

He made it sound simple.

"Except I cannot be in two places at once," Lord observed.

Gideon cleared his throat. The idea he had been giving much thought to on the journey back from Mortlake had come to maturity.

"Yes. About that," he said, and Lord looked across at him with a raised eyebrow. Gideon gathered his courage and went on. "I can get access to the library, but it will need to be alone."

"You have a friend like Ellis who can secure you admission?"

Gideon felt his face colour.

"No. I have another method in mind."

Lord looked doubtful. "If the papers I seek are there—"

"Then I will steal them for you."

Danny was staring at him now as well.

"*You*? Steal?"

"If it is necessary, but…"

Lord laughed aloud.

THE ALCHEMIST'S PLOT

"*Let's handle it with such an excellence as if we would bring thieving into honor...* for surely it must now be an honourable profession now, if Gideon Lennox is willing to undertake it. Though to be fair, let's not forget you have already embraced it as I recall with no less than that theft of a letter from the queen herself. But you seem shy about sharing your intentions, so we should not pry."

Gideon knew he must be bright red. Staring at his plate, he applied himself to the meal and was glad the talk turned to other things—possible ciphers that might have been used by Hester Lovegood and then the troubling details of Danny's encounter with the Covenant. Gideon noticed Danny said nothing about how he came to be taken as their prisoner, speaking only of what they had said.

"They favour Parliament in this war, without a doubt. But then that is no surprise, they can't support a king they seek to supplant, can they? But they still have strength in the king's faction, they didn't say who or how but made it clear they believed they could find Christobel in Oxford and abduct her." There was an uncharacteristically cold bitterness in Danny's tone as he spoke.

"Kate and all her household are well protected as you know," Lord said. "Besides, they would have to get past Shiraz. I think their threat is hollow. What happened with Mags? They let you kill him?"

"That wasn't their plan but I don't think they'll weep that I killed him. But they know I cozened them, so they will see me as a traitor and an enemy."

"Was there some kind of formality, or a..." Lord hesitated as if trying to find the right word. "Was there a ceremony involved with the killing?"

Danny nodded, his mouth full, then sat back and drew the sword he was wearing. It was chillingly familiar. The twin of the one Gideon himself had found on the field at Kineton after the battle. Without conscious thought, his hand went to its hilt. He recalled now the extreme interest that Lord Brooke had shown in his sword, and the way Lord had reacted when he first saw it.

Lord took the sword Danny proffered by its hilt and examined it.

"I have to say I think yours was the better blade, and I am sorry you have lost it in doing my work. This is still a very good sword, however, Gideon can vouch for that."

"I wasn't doing *your* work," Danny said. "I did it for Matt."

"That *was* my work," Lord said, an odd bitterness in his tone.

"So? Matt of all men would have understood it. Would have chastised you if you had dropped your responsibilities in a heap for it. He knew what it was to command. You told me yourself that if anything happened to you my first responsibility was to the company and Kate, not in seeking vengeance. You learned that from Matt."

Lord said nothing, staring at the sword as if unable to meet Danny's gaze. Then he drew a breath and held the hilt towards Danny.

"When you have eaten, we will sleep."

Soon after that, prophecy became fact. Danny managed to change into a nightshirt before crawling into bed and seemed asleep at once. Gideon paused in the doorway, hand on the latch.

"I will be out first thing," he said, "I hope to be able to access the library."

Lord was pulling the truckle out and glanced over.

"You are sure this is something you can do alone?"

Gideon had asked himself the same question a few times and now nodded.

"I believe it's the only way it can be done," he said, expecting Lord to ask the how and why and wherefore of what he intended. Instead, the turquoise gaze held his own a moment longer, then Lord nodded.

"Be back by dinnertime or soon after. The tide will be low in the early afternoon and that is when the horseferry will run."

"I'll be back by then," Gideon promised. Deep within he felt a strange emotion because Lord hadn't asked, just as he hadn't asked Danny how he planned to get to Mags. And just as Danny had succeeded Gideon was determined he would succeed—but he hoped at less personal cost.

THE ALCHEMIST'S PLOT

He woke early and was out at first light as the city he had known so well until a year ago began stirring to life for the first working day of the week. Most were up earlier than usual as they had a little extra to prepare having not done some of the usual daily tasks on the Sabbath. It meant the streets were not empty, even if far from bustling as they would be in a couple of hours.

Deceit wasn't something Gideon had ever been comfortable with. He had been brought up to regard honesty as the most basic principle of Godliness. One of the hardest lessons he had learned was that most people had a much more flexible relationship with the truth. But little as he liked deceit, Gideon was prepared to employ it in a cause he saw as having a greater good.

The house where Gideon had lodged was close to the Inns. Since the death of his mother when he was still a student, his room at Widow Keating's had been as close to home as he had known. When he had left for Newcastle almost a year ago, Widow Keating had promised she would keep Gideon's few possessions safe and his room ready for his return in her spacious house. Of course, at the time he hadn't been expecting to be gone so long and although he had left enough to cover the cost of his lodgings for a couple of months, he was sure by now she would have rented the room to another young lawyer. But, with luck, she might have kept his chest. It was on that his whole plan rested.

With some trepidation, he tapped on the kitchen door. He knew Widow Keating would be there, helping the cook with preparing food for all her young gentlemen, as she spoke of those who lodged with her.

The face that looked out through the window from under a close-fitting coif covered with a neat, embroidered cap was scowling. Then the expression changed to doubt and finally to a smile as the bolts on the door were pulled back.

"And there was I thinking it were some ne'er do well wanting a free hand out, but it is Mr Lennox. And me thinking we'd not see you again."

"You let my room?"

Widow Keating lifted her floury hands and then wiped them on her apron. "Oh no. I told you I would keep a place for you. I did move your things to the small room in the attic as another young gentleman lawyer needed a place to stay. But as it happens, he has told me he is moving out next week, so you can have your old room back if you—"

Now it was Gideon who held up a hand and softened the gesture with a smile.

"You are so very kind, but I came to collect the last of my things that I will need. I am also moving out." He had known he would say this, but when the words were spoken it was as if something deep inside him was cut away. A tight ball of homesickness welled into his throat which had nothing at all to do with this house or Widow Keating and everything to do with the loss of his mother and the final recognition that his life as a lawyer here was never now going to be resumed.

"You're not going for a soldier, are you?" Widow Keating demanded, her face stern. "I wouldn't want any of my young gentlemen getting involved in all that."

How could he tell her he already had done so? He was in the employ of one of the most notorious mercenary commanders and if that wasn't 'going for a soldier' he was unsure what would qualify. But he pasted a bright smile over his face and lied smoothly.

"I am moving to the north," he said, aware that whatever he told her would be repeated around his erstwhile friends and acquaintances in London. "I came to settle my affairs here and take some of my things. Any I leave you are welcome to sell on. You see, I've met someone." And that wasn't at all a lie.

Widow Keating's face lit up at that and she clasped her floury hands together.

"A northern girl has won your heart and your hand?" For a moment she looked as if she might shed a tear. "Let me take you up to the room, though you know the way I'm sure, but the door will be locked, and you must have something to eat before you go. You'll have come in on the tide?"

Gideon nodded and answered her cheerful stream of questions with whatever he could think of in the moment, as she led the way upstairs. Widow Keating unlocked the door to one of the small

THE ALCHEMIST'S PLOT

rooms under the roof, the others of which were where her servants slept. She stood aside, her face flushed and her breathing hard from the effort of climbing the stairs.

"Now don't you mind the other boxes in here, there's yours under the window and here's the key to it you left me."

To be fair it was a proper bedroom, with a proper bedstead and a tired-looking feather bed, but clearly, this was a room where the widow put the belongings of any of her young gentlemen who went away without a word. If like Gideon, they reappeared, she had a room ready for them and their possessions safe. Smiling at her quiet, but kind, subterfuge, he thanked her for her care of his things and nodded as if in agreement when she spoke of him joining the other young gentlemen to break his fast before he took his leave.

Once left alone and with the good widow's footsteps receding down the stairs, Gideon opened the chest, to find all his clothes and small collection of books neatly packed away. Seeing the books made him wish he could take them with him. But perhaps some new law student would soon own his treasured and battered edition of *Perkins Profitable Book*.

Most of the chest was taken up by what he had come for. His formal lawyer's robes and starched bands to wear over the black. He pushed his hair under the dark cloth of the close-fitting cap and put on the soft leather gloves. Within a few minutes, he was transformed from a gentleman to a working lawyer, one who might be about to step into his chambers.

Gideon left the rest and added a crown to the pile for Widow Keating to find so she would know he was grateful for her care and that he wouldn't be coming back and could dispose of what he had left as she might choose. Then he moved as quietly as he could back down through the house and himself out of the main door which had already been unlocked in case any early risers needed to leave.

Once outside he could afford to be seen as no one would think it odd for a properly clad lawyer to be leaving Widow Keating's house.

ELEANOR SWIFT-HOOK

Making his way back to New Place yard, he cut through the passage by Westminster Hall. He passed St. Stephen's Chapel, where soldiers of the trained bands stood guard on Parliament's meeting place and thought nothing of seeing a lawyer about his business. A little beyond that was a narrow turning and steps up to Cotton House. It was an unprepossessing building and looked shut up.

Gideon already knew Sir Thomas Cotton wasn't living there. He had abandoned the place and the library to the care of the Parliament that met not a street away, but the library was still open for those who could justify access. Or it had been when Gideon was last in London.

He had been prepared to wait, but the librarian arrived early and in some state, descending from a coach, two clerks in attendance. He paused, having opened the door, as he caught sight of Gideon.

"Can I help you, sir?"

His tone wasn't hostile, but it was far from warm. Gideon was going to guess that he had to spend a lot of his day turning people away from the library, especially now there would be many seeking to examine old documents here, like the *Magna Carta Libertatum*, to see if there were any words in them to justify their views.

"I hope so," Gideon said, stepping forward to make a polite bow. "I am Lucas Fox, an attorney at law, appointed to act as a solicitor on behalf of—" He broke off and achieved a supercilious smile of the sort he had seen many of his profession adopt when representing wealthy and powerful men who paid them well for their discretion. "On behalf of a client of mine."

The librarian waved the men with him through the door and looked at Gideon blankly.

"I have no notion of what you or your patron might wish with me."

Gideon widened his smile.

"My patron has heard of you and of the sterling work you are doing in the maintenance of Sir Thomas Cotton's library and that is why, in these troubled times, he wishes to bestow some valuable manuscripts here. Amongst other precious gems in his collection,

THE ALCHEMIST'S PLOT

there is an illustrated chronicle of some kind, which may well have come from Monkwearmouth and has some fascinating historical additions. There is also a *Liber Vitae* and a Byzantine psalter. I wish I could give you more accurate details and descriptions but not having seen these items myself I am going only on the rather rough and ready listing I have been given. The family came by them last century, I believe, when the monasteries were dissolved. He has asked me to examine the conditions and care here to see if the Cotton Library would be suitable."

"An *illuminated* manuscript?" The librarian was frowning now, and Gideon worried he might have over-malted the ale of his story.

"So I believe, and I have no reason to doubt my patron's word."

The librarian looked at him, but more through him, his eyes unfocused as if seeing something else altogether. For a moment Gideon was convinced he had made a mistake, either misjudging the man or making too much or not enough of what he had to offer.

"You must come inside, please," the librarian said, coming back to himself with a start. "I will show you what we can offer to both protect these manuscripts and allow them to be studied as historical artefacts." He waved Gideon through the door and murmured to the air behind him. "Illuminated and from Monkwearmouth—could it be?"

Gideon had to suppress a smile. He hadn't over-malted at all.

As he walked in, Gideon was absorbed by the scent of wood and beeswax, old parchment and printers' ink, because this wasn't just a repository of ancient texts but a living library of recently printed codices, letters and even pamphlets. Motes of fine dust danced in the air where the light through the slender windows caught it.

The wooden floored and panelled room that housed the Cotton Library, was a little under ten yards long and about two yards wide and was filled with bookcases that held the manuscripts. Each case was surmounted by the bust of a famous Classical figure— Domitian, Galba, Nero, both Julius and Augustus Caesar, Cleopatra and others. Gideon counted fourteen in all, each giving their name to the bookcase they surveyed. The manuscripts were then catalogued according to the name of the bookcase—as determined by the bust above it—and then which shelf it was stored on, and finally by its position on the shelf.

"You are familiar with the library?"

"I had the privilege to be able to visit as a student," Gideon said. "But of course, then I wasn't paying so much attention to how the manuscripts were kept so much as what was in them and I will admit to having had less interest in the obscure texts of the distant past and the work of long dead monks, and rather more in the inspiring works of more modern writers."

The librarian made a dismissive noise. He walked to a case and gently pulled out a massive volume, opening it with care to reveal brilliant colours and beautifully flushed lettering.

"This might be something like your patron has," the librarian suggested. "This is a copy of the gospels made by the 'long dead monks' of Lindisfarne perhaps nine hundred years ago."

Gideon was transfixed by the freshness and brilliance of the colours. He glanced up and then thought it a great irony that such a book should be set on the bookcase under the rule of Nero. The librarian put the book away and went over to the shelves which were under Augustus and pulled out another document case.

"And here are all our freedoms. Contained in an 'obscure text of the distant past' but one that is still as relevant today as when the ink was fresh on the vellum."

Gideon could see the seal of King John still attached and knew that this had to be one of a handful of copies of the *Magna Carta* remaining, and it carried the king's original seal. The librarian began explaining how the document was being stored and preserved and how Gideon could assure his mysterious patron that the same care and attention would be given to any such he contributed to the care of the library. Gideon nodded at appropriate moments but paid little real attention, his thoughts elsewhere.

He waited until the librarian had finished and then mustered his most calculating smile.

"I can see that from the care you take I might be able to consider recommending that the du—er, that my patron, donates his precious manuscripts to your collection rather than that of the Bodleian or Cambridge libraries."

THE ALCHEMIST'S PLOT

The librarian's eyes widened with horror at the thought of such a disaster then narrowed as he heard something he disliked in Gideon's tone.

"You are not certain you can make such a recommendation?" His voice dropped to a conspiratorial volume. "There is a small fund I have access to for—" He broke off as if unsure of the right word to use and his tongue appeared to moisten his lips, making Gideon think of a snake. "For *assisting* with such things."

Gideon felt a rush of relief. He hadn't misjudged his man.

"That is good to know," he said. "However, there is no need. I was hoping to access papers which are not yet catalogued, for my research. A cache, I understand, that is stored here and might be considered too risky to allow on general view."

The librarian flushed.

"I think you may have been misinformed, sir. We do not keep any prurient material here. None at all."

From the brisk tone, Gideon gathered it wasn't an unusual request. He hastened to clarify.

"What I seek is not prurient in the slightest, indeed it is the opposite. What I seek is to be found amongst the notes, accountancy and high thoughts of a great man."

Now the librarian was frowning.

"I am uncertain that I could think of any—"

It was time to be blunt.

"I am willing to recommend the Cotton Library to my patron as a safe repository for those precious heirlooms if in return you will allow me to have private access today to the papers Sir Robert Cotton found in Dr John Dee's house in Mortlake. There is a client of mine who is in dispute over historic land rights there and it might well be that the cache Sir Robert found will have documents which are relevant to that."

It took the librarian less than a moment to decide.

"They are largely unsorted, and I am told they are more of a record of his religious devotions than anything practical so I think you might be disappointed. But if you wish to look through them, of course, you are welcome to do so." He smiled at Gideon. "Come with me, I will show you."

Feeling a warm glow of triumph, Gideon followed the librarian from the library itself into the rooms beyond which were packed with cases, bags and boxes of books and documents.

THE ALCHEMIST'S PLOT

Chapter Eighteen

Gideon emerged from the Cotton family mansion and walked back to New Palace Yard as steadily as he could. The clock tower opposite Westminster Palace said it was already past eleven and Lord had wanted to catch the low tide in the early afternoon so they could use the horseferry.

Hands shaking, he kept shivering as if the weather was cold. But it wasn't the outside world that made him shiver, it was the turmoil in his mind. He had read the manuscript documents the librarian had described as 'a record of religious devotions'. They gave a staggering account of how Dee, assisted by a man named Edward Kelly, had used a strange crystal and some kind of talismanic table to speak to beings that only Kelly could see and hear, and which Dee believed were angels.

Gideon wasn't so sure. Part of him had been drawn, fascinated, but another part was appalled, and it was that which stayed with him now.

In his hand was a roll of notes he had made, the librarian having kindly provided paper, pen and ink. Beneath his lawyer's robes and inside his doublet, pressed close to his heart, he carried a small packet of papers which he had taken unseen from the documents Sir Robert Cotton had found at the house in Mortlake. They sat heavy as lead against his ribs. He couldn't bring Lord any proofs of his ancestry, but they held, he hoped, the key to where those proofs might lie.

He turned into a narrow alley that ran between two buildings, around the back of some others and then onto Channel Row, a short distance from where Ellis was now living. It was a necessary detour. On the way Gideon made sure he was unobserved and removed his lawyer's gown, cap and neck bands, leaving them there. When he approached the gate onto Kings Street from New Palace Yard, he was dressed much as he had been when he left The Bell that morning. By that time too he was feeling more settled. As if having shed the robes, and away from the rarefied and arcane silence of the library, he could set aside what he had read, and see it as something abstract and academic.

When he walked into The Bell a few minutes later, Gideon was almost restored to himself. Philip Lord wasn't there. Instead, he found Danny in Lord's room, sitting at the table with pen, ink, paper, a loaded pistol and a grin that must hurt.

Danny gestured to two charcoal sketches on the far side of the table.

"Those are the two Covenant men I met. Philip said I should ask if you know them."

Gideon felt a spider crawl of cold down his spine and pointed to the more corpulent face.

"That's Ellis' father. Sir Isaac Ruskin. I've worked for him, I—" He had no words to express the shock, horror, disgust and sheer misery of discovering a man whom he had held in the greatest respect, was not just a party to the Covenant but a key instrument within it. That made him realise how close to home the conspiracy ran. How close he had come to being sucked into its vortex.

"I know. I've been there," Danny sounded sympathetic. "You think you know someone, but it turns out you had no idea about them at all." He had been writing and put down the pen pushing the final result of his deciphering work over to Gideon.

"See what you make of that."

Need urgent instructions on what to do about zephyr. Killed again. Pretending to want money so he thinks he is safe. He found the first channel. Unable to unlock board. Need more suggestions. Lennox was here. HG.

Gideon read it and frowned.

"What is zephyr? And does it mean she killed again or whoever 'he' is did? And what are 'the first channel' and 'the board'?"

Danny laughed.

"It comes to something when I go to all the effort of deciphering a message and it still doesn't make sense." He spread his hands in a helpless gesture. "If you have no idea what she was on about, I don't see how you can expect me to do so."

THE ALCHEMIST'S PLOT

"I'm glad this wasn't delivered. If the Covenant knew I was there they would have investigated."

"And that's the rub," Danny said. "They're going to know something's happened to this Hester. Even if they don't hear she's been killed, and it's not the talk of London so they might not, they will miss her reports and investigate."

That wasn't a comfortable thought.

"True. But it seems to me if they felt able to intervene more in the tapestry works then they would have done so by now. They had to put in Hester Lovegood as a servant to keep an eye on the place. What I don't understand is why they haven't just bought the building themselves."

The door of the room opened as he spoke. Philip Lord came in. He nodded to Danny, who put the pistol down, and then dropped his hat on the bed.

"I would assume that the reason they have not bought the tapestry works is that they cannot do so. Aside from the cost, there has been an ongoing dispute over the ownership of the land ever since it was established. It is difficult to purchase land that is the subject of perpetual litigation—not to mention under royal protection, although such will not count for so much in these current times."

Gideon had a moment to appreciate the irony that the excuse he had offered the librarian was a reality, as Lord took the sheet of paper from his hands and read it.

"That explains a great deal. Now we know who our murderer is at least."

Gideon stared at him.

"Who?"

"Surely," Lord said, "you had some kind of classical education?"

"Of course, but—" Gideon stopped as it hit him. "Zephyrus, the god of the west wind. Hester Lovegood is saying that she thinks the murderer is Richard West."

Lord bowed his head as if in admiration.

"Indeed so."

ELEANOR SWIFT-HOOK

Gideon found himself thinking back over the encounters he had with the man from meeting him in The Queen's Head, through to seeing him outside the tapestry works holding a crow in one hand and claiming to have been there to investigate the possibility of thieves.

"Who's Richard West?" Danny asked.

"He is the man who owns the houses on both sides of the works and has been trying to prove he owns the land between, on which it stands, as well," Lord said.

"He lives next door to the building," Gideon explained, "and—" He broke off as he recalled something else West had said. "And he told me he had purchased some of Dr Dee's books when they were sold off a couple of years after the man died. He must have been in his teens at the time, but he also told me how he used to watch Dee from his window as a child."

As Gideon was talking, Danny got to his feet and picked up the sheets of paper that contained his scribbled notes and tables from the deciphering. He put one in his coat and the rest into the hearth, where the embers of the fire flared to consume them. "So let us hie to Mortlake, drag this evildoer from his den, find out what he knows about the house and its secrets and ensure he signs a confession."

"Oh that it was so simple," Lord said, "But hopefully that will be the ultimate end of this." He pulled his pocket watch from the fob of his breeches and consulted it. "We have time for dinner before the tide is good if you would be kind enough to arrange for that Gideon, whilst I talk of cannons with Danny and break the bad news to him that whilst Wemyss, whilst seemingly little troubled by politics, and happy to talk about his work with great enthusiasm, is not willingly going to leave his present workshop. When you return you can tell me if your morning brought any success or if we are returning to Mortlake more in hope than expectation."

Gideon left the two of them with Lord sketching some diagrams on a sheet of paper and going into an extreme technical detail that meant very little to Gideon's understanding. He spoke to one of the women who was serving to ask for a meal to be sent up to Sir

THE ALCHEMIST'S PLOT

Theophilus' room and as he did so he saw the host of the inn, William Austen as Danny had named him, talking to two soldiers whom he was showing out.

A prickle of cold touched Gideon's skin as Austen glanced in his direction behind the backs of the soldiers and seemed to give him the slightest nod. Wondering and no little concerned, Gideon waited as Austen finished talking to the men outside and then came back into the common room. Grave-faced, he crossed to Gideon.

"Those were men asking me to keep an eye out for someone matching the description of your servant, the one who came back yesterday, beaten up. I promised I would tell them if I saw such a man." He hesitated, then drew a breath. "It was fortunate I intercepted them before they could ask others here, but they seemed more as if this was a call of duty than that they had any notion the man might be found here, so I doubt they'll trouble themselves again."

Considering the state that Danny had been in when he returned, Gideon knew it would be both pointless and rude to deny that he was the man the soldiers were seeking.

"Thank you for saying nothing. I know Sir Theophilus will show his gratitude too. We will be leaving after dinner."

Austen lifted a hand dismissively.

"I am sure he will, he has shown himself a very generous man. But that wasn't why I said nothing. If I had told them the man was here there would have been violence in my inn, which would be very bad for my business, and they would no doubt have found some way to accuse me of involvement. That's what happens in these times. However, I am pleased to learn you intend to leave or I would have asked you to do so."

Gideon went back upstairs, his stomach tight. When he ordered the meal a few minutes before, he had been looking forward to eating it after the trials of the morning, something solid and grounding. But now he no longer had the slightest appetite.

In his haste, he forgot to knock and found himself facing the point of Lord's sword and the round mouth of Danny's pistol.

"I deduce," Danny said returning the pistol to the table which was now also holding several of Lord's charcoal diagrams, "that something has disturbed our Gideon."

"The question is what," Lord agreed. "*Speak, Mephistophilis, what means this show?*"

Their light-hearted response nettled Gideon. "There have been soldiers here asking after Danny. Our host has denied any knowledge of him but is keen for us to leave."

Lord and Danny exchanged looks and Danny shrugged.

"We expected it. I'll have to work harder to disguise my appearance when we leave. But now—" he was interrupted by a polite tap and Lord, hand on sword, opened the door to admit two women bearing the food Gideon had asked for and a jug of ale. "Now, we dine," Danny concluded, as the door closed behind the departing women.

Despite the tightness of his stomach Gideon found the savoury smells enough to allow him to eat, and his was the first clean plate of the three of them.

"So tell me what, if anything, you found in Cotton's lair," Lord said as he filled his cup for the second time. "I believe I have demonstrated the patience of Job on the subject so far."

Gideon reached into his coat and pulled out the two slim packets of pages he had stolen from the cache. The first he unfolded to show what looked to be a series of designs of clockwork apparatus, pulleys, connected cogs, weights and chains. The last of these showed a design which he knew Lord would recognise. It was a panel with the Tudor rose and eagle design, but beneath it, between the splayed legs of the eagle was a chequered pattern five rows wide and high. The central square was occupied by a crown.

Danny frowned at it, but Lord drew in a breath.

"Is that the one in Howe, I wonder? Or is there one also in the Mortlake house?"

Gideon picked up the message that Danny had spent the morning deciphering and put it down between them, pointing to one line.

"*Unable to unlock the board,*" he read out. "*Need more suggestions.* It looks like a chess board, albeit too small and if you

THE ALCHEMIST'S PLOT

recall, in Howe you had to think of the right combination to release the lock it held."

Lord was nodding now, although Danny's frown had deepened.

"I think you have the right of it," Lord said. "And forewarned is forearmed. I will have to consider possible combinations that it could be. The Howe one was easy, it was my name. But this one might be older, so—"

"If it is a name we might not know it." Gideon knew he must sound defeated, but so much had defeated him already that day. He showed them the last of the diagrams he had taken from Dee's papers. Danny realised what it was first and ran a finger along the central spine.

"It's a plan of the house. These rooms are now the weaving room and this," he touched the odd square at the end which represented what was now the artist's room, "is a key point. See? It has a passage that comes up from below here and then another that goes up to here…"

"The rose room," Lord said, a hint of excitement in his tone. "And then there is something from the rose room that goes down very sharply."

"Looks like a vertical shaft to me," Danny said, "into an underground chamber?" He traced a finger over the outline as he spoke. "And here's a connecting rod that runs from your rose room, probably through a rafter, and that is where your board is."

"The staircase," Lord observed, his finger following Danny's. "And would explain why the mantle decoration moves a little when the door is opened. It is connected."

"The stairs?" Gideon was surprised. "There's nothing there."

"There will be," Danny said. "We just have to find it."

Lord clapped Gideon on the back.

"Well done, this is what we needed."

"But it shows no way to access any of it," Gideon pointed out.

Danny was studying some of the strange markings which looked like oddly shaped letters in a strange alphabet that were placed in blocks around the diagram because he put his finger beside one and shook his head. "I am not so sure. This might help. Let me have a go with it."

ELEANOR SWIFT-HOOK

Gideon relinquished the page and Danny bent his head over it, sharpening a quill as he did so, then he began copying the strange letters onto a fresh sheet. Lord watched him for a moment then moved the abandoned plates from the table, so they were not in danger of splashing grease over the pages.

"Was there more?" he asked Gideon. "What else did you learn?"

Gideon described his visit and what he had found in the cache. The manuscripts he couldn't bring out, densely written and annotated, with the initials E.K. featuring heavily. Initials Gideon had learned referred to Edward Kelly—Sir Edward Kelly—the man who had been the seer of the visions that Dr Dee had so carefully recorded.

"I copied a small piece of it out from near the beginning so you could see how strange it all is," Gideon said and unfolded another sheet.

Lord read it aloud.

"*Suddenly, there seemed to come out of my Oratory a Spirituall creature, like a pretty girle of seven or nine yeares of age, attired on her head with her hair rowled up before, and hanging down very long behind...* a child? Not an angel?"

"There is mention of such later by name—I saw Gabriel and Uriel were there," Gideon told him. "Had I longer to study it, I might have found others."

Lord nodded and looked down the page, reading some more.

"*I said, 'Tell me who you are?'*

She said, 'I pray you let me play with you a little, and I will tell you who I am.'

I said, 'In the name of Jesus then tell me.'

She said, 'I rejoyce in the name of Jesus, and I am a poor little Maiden, Madini, I am the last but one of my Mother's children, I have little Baby-children at home.'..." Lord laughed. "This is hardly the most profound communication of spiritual truths I've ever seen."

"And Madini seems not so innocent later." Gideon pushed a copied sheet towards them. It had disturbed him more than the rest.

Lord read it out.

THE ALCHEMIST'S PLOT

"Upon Mr. Kelly his great doubt bred unto me of Madini her words yesterday, spoken to him, that we two had our two wives in such sort, as we might use them in common." Lord stopped reading and drew a sharp breath before he went on. *"It was agreed by us, to move the question, whether the sense were of Carnal use (contrary to the law of the Commandment) or of Spiritual love, and charitable care and unity of mindes, for advancing the service of God."* He paused. "And the answer came it seems. *Upon a Scroll, like the edge of a Carpet, is written, De utroque loquor."*

"I speak of both," Gideon translated.

Lord looked up. "This angel was telling them to sleep with each other's wives."

Gideon nodded grimly.

"There was more on it later. It was presented as some special form of marriage. Dee's wife cried when she was told she had to do it."

There was a stilted silence.

"You would think," Danny said, disgust evident in his voice, "Dr Dee and I would have more in common. After all, we were both mercers and both mathematicians and we both lived in Manchester for a time."

Lord looked at him. "Then perhaps those commonalities will help you work out what those letters are."

"I already have," Danny said. "They are exactly that—letters. There is no code. It's written in plain. Parts of each letter have been removed and then what remains rotated by so many degrees according to its place in the word, then on the subsequent line the rotation is reversed. It's a very simple progression that anyone could work out and why are you two looking at me like that?"

"Because maybe you have more in common with Dr Dee than you realise," Gideon told him.

"Your mind must be a strange and wonderful place to live, Danny," Lord said, then got up and leaned over the table to see what Danny had written. "Hmmm. '*From the first, by the same amount to each as shown here*'. Where was this on the diagram? There? That is the rose room then." He looked pensive and repeated the words quietly. "From the first, by the same amount—

Of course, it refers to the roses on the mantle, they should be turned as the letters are turned. Is there more?"

"There is if I may have a few minutes," Danny said, his tone patient.

"You have very few," Lord responded. "We need to get the horseferry." He straightened up. "You keep on that, and I will get the horses and see that the good Mr Austen is rewarded for both his excellent service and for his keeping of confidences—and is encouraged to continue keeping them and see if he has some clothes I can purchase for you. Then you will need to hide your hair and as much of your face as we can manage. Gideon, fetch your things, then please take mine down to the stables."

In a remarkably short time, the three of them were riding through the gate and into New Palace Yard, past the bored-looking soldiers there and to the broad jetty where the horseferry was already moored and unloading a coach. Danny looked very different. He was wearing a shapeless black coat which concealed his sword well and a hat with its brim broken to hang over his face. That, together with his hair turned lank and a dark muddy colour, meant he resembled himself hardly at all.

They could have found a queue for the ferry but fortunately, there were only themselves and two other riders waiting to step onto the flat, rectangular, vessel. It arrived loaded with a coach and once that was off, Gideon followed Lord aboard, leading his horse onto the wooden planks and soothing it as it felt the unfamiliar movement beneath its feet. The waterman was keen to wait for more custom, but Lord suggested they were full enough and backed up his claim with some coin which the man took and cast off soon after.

The ferry was poled along by the waterman, who moved to adjust the position of the raft-like vessel in the river as it was caught by even the smallest eddies. Gideon knew these ferries were notorious. Dangerous to use except at the most stable points in the tide when there was very little flow, and the water was at its shallowest. The horses were not happy. For most of the way, even Gideon's bay who was untroubled by the sounds of battle misliked the experience. At least the journey wasn't a long one and a few minutes later they were leading their mounts onto the shore at Lambeth.

The next challenge was passing through the new outer defences. There was a fort being built to guard the road at Vauxhall.

"A quadrant, with four half-bulwarks," Danny murmured as they drew near on horseback. "Of course, they have the requisite ditches, scarps and counterscarps. With the right guns, they could hold a while. My only regret is I didn't get the chance to map these defences." He sighed, then fell silent as they reached the barricade where Lord resorted to a mix of bluff, bluster and hard currency to see them through.

After that, it was on to Mortlake, following the course of the river for most of the way. It was strange to approach the town in such a different way, riding past houses and businesses to reach The Queen's Head, with the church and the tapestry works beyond.

Gideon was recognised at the inn from his previous stay but of course, it was Sir Theophilus who was the centre of attention. Lord maintained an appropriate detached and superior manner as Danny made sure the horses were stabled and Gideon organised rooms for them all for the night. He also enquired as to what more had been found out about the murder of Hester Lovegood.

It seemed the inquest had been held that morning and found that she had been murdered by a passing vagrant with intent to rob her. Two witnesses claimed to have seen the vagrant lurking around the church. Gideon wasn't surprised to learn that one witness was Richard West, and another was one of his servants.

By that time the best of the afternoon was over and as he and Danny joined Lord in his room, Gideon wondered aloud if they were being impolite to call on the tapestry works that day.

"Of course, we shall do it," Lord said in his best Sir Theophilus voice, accompanied by a wink. "These people are just tradesmen; they will keep hours to my convenience." Then he switched to his own voice. "I would like to be away tomorrow if at all possible. We have taken too long already. The Covenant will be bound to send someone to investigate. Armed with what you found, Gideon, and with what Danny has unravelled from that, I think we have a good chance of resolving this speedily. Assuming we can get access."

"Then you two can go and see about getting access." Danny sounded stubborn. "I need to see what more I can get from this plan before we go charging in there."

So it was Gideon and Lord who took the now familiar walk from The Queen's Head. Lord nodded towards the house opposite.

"That, I assume, is West's house?"

Gideon nodded. It was more modest than the rambling building that had been converted into the tapestry works, but then that itself had begun life as more than one house. West's was at the opposite end from the limner's house, though of course, from what he had said, West owned the house that was between them too.

By tacit consent, they walked past the tapestry works and headed first to Cleyn's residence. The door was opened by the servant, Simon, but before he had been able to do any more than just open it, Cleyn himself had appeared behind him.

"Sir Theophilus, a pleasure. You will be wanting to finalise your commission?"

Lord nodded. "Indeed so. I must leave tomorrow, and I would like everything to be arranged before I go back to Oxford to continue my contribution to the peace negotiations there."

Cleyn waved his servant away, then changed his mind. "My coat, Simon, and please tell my dear wife I shall be late to supper and not to wait on me to serve it."

A few minutes later they were walking up the stairs of the tapestry works. For once, although the afternoon was advanced and the light less than good, the weaving floor was occupied by half a dozen men and two women. Despite their black mourning clothes, there were even a few smiles to be seen.

"We are excited," Cleyn explained, gesturing at the men who were checking over the looms and made polite bows as Lord swept past them. "The Dutch Church has been talking of commissioning a series of tapestries to help us out here."

One of the women was Jannekin de Maecht and she smiled at Gideon, ignoring her husband's hand on her arm and less than friendly look.

THE ALCHEMIST'S PLOT

Once they were in the chamber at the end of the weaving hall, Lord closed the door and leaned his back against it.

"You have some news?" Cleyn's face was grave.

"We do," Lord said, reaching into his coat. "But first I must return these as I promised." He set the two books that had been Hester Lovegood's on the table. "We have news of more mysteries within the house that we would like the opportunity to uncover. But we also now know who your murderer was. The issue we have is in proving it in a way that would stand the scrutiny of a justice."

"Who is it?"

"For now, I would prefer not to say. But I can assure you that no one in your close community is under any suspicion at all."

Cleyn frowned. "If you know who it is, a confession—"

"I doubt a man facing the gallows for a triple murder will wish to confess especially if there is no other evidence," Gideon countered, an idea forming in his mind as he spoke.

"What can we do?" Cleyn asked. "There must be something?"

Lord opened his mouth, but whatever he was going to say, Gideon cut across him.

"We can trap him. Persuade him to try and kill again and catch him in the act."

Lord closed his mouth and smiled. "As Mr Lennox here says, that is the best solution." He put a heavy hand on Gideon's shoulder. "And Mr Lennox will now tell us how it can be done."

It had come to Gideon in an instant, though knowing the way his mind worked it must have been germinating for a while before bursting into startling bloom.

"Mr Cleyn, would it be possible to arrange a gathering at your house this evening for the entire residential community here? Everyone, even the children?"

Cleyn's eyes went wide.

"A gathering? What for?"

"Perhaps the reason could be to recognise the good news you have just told us about—that and to celebrate the commission from Sir Theophilus."

"We are a community in mourning," Cleyn reminded him. "But I suppose a gathering to bring us together, one of thanksgiving for

God's grace in securing us the commissions and to look to the future. That might be possible." Then his expression soured. "Although I fear that my beloved Sarah will be sorely put out. I take it you wish to give the impression that the tapestry works is empty?"

Gideon nodded. "That is the idea."

"Then perhaps I could be here as—"

Lord had been looking thoughtful and he now spoke quickly. "Mr Cleyn, the man we are dealing with has already killed three people. He would have no compunction killing again if he felt the need. Myself, my servant and Mr Lennox are men well trained to take care of ourselves. As much as I admire your courage and appreciate your offer, the very best way you can assist is to persuade your wife to arrange this gathering, and your colleagues here to attend, without alerting any of them as to the real reason for it."

"And if you could allow me your key," Gideon said. "That would be helpful too. If we have to break in it would be rather obvious."

Cleyn frowned. "So would walking in the front door in full view of the town. Even after dark, some might see. There is the backdoor, but that is not so easy in the dark. No. I will leave a window open for you on the side wall, that way you can get to it unseen as there is a screen of bushes."

Gideon made a bow to Cleyn, impressed by his thinking on the matter. "That would be even better. Then perhaps we can let it be known you have invited us to attend your gathering, something any decent man with polite sensibilities would of course refuse, but Sir Theophilus, lacking any such, would not."

"Sir Theophilus," Lord put in, "will arrange for a firkin of wine to be sent from The Queen's Head so you can toast his good health."

Gideon winced at the notion, but it was the kind of crass deed the character Lord was portraying would entertain.

"I will agree to your plan," Cleyn said, "but with one exception. If this man is to be taken red-handed, you will need more than just yourselves as witnesses. You have already said you need to leave

THE ALCHEMIST'S PLOT

tomorrow—and I am sure you do. But that means you will be unable to testify. It will need to be our men who bear witness."

Lord shook his head. "It is too dangerous. Someone could be killed."

"You must allow us our chance, Sir Philip," Cleyn said. "I promise I will bring the most reliable, capable and close-lipped of men and we will stay concealed until needed."

For a moment Gideon thought Lord's real issue was that with anyone else in the house, his chance to unlock its secrets would be limited. But then he saw the expression on Lord's face, just before he lowered his head.

"You are right. They were your friends—your family. Your community must be a part of this."

After that, things moved very quickly.

Cleyn persuaded Lord that taking both the de Maechts into their confidence would be advisable, so they were summoned to the artist's room, on the excuse of needing to finalise the details of Sir Theophilus Bassington's commission. Jannekin was quick to agree, saying that she and the other women from the works would take food with them and help Mistress Cleyn, whereas Phillips was only persuaded by the promise that the commission was genuine and would bring some much-needed work to his compatriots.

"But who is the murderer?" he demanded as his wife left the room to go to Cleyn's house and persuade Sarah Cleyn into what was required.

"No one of your own," Lord assured him. "It is better that it is not known just yet."

"I don't see why—"

But Lord's patience was wearing thin.

"We need proof to make any accusation," he said, his tone now that of the man who commanded armies. "Until this trap has been sprung, tell no one of it."

De Maecht left the room meekly and, as he shared the news of the new commission and the planned gathering, was greeted with quiet delight by the tapissiers in the weaving hall. Gideon saw them clapping de Maecht on the back, giving him full credit for securing the work.

"I had better go and ensure my Sarah is not too upset by this turn of events," Cleyn told them. "You will come to the house before you return here?"

Leaving the door to his room unlocked, Cleyn escorted the two of them back through the rapidly emptying tapestry works. Whilst it was, as he said, a place in mourning, the mood was lighter. They had the certainty of the commission from Sir Theophilus and expectation of a much larger one for a sequence of tapestries, Cleyn had said, from the Dutch Church in Austin Friars. There was a feeling that whatever dark shadow had been over them was lifting. Gideon just hoped that this evening he, Lord and Danny would be able to close the door on it by bringing both answers and justice.

Back at The Queen's Head, they held their own, brief, council of war in Lord's chamber. Danny had the original plan of the house open on the table and one he had copied, which was written in plain and, unlike the original, designed to explain more than conceal.

"I think I have found how your man West gets in and out unseen." He pointed to some lines drawn touching the artist's room and extending back along the side of the house. "There's a cellar that looks on the plan to have steps up. Inside-the-wall steps like those you found going to your rose room, marked in the same way. The entrance is along a passage here." He traced his finger on the plan, "which looks to me as if it can be reached through one of the outbuildings. It wouldn't be hard for someone to get in that way unseen."

Lord nodded. "I could see why Dr Dee might have wanted to have an entrance that didn't require access to the main part of the house. Besides," he put a finger on a strange symbol that was placed on the cellar. To Gideon, it looked like a flower with six pointed petals and a squared centre, or perhaps a star. "That is an alchemical symbol, perhaps he had a laboratory there. Some alchemical operations are said to work best beneath the earth."

"But if that is how West gets in that makes no sense," Gideon said, confused now. "We saw someone walk along the length of

THE ALCHEMIST'S PLOT

the weaving hall with a candle the night we broke in and then when they ran off, they went down the main stairs."

"I still think it was Hester Lovegood we saw," Lord said. "We know from her ciphered message that she was trying to solve the puzzles as well." He tapped the sheet with the original diagram. "I think this plan must have been lost to the Covenant at some point."

"We have the key now," Danny said. "The rose room has a vertical shaft down to what looks like…"

Gideon drew a breath, hoping he was wrong in his thoughts.

"A crypt," Lord said. "I wonder who is buried there? Christian Rosenkreutz perhaps?"

Danny narrowed his eyes. "Isn't that the tomb of the man who was supposed to start a new age of enlightened religion?"

"According to the Rosicrucian pamphlets that were all the rage twenty-five years ago," Lord agreed.

"You don't sound very convinced," Gideon said.

"I think a lot of people believe a lot of things that are not true. I also think it suits some to have that happen. The Covenant, if you recall, was set on creating a reunification of religion. I was brought up to hold a very similar view, so I think it is safe to assume they were behind that. Perhaps had it worked…"

"Had it worked we'd not just have had the last twenty-five years of war in the Empire," Danny said. "Then who'd have paid our wages?"

Gideon was studying the plan as they spoke, trying not to think about the heretical beliefs Philip Lord had been raised to profess.

"Does it say how we get down the shaft?" he asked, keen to move the conversation on and back to what they needed to do.

Danny pointed to a small area of cross-hatching where two vertical parallel lines were connected by horizontal ones. "I would guess there's a ladder."

"Then let us hope it is a safe one," Lord said. "If not, the crypt might gain a real body or two."

"But before we can investigate that we need to trap our murderer somehow," Gideon pointed out.

Danny pushed a finger at the artist's room on his version of the plan.

"I'd say we try here. If Zephyr has made it that far he's committed and whichever way he tries to leave he has ground to cover. I could be out the window and..." He broke off. "Philip could be out the window and to the outbuilding entrance before him if he tries to retreat that way."

"*If* he comes," Gideon said.

THE ALCHEMIST'S PLOT

Chapter Nineteen

Lord insisted they ate supper in the common room, so they could be seen to do so. As they waited for the meal, Gideon caught sight of Richard West. Glancing at Lord, who gave the slightest of nods and on the excuse of needing a piss, Gideon went past where West sat and exchanged polite greetings.

"I am leaving tomorrow," he said. "Sir Theophilus has arranged his commission. It seemed to be a great relief to the weavers, I must say."

West nodded. "They have been having a hard time of it these last weeks, what with the war drying up their work and now these terrible murders."

"Still, I believe they feel things are improving. This evening they are to be gathering at the limner's house, women, children and all, and Sir Theophilus has asked the host here to send along some Rhenish so they can drink his health. I fear he will wish to intrude on them as well after we have supped." He sighed and exchanged a knowing look with West, a man who was painfully aware of his employer's shortcomings but was unable to voice them.

"I will wish you Godspeed on your travels then, for tomorrow," West said, and Gideon thanked him and bade him farewell.

When he got back to his table it was to find Lord again enjoying himself in his role as an obnoxious, but generous and condescending landed gentleman. He was opining loudly and fulsomely on the war, the state of the nation, the evil advisors about the king and his hopes of helping bring the king to see sweet reason.

Fortunately, all Gideon had to do was nod now and then. Danny was nowhere in evidence. He had slipped away as an anonymous servant could, without attracting any attention, to keep a watch on the house. A little later, making a great show of his going, Lord left the inn, taking with him Gideon and the mixed feelings of the people of Mortlake.

"West went back to his own house about half an hour ago," Danny reported quietly, joining them as they walked along the edge of the churchyard, past the lych gate. "I haven't seen him leave it since."

Which meant West must have left right after Gideon spoke to him. Surely that was a promising sign? Gideon's greatest fear was that they had made a mistake in identifying West. Or that they were correct, but West wouldn't rise to the bait. He was counting on the idea that given the knowledge the house was empty for a time, West would be keen to use that to further his explorations. West had got as far as the rose room and presumably had some notion that the fireplace was the way on, but the time he could spend working on it with no worry about being discovered must be very limited. No doubt when Gideon had seen him the previous day, he had been hoping to use the absence of the tapissiers and their families to further his investigations.

So why, Gideon had to wonder, had he risked so much by investigating when there were people in the house? The answer came to him with the question. If Hester Lovegood had discovered West's nocturnal activities, maybe he had seen signs that someone else was looking at the same things as he was and felt time pressing to get to it first. Or perhaps he had become used to being able to sneak in and out when he knew Cleyn wasn't working. The only way to know for sure, of course, would be to ask the man himself. With a modicum of luck, Gideon would get that chance at some point in the next few hours.

They didn't need to go as far as the Cleyns' house, because as they crossed the road one of the men they had seen earlier in the weaving hall was waiting to show them how to get into the tapestry works. Cleyn himself was inside with another two of the weavers. Both were burly men, as was their guide, and grim-faced by the light of the shielded candle.

"You must all stay here," Lord told Cleyn, his voice brooking no argument. "Unless I call your name or send one of these two to find you." He gestured to Danny and Gideon. "I need to know that any footsteps or movement I hear are our murderer's and not mistake you for him." As he spoke, he was shedding the stuffed

THE ALCHEMIST'S PLOT

cloth that he had been wearing to create Sir Theophilus's paunch. "The man you should be wary of if he comes to you, is Richard West. If he does, then lay hold of him and find me."

That elicited less surprise than Gideon had thought it should. The tapissiers looked at each other and Cleyn nodded.

"Somehow that is not unexpected," he said, sounding almost sad. "I have seen the man loitering around the house and grounds at odd times for years. I always had it down to his obsession with the notion that he owned the land. But to kill? How would that help his cause?"

"I think it's the other way around," Gideon said. "His desire to prove he owns the land is more about his obsession with this house. I believe he seeks something here." Another answer they could hope to provide soon.

Leaving the tapissiers and Cleyn, Lord led the way through the building. They reached the artist's room and after listening for a time, Lord eased open the door. The room was unoccupied. The secret stairs on both sides were still concealed behind their closed panels.

"We wait." Lord breathed the words into the stillness, then he and Danny moved briefly before being absorbed into shadow. Gideon leaned against the wall between the door and the shelves. He was the goat staked out to distract. When there was any noise from the walls, he would bend to open the panel so West would be tempted to attack him.

The wait was a long one.

Too long.

Gideon had to move a little to keep his body from cramping and he wondered at the silence from the other two. Had he not known they were there he would have thought himself alone in the room.

It must have been well over half an hour after they had arrived that Gideon realised they were running out of time. The gathering in the limner's house wasn't going to last all night. Through the window, Gideon could see that the lights in West's house on the other side of the alley had all gone out.

As time crawled on, Gideon realised that for whatever reason, West had decided not to try a nocturnal investigation that evening.

"I don't think he's coming," Danny whispered. "The Dutch weavers will be coming back in an hour."

Lord's sigh came from the darkness so close to Gideon that he started.

"Then, gentlemen, we have given enough time to the commonweal and the service of justice. We will pay Mr West a visit when we are done here. But for now, let us use what time remains for our own investigations."

As he spoke, he stepped forward and crouched to reach for the catch that opened the stairs. The panel opened with the now-familiar whirring and heavier sounds of chains. Uncertain it was the right thing to do, Gideon allowed his conscience to be silenced by Lord's promise to attend to West later,

"Now that," Danny said, "is impressive." And he followed Lord up the stairs, which were enclosed in complete blackness, counting in an undertone. Then he stopped suddenly and Gideon, who was right behind, nearly tripped. "It should be here. There is something... I need a light."

It took a few moments for Lord to light a candle and its glow revealed Danny running his hands over one of the wooden panels that lined the walls of the narrow staircase.

"See this mark on the wall?

The mark was small and hard to identify in the scant light, but it was Dee's *monas hieroglyphica*. Danny ran his fingers around the panel.

"This should open according to the plan, but there's no obvious way."

Gideon thought of the doors here and in Howe. He retreated a couple of steps, as it was impossible to bend down because the stairway was so narrow. His fingers probed beneath the beading, finding a small, familiar recess. There was a click from the wall where Danny was still studying his panel and a moment later it opened.

"Well done," Lord said. "Your lawyer's wit once more triumphs."

The candlelight revealed a metal panel behind the wooden one. It had the same Tudor rose and eagle design that was above the

THE ALCHEMIST'S PLOT

fire, but beneath it, between the splayed legs of the eagle was a chequerboard design with a rose in the central square, as illustrated on the documents Gideon had found in the Cotton Library. For a moment Gideon was back in the claustrophobic secret rooms in Howe, with the same chequerboard design.

Lord reached out with rapid fingers pressing the first tile in the third row, which gave beneath his touch, then the last tile in the same row, the third tile in the fourth row and then, the fourth tile in the first row. Then he drew a breath and held it as he depressed the centre of the Tudor rose.

Nothing happened.

"We couldn't expect it to be *that* easy," Lord murmured. His fingers moved again and again when he pressed the central boss nothing happened. "Not Tudor, then. We have some slight advantage in that we know it cannot be 'Philip' or any name in which a letter is repeated."

"I want to see how this is made," Danny said, his tone close to reverential.

"Let us make it work before you try to pull it to pieces," Lord chided him, "I am going to guess that this is the panel Hester Lovegood wanted help to open, so if we can indeed master it, we will be ahead of the game." He tried another combination without success.

"Mary," Gideon suggested.

"Good idea." Lord's fingers moved, pressing the square to the left of the central one, the first square, the one below the central square and then the second to last of the bottom row. But again, when he pressed the centre of the rose in the middle, nothing happened. He stood lost in thought for a moment. "This is designed by Dr Dee who had his eye on a new Holy Roman Empire, we saw how he addressed the emperor with his hopes that one of his line might take on that role, and since it cannot be Maximilian or Ferdinand, so…"

His fingers moved again. The third square on the fourth line, which Gideon by then realised must be an R. The first letter of the last line—a U. The fourth letter of the first line—a D. And on until he had spelt out RUDOLF. Rudolf, Gideon knew, had been the son and successor of Maximilian, who had ruled as Emperor for over thirty years but never married. From what Gideon had seen of the notes in the Cotton Library, he had been visited by Dee and Kelley in their travels around Europe.

Lord pressed the heart of the rose, and it sank inwards. The metal panel opened to reveal a brass handle which was pushed to one end of a runnel.

"Is that all?" Danny sounded disappointed. "I was hoping for gold or gems or at least your papers." Then his voice shifted, and he put a hand out. "I wonder what it does?"

Lord caught his hand before he could move the thing.

"I'm not sure that is wise."

Danny shrugged, then winced. "I am not sure any of this is wise, but we can leave it for now and go and see your rose room."

"Now we know why the stairs had to be left as they were and not filled in," Gideon said. "That must be something important."

"I want to look again at the plan to see if it is on it," Lord said as they followed Danny up the last few stairs.

The rose room was peaceful, and a stray moonbeam had found its way through the window to light upon the bar that held the roses and was set into the mantlepiece. Lord put his candle where the shaft of moonlight fell and used it to study the sheet that showed the secret passages in the house. Danny poured over it with him.

Gideon, meanwhile, took the sheet Danny had copied from that original plan and addressed himself to the row of roses. At first, he wondered how one could know how far each had been turned from its starting position. The roses looked symmetrical with the five white petals within the five red and the five small green pointed leaves behind. It took him a moment to see that one leaf behind the petals was slightly larger than the other four, almost like a pointing finger…

By the time Lord and Danny had decided the device they had found behind the panel was for unlocking something to do with the hearth, Gideon was turning the last rose to the position Danny had worked out it should be, if his understanding of the text was correct. But once all were set, nothing changed, and nothing moved.

THE ALCHEMIST'S PLOT

"Perhaps now you should indulge your curiosity, Danny," Lord suggested. "If we are correct…"

Danny needed no other invitation and gave a painful grin as he stepped back behind the panel door to the stairs. A few moments later there was another grinding noise and when Gideon pushed again on the mantelpiece, the whole thing seemed to shift back into the woodwork and as it did so, the plain cast iron fireback opened like a door.

This time though, the candle flame didn't reveal a staircase, it revealed what looked more like a well. A rectangular well perhaps one yard wide and one and a half long, the length being behind the wall panel. The smell from below was musty and dry.

"Did it work?" Danny asked, rejoining them.

Lord's grin was made sinister and feral in the flickering candle flame.

"It worked indeed. *We are the Jasons, we have won the fleece.* Though perhaps we should wait to celebrate until we see what we have indeed won. Oh, look, there is a ladder."

There was indeed a ladder, its bars set into the wall, starting a good yard below the top of the shaft. Braced by Danny for the awkward first part of the descent, Lord tried his weight on the rungs.

A shout came from the artist's room, brief and cut off. With Lord being held by Danny in the shaft, Gideon was the nearest and without thought, he turned and ran down the stairs. There was a candle now on the artist's desk and as Gideon came out of the panel at speed, he saw West lying on the floor, face down and unmoving. Beyond him, in the opposite wall, another panel stood ajar.

As Gideon barrelled into the room the panel to the stairs up closed behind him with a definitive clunk. He spun around, hand reaching to draw his sword as he did so, but before he could complete the move and bring his blade free, a sword point at his undefended throat made him freeze.

"Fought like a true lawyer."

The man who confronted him was a face from Gideon's past. Sir Gilbert Brandon, once a man who he had thought of as one of his father's friends, but now the man he knew was called Michael by the Covenant. He held his sword with the same easy grace Danny displayed with a blade and his free hand reached in and claimed Gideon's. He glanced at it and his expression changed.

"Where did you get this?"

Gideon opened his mouth but had no chance to answer.

"I suppose you'll claim it as a family heirloom, eh?"

"I found it on a battlefield," he answered honestly.

"Swords like this are not abandoned on battlefields. But you can keep the secret, it makes little difference. Who told you the trick of this place?"

It was then Gideon realised that Sir Gilbert believed he was on his own and the faintest spark of hope kindled deep in his chest.

"No one," he said quickly. "I found some documents in the Cotton Library. They showed me how to open this door."

That sparked a sudden interest.

"The Cotton Library? What documents were there?"

Something in his tone made Gideon wary of revealing too much.

"Some household account ledgers and a few astrological charts. There was a plan of the house and some details on the secret passages and rooms thrust into one old ledger."

"Where are they?"

For a moment Gideon thought he had a way out.

"I left them upstairs—on the mantle. I can show you. I was looking at them when—"

"Good," Sir Gilbert's voice was sharp. "When we're done here, I'll find them. I have a few more questions first. Was it you who killed Peters?" He aimed a kick at the unconscious West. "That piece of filth denied it, though he admitted he killed Maud."

"If Peters was the man who attacked me in Mortlake four days ago, then yes." Gideon wondered why Danny and Lord were taking so long to get to the door. Then he realised Brandon—or perhaps even West—must have locked it. The thought made sweat bead on his brow. He was truly trapped now.

"Good man, Peters, loyal." Sir Gilbert said. "If he attacked you, it will have been for a very good reason. What were you doing?"

"I saw him pass on a note to Hes—Maud."

THE ALCHEMIST'S PLOT

"Who else knows what you know about this place? The buffoon you have cozened into buying a tapestry here?"

"No," Gideon said, hoping he sounded like someone trying to keep an innocent from the line of fire and desperately trying to think how to keep Sir Gilbert talking to buy time. "Sir Theophilus knows nothing. I have told no one else."

"Then let us be grateful for small mercies." Sir Gilbert's face wore a tight smile. "I was told you were supposed to have died in Durham. Though that was in some dispute even at the time. Now we will make sure it is done. I have no wish for any loose ends left lying around and that is what you are, Lennox, a loose end. Though I suppose you have no idea why do you?"

"I have never understood why the Covenant wanted me dead."

Sir Gilbert made a dismissive sound.

"I'm not here on behalf of the Covenant. They would probably be appalled to know I was here. The fools are quite happy to leave whatever documents might remain in this place and trust in whatever protection it has. They don't understand the damage that could be done if our founder's spiritual diaries ever came to light."

Gideon was very glad he hadn't mentioned finding them.

"Fortunately, they never will," Sir Gilbert continued. "I'm here to gather and protect them, you and your kind are simply an obstacle to that."

"My kind?"

"As I said there is much you don't understand."

"You could explain," Gideon suggested quickly, feeling the sand slipping through the glass.

"Perhaps if I had greater leisure, I would indulge you. It would be interesting to see how you took the truth."

"Then why not tell me?"

Sir Gilbert shook his head, lifting his sword.

"It hardly matters now. I have learned from you all I need, and I have things to—"

The sword thrust, but a moment before Gideon had seen that it would. Something in Sir Gilbert's eyes betrayed by the slender candle flame, or the slight tensing of muscles, and Gideon moved at the same time, so the edge skimmed the flesh on his neck, drawing blood, but this man was a master with the sword and the blade was already turning to cut down, as Gideon threw himself sideways to avoid it.

The problem was the room was small and cluttered and whilst that meant Gideon could get behind the table and use it as a shield, it also meant he had almost no space and had cut himself off from his only possible escape through the other secret panel. In desperation, he seized the edge of the table and heaved it. But all overturning it did, aside scattering paper, paint pens and ink, was cause Sir Gilbert to dance back a pace.

"You are making such a mess," he said and tutted in irritation as he moved in to cut again.

What saved Gideon that second time was West, who groaned and lifted his head just as Sir Gilbert sliced at his exposed side. The distraction made Sir Gilbert divert his attention momentarily, and Gideon dodged aside. But the reprieve was little more than passing. Sir Gilbert sidestepped and the sword slashed in the candlelight. Gideon saw his own blood still sheening the edge and tried to throw up a hand as a last desperate defence. Then suddenly there was another sword there. A sword already tinged with blood.

"You!" Sir Gilbert lost all interest in Gideon in a moment.

"The Archangel Michael, I believe," Lord said, his voice colder than arctic air. He was slightly breathless, and Gideon realised that he must have run to the outhouse and found his way up through the staircase in the wall, the door to which now stood open. "I wonder how good you are with that sword when not fighting an unarmed man."

Sir Gilbert lunged without warning.

"Ever the gentleman," Lord said, parrying high with obvious ease so the tip of his blade nicked Sir Gilbert's ear lobe, whose breath hissed as he lunged again. Lord's blade moved like a striking snake, catching and deflecting the older man's sword before slashing his face, leaving another trail of blood.

"Let me know when you have had enough," Lord said, stepping back, his teeth bared in an ugly grimace. "I'd like a chat before you die."

THE ALCHEMIST'S PLOT

Sir Gilbert, outclassed and outfought, snarled something incomprehensible and pressed his attack harder. Lord seemed unconcerned. His focus was absolute and despite Sir Gilbert's best efforts, he managed to inflict several cuts. It dawned on Gideon that Lord was playing with his prey like a cat might a mouse—and he was enjoying doing so.

Gideon looked around for something he could use to strike Sir Gilbert with from behind. Then became aware that Richard West was stirring and, in a moment, would no doubt try to sit up. Lacking any other way to stop him doing so and either distracting Lord or getting in the way of the fight, Gideon sat on the man, pinning him to the floor.

He had barely done so when the door beside him was unlocked and burst open to admit a bristling Danny. It was just as Lord had lunged and Sir Gilbert turned sharply to the new threat, so he caught the blade below his ribs. He folded to the floor, heaved a couple of choking breaths then shuddered and was still.

Lord cursed.

"I wanted him alive." He looked at Danny accusingly. "You have bad timing."

"For all I knew you were being massacred," Danny said. "But next time I'll wait until I see blood seeping out from the room."

Gideon got up and West looked blearily at him.

"Lennox? What are you doing here? That man was insane, made me write a confession to murdering the weavers and Hester Lovegood, said he would kill me if I didn't, then brought me here through some secret passages. He was going to hang me on one of the looms, make it look as if I had killed myself in remorse."

There was something in his outraged innocence that was more than hollow. Danny crouched beside Sir Gilbert and began searching his body. Gideon shook his head.

"I think you are lying to say you didn't know of them," he said.

"I've never seen them before. This is all some mistake."

Lord gripped Gideon on the shoulder.

"It makes no odds, no one will believe you if there is a written confession. You will hang anyway." Lord gestured to Danny who held a sheet of paper he had just taken from Sir Gilbert. "However, we have no real interest in the fate of a couple of weavers and a servant. Like you we only care about the secrets this house might hold. In exchange for answering some questions, Danny there might be persuaded to drop that confession in the fire."

A gleam of hope sparked in West's face. "Anything, ask me anything."

"Honest answers, now," Lord said. "We know you killed them, and the confession proves it to the world. Your way through this is to tell Mr Lennox here whatever he wants to know."

West nodded. "Yes. Yes. I understand."

Lord smiled and stepped back making a gesture to Gideon that he should take over. It was the opportunity he had hoped for.

"Hester Lovegood was blackmailing you, wasn't she? She must have found you in the house and said she would reveal the secret places you had found." It was an old barristers' trick, make an accusation you know to be false to try and shake out the truth.

West shook his head.

"No. It wasn't like that. She said we should pool what we found—share our knowledge. I swear it. It was never blackmail."

"You killed her because you feared she might tell what she knew?"

But now West was beyond denials.

"I'd seen her talking to some people from London, I was sure she was going to sell what we'd found. I couldn't allow that, not after so many years. Being so close to success."

It was a confession to murder, but Gideon gave West no time to reflect on that.

"I don't understand why the weavers needed to die. Why take the risk of looking around the building in broad daylight with people in the building?"

West shook his head.

"I had no choice. No time. Once I knew Hester Lovegood was poking around as well, I had to take every possible opportunity. Besides I had the key to this room which I'd come by years ago and I knew anyone trying the door and finding it locked would assume it had been locked by the German. No one was using the

THE ALCHEMIST'S PLOT

loom in the room upstairs so no one had cause to go there. It seemed perfectly safe."

"Why kill the tapissiers?" Gideon asked. "You could have just gone back down the stairs, and they wouldn't have seen you."

"But there was a chance they might and besides, they had seen things move on the hearth. I didn't realise before the old man stood there talking to himself about it. After that, I had to kill him. He would have told other people and started others looking. It wasn't a risk I could take." There was an edge to his words, something almost fanatical. "You must let me help you. I've found out a lot over the years. I am sure the rose room is the key. The hearth. That's where it'll be. There's a shaft in the walls going to a secret room lined with gold."

Gideon stared at him. The man actually believed that.

"Is that what this was all for? Gold?"

"Of course not," West was almost contemptuous. "Dr Dee was an alchemist. What he hid there was the philosopher's stone—that which bestows immortality and changes base metal into gold."

Lord laughed aloud.

"If so, it failed him. He died and had no great wealth when he did so. Danny, please go and fetch Mr Cleyn and the men with him. I would have their opinion on this."

Danny gave a stiff bow and handed the confession to Lord. Then he opened the door as if to go through it, but instead stood there and held it open. "If you would join us, please, gentlemen."

Cleyn came in and the three men with him. Lord frowned at Danny who shrugged. "It was quicker to fetch the man who had a key."

Lord looked at Cleyn. "Then you will have heard something of what this man West said. Here is his confession. He admits to killing your friends." There was a marked tension of anger in the men now. "We can, if you wish, turn him over to the courts and trust that justice will be done. Or…"

"There is an alternative?" Cleyn was frowning at the confession Lord had given him.

"Yes, there is. This confession finishes by saying that West has killed himself from remorse. If you wish to be sure justice is done, do it yourselves."

Even in the candlelight, Gideon could see West become deathly pale. There were muttered voices in Dutch.

"Either way I leave him in your custody."

Cleyn bowed his head.

"I think you know our minds on it. A confession can be denied as you say." The men behind him nodded, faces grim. Cleyn gestured to the corpse of Sir Gilbert. "And that man?"

"Will be gone soon as will his man who is dead in your cellar," Lord assured him. "But first I have some business in the rose room, and I will leave you, gentlemen, to yours. Be quick, your fellow workers and their families will be returning presently."

"They will be a while yet and have no reason to come up here," Cleyn said. "No one has until tomorrow."

Gideon knew he should object, should protest that yet again Sir Philip Lord was allowing wild justice to reign over true justice. But he knew he would get no hearing. Not from Lord or from the Dutch tapissiers who had lost two of their own to this man. He could speak of the need to allow West time to repent for the sake of his immortal soul but knew it wouldn't reach any of these men for very different reasons. The very worst part of it all was that Gideon knew a corner of his own soul was in accord with them.

For true justice couldn't be assured. Cleyn might be a denizen and the weavers accepted in the Mortlake community, but they were still outsiders, foreigners. An English judge with an English jury might well favour the word of a stalwart of the English community over theirs. So Gideon said nothing as they went back up the stairs to the rose room. But his heart was darkened.

He knew he would never match the cool-blooded reaction of Lord and Danny to whom sudden and devastating violence was an event no more or less impacting than any other. To Gideon, it was always going to be something profound and altering. No amount of experience seemed to be changing that. He could never step away from it once it was over. This time the stickiness of blood from where Sir Gilbert's sword had brushed the flesh of his neck

THE ALCHEMIST'S PLOT

was an ongoing reminder of just how close it had come to himself being the one lying dead on the floor of the artist's room.

Danny was talking as they reached the room again.

"As I see it this entire set-up—the doors to the stairs, the brass rod in the wall, the roses on the mantle decoration—are a giant mechanical lock established to prevent accidental access to whatever is in that crypt below. I would very much love to have the opportunity to take all the panelling and the brickwork down so I can see how it was achieved. Whoever designed this must have been a genius."

"I can think of a few candidates," Lord said. "But let's not forget Dee himself once awed an audience with a flying mechanical beetle so perhaps we need look no further than the owner of the house himself. Either way, I regret you cannot be granted your wish, Danny. We need to leave things invisible when we go. The people for whom this house is both workplace and home deserve that from us."

The rose room was as they had left it and Gideon looked into the dark hole behind the hearth and shivered. But he was given no time to dwell on that as Danny and Lord were once again attempting a descent. Lord's head vanished from sight into the dark and for a short time, there was silence. Then Lord's laughter came up to them.

"It seems secure enough, you could join me here safely."

Danny gripping his arm to brace him, Gideon slid into the hole until his feet and then his hands found purchase on the metal rungs. As Lord had said it seemed set firmly into the wall and after about ten or twelve feet was free of the shaft and set on the wall of a chamber.

The first thing that struck Gideon about the room was its small size and odd shape. It wasn't a big room. Brick walls stood not quite three yards high and at its widest point, it was almost as wide as it was tall. It was seven-sided. Seven walls, all of the same size. In the middle of the chamber was a round stone pedestal and above, set into the ceiling was an unfamiliar version of the eagle and rose heraldry.

This had the background of a blazing sun, upon which the black eagle was set so its head, outstretched wings, feet and tail feathers touched the circumference. Upon its chest, just behind the expected five-petaled and leaved Tudor Rose extended four rectangles representing an equal-armed cross.

Lord spoke softly from beside him. "*Dieses Gewölb, ob es wohl von der Sonnen niemahls bescheinet wurde, leuchtet es doch helle von einer andern...* I should feel flattered being compared to an enlightening sun." He chuckled and Gideon looked at him blankly. "Oh, I forgot you have no German, though I am sure someone will put it into English one day soon. It is a quote from the first of those Rosicrucian tracts I mentioned. It describes the discovery of a vault of seven sides and corners, every side five feet broad, and eight feet high, lit not by the sun itself but by another sun. One set in the ceiling and with a round altar in the middle instead of a tomb." He broke off and gestured to the space around them. "I have jested about it before, but it seems we really have found the tomb of Christian Rosenkreuz—or at least the room that our Covenant friends planned to make such. But it looks as if they didn't get very far with their efforts. I doubt many would be fooled by this."

Danny had joined them but stayed by the ladder. Gideon looked at the ceiling piece.

"Then how would they explain that?"

"Prophecy," Lord said firmly. "These Rosicrucian publications were all about prophecy. Prophecy is pretty easy after the fact." His cynicism was clear, but then how could it not be when he was the one indicated by what was depicted on the ceiling? "There are two kinds of men of learning in this world, those who look forward and those who look back. Those who believe all must be novelty to be of value and those who believe everything in the distant past was the truest wisdom. Then there are the handful who stand on the line between the two and to convince others they must represent the new as being ancient in origin and the ancient as—"

Danny interrupted him. "Intriguing as this all is, the weavers and their families are coming back. I can hear them."

THE ALCHEMIST'S PLOT

"We will need to be quieter then. I hope Cleyn and his men have finished their work." He gestured towards Danny. "If you have seen enough to satisfy your curiosity, you could go and ensure they have."

Danny looked up at the ceiling and then gave an exaggerated shiver.

"I've seen enough. I'll look to the weavers and keep them away from here."

He vanished from sight up the ladder and his footsteps retreated.

If Danny had been troubled by what was there, Lord was undisturbed. He turned his attention to the rounded raised plinth in the middle of the room and Gideon joined him. The top part appeared to be a stone lid and it had a slight, rectangular indentation indicating a metal plaque had been set there once—or had, perhaps, been intended but never put in place.

"As I recall we had scything blades in the lid of the one in Howe. I wonder what they put here?"

The answer, as they moved the stone lid with care, was nothing. If there had been any traps another had sprung them. The first thing Gideon noticed as they eased the lid back was the smell of charring.

Inside, set on a bed of ashes and curled and crisped parchment was what looked like a small manuscript. Lord's breath was released in a sigh.

"I might have guessed." The disappointment and frustration were well hidden. Lord lifted the manuscript from its bed of charred documents and started leafing through its few pages. "This looks to me very like a first draft of a work on alchemy by one Sir Edward Kelley, and yes there is his name. You will like this, he writes: *the saying that none but fools and lawyers hate and despise Alchemy has passed into a proverb.*"

Gideon looked at the blackened mess that remained in the hollow. Whoever had burned what was here had done so well. Then he saw a scrap of cream, lost against the grey of the stone and gently pulled it free. Part was so burned it fell away as he did so, but perhaps a quarter of the original was still uncharred.

It was the remains of an ancestor chart, an ahnentafel.

ELEANOR SWIFT-HOOK

Gideon held it to the light and studied what was there. It was written in a scrawling hand and lacked all but the bare bones of detail. He could make out the name of Ferdinand and his wife Anne, Maximilian and his wife Maria and then beneath that Rudolph who was shown married to someone, but only the letters '-et-' remained of their name and of whoever she was, her ancestry was gone. All that remained of it was two generations before: Charles, who had been both King of Spain and Holy Roman Emperor, and father to King Philip who had married Mary Tudor. But if they were ever on the ahnentafel, their names had been destroyed by the flames.

The final name, the name this document was focused on, was just visible though blackened. Gideon made it out to read 'Madinia'. Of the date, he could only see the year—Fifteen Ninety. He felt a lump in his throat.

It was too much and not enough. He had seen that name before but couldn't recall where or when.

His stillness must have drawn Lord's attention.

"You have found something? Something in the ashes? A phoenix feather? A—" He stopped talking as he saw what Gideon held out. Then, placing the manuscript on the edge of the stone he took the charred remains of the sheet from Gideon's hands as if it were a holy relic. His eyes, fluid in the candlelight, fixed like gemstones as they saw what was there.

He looked at Gideon and his face had blanched whiter than parchment. Despite that, he still managed a thin smile.

"It seems my mother has a name and even, perchance, that she may yet live." He bowed his head for a moment and drew a breath before going on "But if I have a name, it is not 'Habsburg' and not 'Tudor'. Perhaps it is yet 'Lord'."

"It is not the proof you—"

"No. But it is more than I had before. Much more. And perhaps even a way forward." Then he placed the fragile fragment almost tenderly on the stone and picked up the manuscript. "This was left here by Thomas Kelley, the younger brother of Sir Edward who was with him and Dee in their travels and even tried to help his brother escape captivity after he fell out of favour with the emperor. I think Sir Edward must have revealed the secrets of this house to him and when, after Sir Edward's death, he fell on hard times he came here. I would suspect by then Dee had gone to Manchester."

Lord turned to the back page of the manuscript. There was a complex table of letters and symbols drawn on it and beneath was written in a different hand from the rest.

For my dearest sister Lydia, to whom all secrets are revealed and from whom none are hidden—to her profit. Th.K.

Gideon frowned at the words. "What is that supposed to mean?"

"I could be wrong," Lord said, "but I think it is by way of threat and extortion. You see, most of these pages burned here are blank."

"Thomas came here, broke into this chamber, took the documents that were here and left that manuscript and the burned papers? Why?"

"Because he couldn't challenge Dee directly. This way he was sure Dee would find out and then he would have to pay up to get his documents back. However unfortunately for him and perhaps fortunately for us," Lord picked up the burned fragment of the ahnentafel and placed it in the manuscript and slipped both inside his doublet, "Dee never came. Perhaps he was too old by then to make the climb or saw no reason. Perhaps there was no longer a way to access it unseen. He must have opened the rose room by then."

"You think we can trace the documents? Or do you think the Covenant will have long since claimed them? After all, they will have known of the Kelleys' involvement from the first."

There were voices faint but audible. Lord gestured to the ladder.

"We should go. We have seen all there is to see here, and we have bodies to dispose of before bedtime."

Gideon nodded and turned to the ladder, climbing as fast as his limbs allowed, relieved to be leaving that place of darkness and enlightenment. They reset the rose room to its pristine state, reversing the use of rose rotations and the lever on the stairs, closing the panel so no trace remained, and the secrets of the house were once more concealed from view.

The rest of the evening passed quickly. The Thames would take the dead. But as not even the Covenant knew Sir Gilbert and his man had been in Mortlake, no link should be made with the tapestry works when their bodies eventually surfaced.

Cleyn was waiting as they came back to the house. He thanked Danny for his specific help and Gideon was glad there was no further explanation added as to what that help had been. Perhaps faced with the reality of taking a life, Cleyn and his fellows had found it harder than they thought. Then Cleyn addressed himself to Lord. "You will be returning to Oxford tomorrow, Sir Philip?"

"That is my intention," Lord said.

"If you don't mind, I will ride with you. I've been offered some commissions in Oxford through a fellow artist. There is little enough work for any here with the war and I can create any cartoons needed there as well as here. I had been looking to travel when the opportunity arose and you offer me that."

"There is another reason?" Lord surmised and Cleyn smiled.

"Yes. I need to be out of temptation's path. Tomorrow they will find the body of Richard West who hung himself in remorse for his evil, on one of the looms in the weaving hall. Once all that he did has been set straight I know I would be tempted to look again in those passages and that would be unwise. Besides," he added in a different tone, "although I'm not sure my wife will wish to come with me, I know it would help at least one of my daughters to be away from Mortlake for a while."

By the time Gideon was able to seek his bed in The Queen's Head, having walked in under a borrowed cloak to hide the blood on his clothes, he was so exhausted he cut short his usual prayers for the safety and wellbeing of Zahara as sleep claimed him. But his last thought was to remember where he had seen the name Madinia. It had been the name of the child in Kelley's vision.

THE ALCHEMIST'S PLOT

Oxford, 25th March 1643

As England celebrated the change of years, Sir Philip Lord finally and finely silenced the gossip of their union's irregularity, taking to wife Lady Catherine de Bouquelemont with full priestly blessing in Christ Church Cathedral of Oxford. It was as extravagant as the strictures of war might permit. The king himself was in attendance as were the Palatine Princes and much of the nobility resident at that time in the city. Sir Philip distributed largesse to the people of Oxford who were little compensated for the inconvenience of having the court and—surely—half the king's army inflicted on them.

Immediately after the ceremony, the happy couple received a visit from one of their guests, Lady Frances Coke, Viscountess Purbeck, daughter of the late Sir Edward Coke. She gave them an unconventional wedding gift in the form of a bundle of documents. These, Sir Philip and Lady Catherine looked through. Having shown them to Gideon Lennox, who avowed that they were indeed genuine, Sir Philip sent them to the king with the humble request that his majesty might take the time to peruse their contents.

Before they had commenced the dancing, the king sent for Sir Philip and was closeted with him privily for almost half an hour. At the end of that time, his majesty had issued a command to strike down and annul the attainder that had been issued against Sir Philip twenty years before. He was no longer pardoned for treason as he was no longer deemed to have ever been a traitor.

When he left the king, Sir Philip returned to the cathedral and, ordering his men to wait without, entered alone. He walked to stand before the high altar, glorious below the rose window, where candlelight cast a nimbus around the tormented figure of Christ on the altarpiece. He held his head lifted, gaze defiant, almost as if in challenge. Then with a single movement he drew his sword and dropped to one knee, the basket hilt gripped between his finger-locked hands and the point of the blade to the stone floor.

He bowed his head briefly, as he might to a social superior, then lifted his gaze again. His voice was clear and quiet.

"I swear before God, by my soul, by my heart that if you still live, wherever you may be in this world, I will find you, my mother, so you can embrace your son who I know you will have never forgotten." His voice caught with a tug of emotion unfamiliar to it and he had to swallow before he could go on. "And so you may have the protection of your son, who has never known you, but has always loved and honoured you."

He stayed there unmoving for a few minutes as if awaiting an answer or a sign. Nothing happened and the air about him remained still, quiet and empty. Then he got to his feet, sheathed his sword by his thigh, and walked from the building. His men saw his face as he emerged and knew it best to say nothing.

But the Sir Philip Lord who rejoined his wife and his friends at the celebration showed no trace of anything except the undiluted happiness expected of a man on his wedding day.

THE ALCHEMIST'S PLOT

Author's Notes

This book is dedicated to the late Dorothy Dunnett; indeed, the entire series is my tribute to her. I owe so much to her inspiration I will never match her peerless prose or be worthy to touch even the hem of her literary skirts but striving wholeheartedly to do so has made me the writer I am today.

There are many people and places in this book who are drawn from history and as far as possible I have had them all be in the place history placed them at this time. How they behave and what they say is almost entirely my invention.

A few deserve specific mention.

Queen Henrietta Maria did indeed courageously endure the sea crossing as described and her landing at Bridlington Bay, together with the subsequent attack, is very close to my interpretation of it

Sir John Hotham asked for precisely the things I mention to switch sides, but his offer was made through the Earl of Newcastle Later that year his own and his father's wavering loyalty was to lead to their arrest and execution by Parliament.

The Royal Tapestry Works at Mortlake certainly existed. In them, England held an artistic jewel beyond price and the works it produced are seen as amongst the very finest in the world for that era. Whilst, to my knowledge there were neither murders nor secret chambers there, the works were indeed set up in the house that had previously belonged to Dr John Dee and was the subject of an ongoing land ownership dispute.

The works operated at this time much as I have described Records point to the house (or perhaps more accurately interconnected houses) being both workshop and home to the Dutch and Flemish weavers who produced the tapestries. Phillip de Maecht was a Flemish weaver brought from Paris to manage the works. Francis Cleyn was poached from the Danish court, and he provided the design for the tapestries. Near the start of the war Cleyn moved to Oxford and produced several portraits there.

could not find any information regarding his wife, so the suggestion of a familial link with the de Maechts is not historical, though Cleyn did have daughters called Magdalen and Penelope, who went on to become painters themselves.

I have done my best to be accurate in presenting London and its environs as it was at the time. Whilst The Crown and its location is my invention, Hanging Sword Alley did and does exist. The story of how it got its name is as I have described. The liberty of Whitefriars had been renamed Alsatia after the province of Alsace, devastated in the Thirty Years War, because it was such a lawless slum. Its charter granted by King James in 1608 was opaque and left it both largely self-governing and with the archaic right of sanctuary which had belonged to the Carmelite monastery. As a result, it became a haven for debtors and other criminals.

John Dee was a controversial character in his lifetime and ever after. He is a fascinating historical figure. If you have the time and inclination, I recommend picking up one of the more recent available biographies about him.

He was much concerned with the idea of an empire centred on Britain and his religious inclinations seem to have been very flexible, more driven by his idea of direct communication and revelation than by following any specific creed. Indeed, he was to face accusations of heresy on and off throughout his life. He was also a great mathematician and cryptographer, involved himself in experiments, studied astronomy as well as astrology and, like Isaac Newton a century later, saw no hard line between science and the spiritual.

The quotations taken from his spiritual diaries are his account of his interactions with what he believed to be angels and spirits. However, he couldn't see them himself. For this, he relied upon Edward Kelley, a rather dubious individual with whom Dee had an often stormy relationship. There is no doubt that, according to Kelley, the angels insisted that he and Dee slept with each other's wife—and that they did so much to the immense distress of Dee's wife, Jane. It is possible her son, Theophilus, born about nine months after their 'cross matching' was Kelley's. Soon after that event Kelley and Dee broke up their partnership and Kelley went on to gain first a knighthood from, and then an ignominious death as a prisoner of, Rudolf II. Kelley had represented himself to Rudolf as an alchemist but failed to deliver on his claims.

As for Dee being involved in a secret conspiracy, being the man he was, it is a given he would have been involved with several in his lifetime—quite possibly beginning with one to place Elizabeth on the throne, whilst being a chaplain in the service of the Catholic Bishop Bonner. However, whether he was ever involved in a plot that focused on maintaining a bloodline of descent from Mary Tudor and Philip of Spain, is a matter upon which the historical record is silent…

If you have enjoyed The Alchemist's Plot, I would love to hear what you thought about it so please do leave a review. You can also follow me on Twitter @emswifthook or get in touch with me through my website www.eleanorswifthook.com where you can find more about the background to the book including the origins of the various quotations in the text.

Meanwhile, you will be pleased to know The Alchemist's Plot is the fifth of six books in the Lord's Legacy series, which follow Gideon Lennox through the opening months of the first English Civil War. As he unravels the mystery of Philip Lord's past, he finds himself getting caught up in battles and sieges, murder investigations and moral dilemmas as all the while he bears the heartache of his seemingly impossible romance with the beautiful Zahara.

Printed in Great Britain
by Amazon